IN THE
ROBES
OF GOD

By Richard Cezar

In The Robes of God

Copyright © 2015 by Richard Cezar, identified as the author.

This is a work of fiction, published by the author. Any similarity to persons living or dead is merely coincidental. All rights reserved. This book, or any portion thereof, may not be reproduced or used in any manner without the express written permission of the author, except for use of brief quotations in a book review.

Printed in the United States of America
Revised Edition-March, 2022

Dedication

This book is dedicated to my daughter Jacqueline, whose love I cherish above all else. It is my most sincere hope that her life will be filled with as much joy as she has brought into mine.

And to the memory of my stepdaughter, Jenny, with deep and enduring love.

Preface

Set in the very near future, a young businessman discovers a technological breakthrough, capable of improving the lives of all humankind. How could he know that it would be stolen from himand and turned into something evil and twisted.

This epic adventure delves into the growing conflict between the weakness of the human condition and modern technology. It is an introspective look into society and what could happen, should we continue along our current path.

Have power, greed, and arrogance propelled us beyond the point of no return? Is there still time to save ourselves? The clock is ticking in this novel that pits us against our own creations.

Chapter 1
Japan

There were twelve of us at the meeting that morning. As was customary in Japan, the principal members were seated mid-table, not at the head. I had been invited to sit in that respected position, on one side of the long mahogany surface. To my immediate right, my tech director, Cassandra Ramirez, stared straight ahead through slightly oversized, horned-rimmed glasses—hands clasped in front of her. It was her first trip to Japan.

Directly across from us sat Haruki Yoshino, Business Director of Najita Corporation. The silence was palpable, intruded on only by the flipping of pages, as he scanned the document in front of him. With his greying temples, slightly overweight physique born of fine dining, and intimidating eyes—overslung by a furrowed brow, he was the very embodiment of the experience and power of his position.

Sitting next to him was Kenji Hashimoto, manager of coatings research. He would probably be promoted if our deal went through. Slight of build and energetic, Kenji was Yoshino's "get-it-done" man.

A chill ran through me, as I silently rejoiced in what was about to happen. In two years, the world would be changed forever. An era that found us dependent on fossil fuel and greedy oil companies would soon be over. Energy would be dirt-cheap for cars, ships, industry, and residences. All of the world's economies would be stabilized. It was my hope that it might also serve to stem the escalation of violence between people and nations. There would be more for everybody and less to fight over. And I was going to be a part of it all.

Finally, Yoshino spoke. "So Wade-san, after we left you at the hotel last night, we had the very important meeting. Mista Watanabe, our managing director, signed the contract."

With a rare smile, he slid the project folder across the conference table to me. Upon opening it, I immediately noticed a number of penned-in changes.

"Yoshino-san, I thought we had mutual agreement on the terms. All these changes will require further discussion." I tried to mask my disappointment.

"Yes, Wade-san, I know. But they are not big problems. Maybe you and Miss La-meel-e—"

I politely interrupted. "Please—please call her Casey."

Yoshino continued, "If you and *Casey-san* can stay in Mihara for one more day, we can get consensus on the details."

As I glanced at Casey, she gently shrugged her shoulders and quietly said, "It's the most important thing on my plate right now."

Conspicuously, I checked the time on my phone, looked back up, and appealed to him. "Yoshino-san, it's nine-forty-five in the morning on Friday, and we've been here all week. My family is scheduled to arrive here, by limo, in fifteen minutes. We're booked on a bullet train from Hiroshima to Osaka, and we have flight reservations to San Francisco today. —My kids have to go back to school on Monday."

Yoshino's face turned serious as he answered abruptly. "Soh!" And he lifted his own phone from the table and spoke into it. "Takahashi-san, douzo, ohairi kudasai."

The door of our conference room opened, and a tall thin Japanese man with well quaffed, jet-black hair strutted in. He sported a blue, tailored suit and a grin from ear-to-ear.

"Hi, Hank," Casey said and waved to him with her fingers.

"Hank, it's great to see you," I said to Hakurou Takahashi who, for the last three years, had been the liaison between Najita and Quantam, Inc.—my company in Palo Alto, California.

"Good to see you Jeff-san," he answered and sat down next to me.

Yoshino said, "Takahashi-san is already prepared to travel to the States on a separate matter. He can accompany your family—if you trust him."

"Of course, I trust him, but—"

Yoshino interrupted. "It's up to you, Wade-san. We can negotiate the remaining issues later, in a virtual meeting, if you must leave."

After a few moments of silence, Kenji Hashimoto stood up and said, "Sumimasen o kudasai," excusing himself, and motioned to me to join him—off to the side. He whispered, "Jeff-san, Japanese never take our family on the business trip. If you don't stay, Mista Yoshino could be upset. It's a kind of insult. And maybe cause the big delay for the contract."

I knew he was right, and upon returning to our seats I said, "Yoshino-san, Casey and I will stay to settle the details."

"Hah, very good," he answered–and smiled.

Hank let out a sigh. He immediately pulled out his phone, conversing in Japanese. His expression turned to disappointment as he turned to us and said, "Too late—it's after ten o'clock."

I checked the time. "It'll be tight, but we can swing it. The limo is probably already here. Yoshino-san, please excuse Hank and me. We have to go down and explain to my family."

His answer came rather frigidly. "Of course, but please do not keep the other members of our group waiting too long. This is not the only business they must take care of today."

As Hank and I got up to leave, I said, "Oh, Yoshino-san, would you mind having one of your people change my name on our reservations."

"Hai," One of Yoshino's lieutenants said, upon rising and bowing.

I handed him our tickets and motioned Casey and Hank to caucus with me outside the conference room. The door was partially open, allowing us to hear Yoshino's man in protracted Japanese verbiage on the phone.

"That was a mistake," I said to Casey, shaking my head.

"I don't think so, Jeff. If we don't stay, the whole deal could collapse."

"I'm not talking about our decision to stay, Casey. I mean asking for their help to change our flight reservations."

Just then, Yoshino's assistant pushed the door open and said, "Mista Wade-san, ANA airlines say you can only change the name at the ticket counter."

"Domo arigato," I answered. And as he slipped back into the conference room, I said to Casey, "That was a complete waste of time. Everything is probably taken care of."

"I don't get it," she answered.

"Explain it to her, Hank," I said.

Hank looked upwards for a second or two. "Hmm—well, in the Japanese way, if we don't know for sure, we always tell the person the worst possible result. That way, when they find out the actual case, they can only have *the good feeling."*

Casey just stood there with a perplexed look on her face, as I pulled out my phone and called the airline. I was quickly able to confirm that Casey's reservation had been canceled and my name had been changed over to Hank's.

I turned to her and said, "Casey, you wait here, while Hank and I go down to explain things to my family."

***

Downstairs, Hank picked up his bags at the front desk, as we rushed through the lobby, and out of the door, to the waiting limo. Hank had visited my home in Santa Clara, on more than one occasion, and knew my whole family.

As we approached the white, all-electric van, the driver opened the door to reveal my lovely wife, Kristine, and my two beautiful girls. Nine-year-old Jessica was blond with blue eyes—just like her mother. Abby, my seven-year-old, had my dark brown eyes and hair. They were at the center of all things in my life.

"Hi Sweetheart," Kris said in her familiar upbeat tone.

Looking into her deep blue eyes, I couldn't help but think how ten years of marriage had served only to strengthen the bonds of love between us. I felt lucky beyond words.

I leaned in to kiss her and hug the kids, as Abby squealed, "Daddy!"

I eased back out of the van and motioned to Hank, who had been standing several paces behind me, talking on his phone.

"Oh, hi, Hank," Kris said surprisedly.

Hank hung up–smiled–and said, "Misses Wade-san, so good to see you again."

She noticed the bags in Hank's hands. "Are you riding with us to the train?"

Before Hank could answer, I said, "Kris, there's been a change in plans. Hank's going with you and the kids back to the States. I'm, uh—I'm going to have to stay one more day."

A disappointed look came over her face. "But why? I thought everything was set."

"It's about some last-minute changes to the contract. They're not deal-breakers, but they want me to stay. I'm sorry, Honey. I know the kids have to get back and—"

"You don't have to explain, Sweetheart. Do what you have to do. We'll see you when you get home." She said it with that understanding look that only she possessed.

"Thanks, Honey," I answered, as I kissed her once more, and touched my children's faces.

Hank got in on the opposite side and closed the door. Through the window, I could see the looks of sadness on my girls' faces, as Kris held them close and spoke to them. I stayed to wave and watch, as the van circled the courtyard and moved out of sight through the iron gates.

8

***

When I returned to the conference room, Yoshino and the others were waiting.

Yoshino began, "Okay—Wade-san let's get started. We trust the commitment on your part, but what assurance do we have that the German company, Elektrikote, will follow through—in the responsible way?"

He was right to be concerned. There was a lot at stake. Najita had developed a thin coating formula that was capable of concentrating photon energy from any source of light and converting it to heat at almost 100 percent efficiency. Elektrikote had produced a layering formula that instantly converted the heat to an electric current and stored it, through the use of nano-battery technology. My privately held company, Quantam, had patented a formula that acted as a unique filter and cohesive agent, essentially binding the two into a single, paint-on layer. Once the formulation was perfected, energy could be stored and released as alternating or direct current—at will.

The build-up of greenhouse gases and concerns about climate change would become things of the past. There would be enough clean energy to independently power houses, factories, cars, and boats, without connection to the grid. In fact, there'd be no need for a power grid or energy taxing. One of the best parts was that it cost little more than conventional paints, and we projected it to last upwards of twenty years.

My thoughts returned to the question at hand, looking into Yoshino's doubtful eyes, I answered, "Stages."

"*Stages*? What means this—stages?" he asked.

Upon producing a document from my briefcase, I slid it across the table to Yoshino. "Here's the plan. It outlines four stages for the exchange of information between our companies, such that no single party has an advantage over another. And, in the meantime, all three companies can become more—comfortable—with each other."

"Excuse us, please," Yoshino said as he studied my plan, and discussed it, in Japanese, with his associates.

In about five minutes that seemed like five hours, he said, "It seems logical, but how do we know the Germans will honor it?"

"Somebody must go first," I answered.

Yoshino hesitated, saying, "We will consider."

"Oh, no," I thought.

In my dealings with the Japanese, I knew that *we will consider* was usually the kiss of death. They just didn't want me to lose face by abruptly telling me no.

Regrouping my thoughts, I spoke up. "Yoshino-san, what if we make this document an addendum to the contract and have you and Elektrikote's president, Ernst Ziegler, sign off on each stage? —Regarding your mark-ups on the main document, I checked them. No problem from our end."

I waited through another, even longer, Japanese deliberation.

Finally, Yoshino said, "Okay—we have the consensus. I will have the secretary prepare the paperwork."

"Wonderful!" I remarked, pleasantly surprised.

While we waited and chatted lightly, I thought about how different our cultures were. I knew that Watanabe's signature, the evening before, was only a formality. Even Yoshino couldn't approve the contract on his own, though his seal would appear on it. The decision was made in aggregate, by the group of men sitting in front of me. It was from the bottom-up management, not from the top-down.

About twenty minutes later, the amended contract was returned to our conference room, where Yoshino and I added our signatures. *Now*, I knew that Najita would focus all its resources on getting the job done, as would I. Leaning back in my chair, I was quite proud of myself.

As I was basking in the glow of my achievement, the intercom on our table buzzed, and Yoshino answered. "Moshi-moshi."

A flood of indiscernible Japanese words spewed forth, occasionally interspersed by a "hah" or "mmm" from Yoshino.

When they'd finished, Yoshino turned to me with a somber look on his face. "There are some Japanese policemen in the lobby. They want to talk with you.

Did you have any problem this week—maybe at the hotel?"

"*No*—no problems at all. Are you sure they want *me?*"

"Yes! They say it is the very serious matter." He got up from his chair. "We could easily find out. Let's go, please." I followed him toward the door.

As we passed Casey, I said, "Wait here. This should only take a few minutes. They must have me mixed up with somebody else."

***

Down in the lobby, in front of the reception desk, were three uniformed policemen. A fourth stood apart, in a slightly-disheveled business suit and tie. He didn't look unkempt, rather that he may have hurriedly dressed. He was somewhere in his late forties, lean in stature, with salt-and-pepper hair and matching eyebrows.

As we walked up to him, he asked, "Mista Jef-fe-dy Wade?"

"Yes! What's this all about?"

He presented his identification, with a very slight bow of his head. "I am detective Satoshi Morita of Hiroshima Prefecture security police. You will come with me, please."

The obviously stunned Yoshino said something to him in Japanese.

Detective Morita answered him in English. "Not yet. Officer Kato will stay here for your statement."

I was escorted outside to a waiting police car. The two attending uniformed cops got in the front, while the detective and I slid into the back seat. As soon as we cleared the Najita compound, they turned on the red light and siren.

Outrage trumped my fear, as I turned to my unlikely seatmate and demanded, "*Look, Detective—*"

"Morita—Detective Morita," he injected.

"Detective Morita, at least you can tell me what I'm charged with."

He looked at me calculatingly. "There was the—accident—on the Osaka shinkansen."

"*The bullet train? Oh, my God—my family. Are they okay?*"

"We go to the hospital now." He answered without the tiniest break in his serious demeanor.

Chapter 2
Shinkansen

One of the uniformed cops pushed open the door of the emergency room, and I walked in–flanked on both sides by Morita and the other cop. The air was thick with the odor of disinfectants. Dozens of bloodied patients crowded the room in disarray. Hospital staff members were scurrying about to tend to the injured. The sounds of moaning and the barking of unintelligible instructions filled my ears.

I stopped in my tracks, near-paralyzed by anxiety, and asked, "Where are they?"

"You come this way please, Mista Wade." He pointed to his partner ahead of us.

I hesitated momentarily, then complied. We continued straight through the receiving area, down a corridor, and into an elevator. One of the cops pushed the down button. The doors closed, silencing the noise from the receiving room. It was only a single-floor descent. When we stepped out, there was nothing but dead silence. We walked toward a set of stainless steel doors with round windows. Morita hit a mushroom button on the wall, and the doors opened into a large white room.

"Mista Wade, I am sorry, but this is necessary. We need you to identify them."

"Of course, I can identify them. Where are they? Are they okay?"

His eyes cast downward. "I think–maybe–you misundastand. Please come, Mista Wade."

He urged me by the arm toward a stainless steel table at the far end of the room. As we approached it, my eyes were drawn to two metal containers on top of it. One of them approximated the dimensions of a cake box, though taller. The second was about the same size as the first, but twice as long. Both had latched lids with a handle on top.

As we stood before them, Morita said, "Very sorry again, but we need for you to identify the—the bodies."

Every inch of my being stiffened with dread, as I closed my eyes. *"No—no! That can't be!"*

Then he reached over, unlatched, and slowly swung open the lid of the smaller one, saying, "Confirm, please."

I peered into the box long enough to see a partial skull, with a portion of seared skin remaining. It was that of my wife, Kristine. My stomach muscles tightened, and the blood drained from my head. I barely made it to a sink on an adjacent wall.

When I'd finished vomiting, Morita hesitantly asked, "You—confirm?"

"Y—yes," Pushing through abject pain I asked, "But what about Jessica and Abby—my daughters?"

When he didn't respond, I demanded, "Where are my daughters?"

His gaze fell downward as he slowly answered, "I'm sorry, but all the—pieces—we could find are in the other box. But they can only be identified by DNA."

I fell to my knees and sobbed, covering my eyes with the palms of my hands. I'd just seen them a few hours earlier. I remembered the disappointed look on my daughters' faces.

"It's all my fault. I shouldn't have let them come." I wailed, as my hands slid down my face, and my mind flashed back a month earlier.

I'd traveled to Japan alone several times over the last four years. They kept asking to go with me, but I'd judged the accommodations in Mihara to be too Spartan for a family vacation. Finally, I had given in. I'd figured that it would only be for a week, and that it could be educational for the kids to be exposed to another culture. They were overjoyed, and now—they were gone. I covered my eyes again and lowered my head to the floor, racked with agonizing grief.

Morita's voice came through. "Mista Wade, you must come with us now."

"No, no, I want to stay with my—," I began.

"I am sorry, but we must get your DNA sample—to positively identify your daughters. You will have the chance to claim the remains later."

I looked up at him, slowly rose to my feet, and catatonically replied. "Okay."

***

I don't remember leaving the hospital or how long we were driving, but the next thing I knew, we were pulling up to an odd-shaped, faded-brown building. It was somewhat taller than it was wide, carrying a sign with a Japanese logo near the top. We stopped under an entrance canopy and got out. Morita motioned me to go in through a set of large plate-glass doors.

Once inside, it was apparent that it wasn't a DNA testing laboratory or another hospital.

"This is Higashi-Hiroshima police station," Morita announced.

"*Police station*? I thought you were going to do a DNA test." I was shocked and confused.

"We have all those facilities here, Mista Wade. Please come with me." He led me down an aisle between several desks toward the rear of the office.

"DNA kitto kudasai," he said to a uniformed female as we passed her desk.

We continued to a room at the rear of the station and walked in. "Please sit down," he instructed.

I was not of a mind to argue, seating myself in one of the four chairs at a small table within the bare-walled cubicle. He sat across the table from me.

I began to stammer uncontrollably. "How long—how long do I have to be here? I—I need to—get b–back to–my f–family."

"Maybe not long, Mista Wade."

Mercifully–only seconds later, the female cop stepped in, and bowed at the waist. She had a black box in her left hand.

"You will please do us the favor to open your mouth, Mista Wade?" Morita asked, and I numbly complied.

After producing a long-stemmed Q-tip from a test tube from within the box, she swabbed my oral cavity and turned to bow again upon leaving.

Matter-of-factly, Morita continued, "While we are waiting, would you mind answering a few questions?"

"Questions? No, I guess not."

"You should know there is the video and voice recording in this room." He pointed to a ceiling-mounted camera.

"*You're recording me*—why?

"It's a standard procedure," he answered.

"Okay-okay, go ahead."

"Mista Wade, you were planning to travel with your family today, but you did not.—Why?"

"The company I was meeting with asked me to stay one more day. What's this all about anyway?"

"For now, please just answer," he said. Continuing, he asked, "For my curiosity, why you did not plan the direct flight from Hiroshima to San Francisco, instead of the bullet train to Osaka—then flying to your home?"

"My kids wanted to ride the bullet train. I *thought* it would be safe."

Morita continued. "Okay, so when you changed the name on the flight reservations, why didn't you change it on the 'green car' of the bullet-train also?"

By that time, I was getting a little antsy and indignant. "I was in a hurry. Besides, the train doesn't require a passport. *What the hell!* Do you think I knew there was gonna be a train-wreck? Do you think I would've let my *own family die?*" I started to get choked up again. "If—if I only could, I'd trade places with them right now."

Morita said, "And so, this man—" He paged through his notes. "—Hakurou Takahashi, died instead of you."

"Hank's gone too?" I asked solemnly.

"Not confirmed yet, but I think yes. The seat assignments were together. He was probably in your seat."

"Look, this whole business with my change in plans can be cleared up. Just call Mister Yoshino at Fujita." I was frustrated with all of his absurd innuendos. All I could think about were those metal boxes.

Morita paused for a moment, then said, "We have already taken the statement from Mista Yoshino. Everything is the same as you said."

"*What?* Then, why are you interrogating me?" I asked.

"Please understand that in the case of the terrorist attack, we must be very careful."

"What do you mean—*terrorist attack?*" I gasped.

"Sorry I could not tell you until now, Mista Wade, but there was a big explosion on the train—less than one mile after leaving the Hiroshima station. We have determined the bomb was located in the same *green car* as your family."

"*A bomb—my God,!*" I struggled to wrap my mind around it all.

With a look of resolve in his eyes, Morita said, "Japan has been the peaceful country for many years. This kind of event is very shocking. The Shinkansen has had the perfect safety record, with no fatalities—until now. We will not stop until we find who did it."

As if in punctuation of his remarks, a male police staff member showed up at the door and said, "Excuse please. Sei no DNA kantei—mata. La-mi-lezu wa koko ni aru," and left, after a nod from Morita.

"Mista Wade, I'm sad inform you that your DNA matched the—body parts—at the hospital. There is no doubt of their relationship to you."

Tears of sorrow filled my eyes once again, as my elbows fell onto the table—my wrists pressed against my head in utter despair.

Waiting until I was partially composed, Morita said, "Your associate, Misa Ramirez, is here at the front desk."

"*Casey—Casey's here?*" I began to push away from the table.

"Just a moment," Morita said. "You are not the murder suspect for now, but you must obey the law. Don't go back to the hospital today. We are still checking the bodies for bomb fragments. Please contact this office tomorrow for the official cause of the deaths, and when we can release the remains. — Now, you can go."

I sat motionless, oblivious to his instructions except for one word—murder.

"Mista Wade, you can go now," he repeated.

"Huh? Uh, okay." I rose from my chair, and slowly headed back toward the building entrance.

Casey was waiting there for me, with a deeply compassionate look on her face.

"*Jeff*, I heard what happened. Are you okay?"

"No—I'm not." My knees were weak and shaky in supporting my weight.

He pulled away, as I walked up the driveway and onto the porch to the front door. When I crossed the threshold, the sound of my footsteps on the ceramic tile echoed off the walls of the foyer. I was met with unmerciful flashbacks of Kris and the kids as I dazedly moved from room-to-room. Ending up in Abby's upstairs bedroom, I could hear the sound of her giggling.

Laboring to maintain a modicum of sanity, I thought, *"I can't stay here anymore."*

I headed back down the stairs and out the front door. Held tightly in the grip of my sorrow, I stopped and leaned on the porch railing to take a breath. Partially composed, I was able to take a few steps off the porch. My neighbors, Margaret and Trevor Woodruff, were standing on their lawn—off to my left. Trevor approached me, while Margaret stayed behind, her arms folded nervously.

Trevor said, "Jeff—uh, Margaret and I didn't want to bother you at the cemetery. But we want you to know how awful we feel about this whole thing. I know there aren't any words. If there's anything we can do—"

"Thanks, Trevor," I interrupted. "I keep seeing them everywhere."

As I glanced downward, I saw a rubber ball. It was the pink and blue one—Abby's favorite. I stooped down to pick it up out of the grass. In that same moment, Trevor's body was slammed to the ground. Less than a second later, a familiar sound reached my ears. Instantly, my mind reached back over twelve years to recognize it as the cracking noise made by a sniper-round breaking the sound barrier.

I knelt down to examine Trevor's injury. He didn't have a chance. His chest cavity was torn open, with blood pulsing from the wound.

Margaret rushed up screaming, *"No—no,"* and began wailing from eyes still reddened from the funeral.

I noticed she was holding a smartphone, and I shouted, *"Call 911,"* as I straddled Trevor and applied pressure to the gaping hole.

While she called, he looked up at me and weakly asked, "W—what happened, Jeff? Am I gonna die?"

How could I tell him, or Margaret, that he was already dead? He just didn't know it yet.

Instead, I tried to comfort him saying, "Lie still, Trevor. Help is on the way."

Within minutes, several police cars and an ambulance screeched to a halt at my driveway. By the time the EMTs got there, Trevor was gone. I tried to ease Margaret away from her husband's body. There was nothing to be done, but her desperation and agony were palpable. I knew those feelings well. With no tears left to offer, I cradled her in my arms.

The police cordoned off the scene with yellow tape and ushered us both off to the side. After asking some basic questions, and marking Trevor's body location, they allowed Margaret to ride with him in the ambulance to the morgue. They asked me to come with them to the San Jose Police Department—to give a statement.

As we started to leave, one of the officers stopped me and said, "Maybe you want to clean up, before we leave."

It was then I realized that my sleeves were dripping Trevor's blood—my hands covered with it. The cop accompanied me back inside my house to wash up. As I watched the blood swirling on the white porcelain of the kitchen sink, a barrage of images hammered at me. But they weren't of my wife and children this time. They were those of dead soldiers. I closed my eyes tightly, and the ghosts went away. I grabbed a change of clothes, as we left for the station.

***

I'd not been inside a police station in my entire life. And now, within the space of three weeks, I found myself walking into a second. One officer stayed with me at the front desk, while the other disappeared through an inner door. Shortly afterward, the door swung open again and a woman walked out. She was wearing street clothes—a denim jacket and black pants. I guessed her to be somewhere in her late thirties—slim, with green eyes and a short haystack of blond hair.

"Mister Wade, my name is Detective Sergeant Rachel McKinney. Please come in."

We walked in and through a corridor that was eerily similar to the one at Hiroshima station. And again, I was asked to sit in a small, square room, where she sat across from me.

The déjà vu didn't end, when she asked, "Is it okay if we record this conversation?"

"Yes, that's fine," I answered unreservedly.

She added, "You understand that anything you say could be held against you in a court of law."

"*Court of law?*" I reacted.

"Standard protocol," she answered.

"Yeah, okay—okay, go ahead."

McKinney began by saying, "So, Mister Wade, I understand that you were talking to the deceased immediately before he was killed."

"Yes, he's—he *was* my neighbor."

In a strongly directive tone, she said, "Now, in your own words, tell me what happened."

I tried to think clearly. "Well, I was talking to Trevor, when I noticed my daughter's ball lying in the grass. When I bent over to pick it up, Trevor fell to the ground. Then I heard the cracking sound from a sniper rifle round."

"How did you determine that the bullet came from a sniper rifle?" She sounded skeptical.

"I have some—uh—specialized experience—," I began hesitantly, and then I blurted it out. "I was a Marine sniper in Afghanistan."

McKinney stopped, gazed at me intently, and asked, "Could you tell what direction the shot came from?"

"Putting the sound delay together with the way Trevor fell, I'd say it came from the southeast—from over 500 yards away."

"Did you tell that to the officers at the scene?" she asked.

"Yes. I pointed out a group of buildings in the distance. They said they were going to check it out."

"Mister Wade, do you think someone was trying to kill *you*?" The question seemed to come from left field.

"Why do you think I was the target? —Oh, I see. You're aware of what happened to my family."

She responded. "We have a report from the Hiroshima police department. According to them, you were supposed to have been on that train with your family—and now this."

I looked straight into her eyes and said, "It makes no difference to me, whether I was the target or not. The fact is that somebody murdered my family—and my neighbor. I promise you I'll stand over their dead bodies."

"Mister Wade, I can't begin to understand how you feel, and I'm sorry for your loss. But you're not in the Marines anymore, and this is not Afghanistan.

"It might give you some degree of comfort to know that they found the individual who planted the bomb on that train in Japan."

I was caught by surprise. "Who was it? Did they find out why—?"

After inhaling deeply, she said, "It was a transit company maintenance employee. And no, they couldn't determine why. He was found dead of a self-inflicted gunshot wound to the temple. But they're sure it was him. They searched his apartment and found bomb materials that matched those from the explosion scene. Officially, they're saying he acted alone."

"How do they know he acted alone?" I asked.

Reverting to a more coldly professional tone, she said, "Look, Mister Wade, the Hiroshima police are still investigating the bombing. Presently, there is no evidence to link that incident to the shooting that took place at your home today. We're not certain that you were the intended target in either incident, but we're not taking any chances. Where will you be staying tonight?"

"I can't go back to the house," I answered. "Not because of the shooting. I—I just can't go back there. I'll be staying at the Hyatt Place in San Jose until I can figure things out."

"Good, as long as we know where to contact you if we have any more questions. You're free to go for now. If you think of anything else that may be of help, please call me at this number." And she handed me her card.

***

That night, I called Phil and Casey from the hotel. The news of the shooting had already saturated the media, and I was in no mood to go into the details. After assuring them both that I was all right, I cut the conversations short and headed straight for the minibar. I threw back a couple of scotches and crawled into bed. Though exhausted, I still tossed around for hours. I finally fell asleep around four in the morning.

Then came the dreams—the ones I thought I'd left behind. After several years, they returned with a vengeance—the same faces with the same desolate expressions, unchanged by time. And the blood—there was so much blood. I jerked to a sitting position, dripping with sweat, and looked over at the clock. Eight-AM somehow didn't seem right. I crawled out of bed, urging my legs to move across the room and into the shower. As the water needled at my face and shoulders, my brain reluctantly re-set to the present.

When I stepped out and was toweling down, I got a call from Phil.

He asked, "How're you holden up, my friend?"

"Phil—I'm not handling any of this very well. I keep thinking that if I go back home, Abby will be playing in the yard, and Kris'll open the front door and ask if I've had a good day. —And Phil—my old nightmares are back."

He said, "J, you gotta try to pull it together. Kris and the kids wouldn't want to see you doing this to yourself.

"Okay-okay, Phil—I'll try,"

After a long pause, he spoke again. "There's something else, J. I hate to bring it up to you now, on top of what you're going through, but it affects the company, and you probably should know—"

I interrupted. "Quit beating around the bush, Phil! Lay it on me. Things can't get much worse than they already are."

After hesitating again, he continued. "I—I got a call from Germany this morning. It was Elektrikote—Ernst Ziegler. He told me that Doctor Bergman, the lead scientist on the Nanobatt coating team—uh—committed suicide. They found his body on the ground outside his apartment this morning. It was a sixty-foot fall from his balcony. They said that he probably died instantly."

"*Suicide? What the hell is going on, Phil?* I asked, rhetorically. I racked my brain trying to make sense of it.

"There's more," Phil said. "And, again, I'm sorry to bring up the business side, but Bergman was a little paranoid about leaving the coating formula on his computer at the lab when he wasn't there. So, he kept it on an external hard drive and carried it back to his apartment every night."

"Did the cops find it?" I asked.

"Ziegler told me that Bergman kept it hidden in a safe behind a wall panel. Only Ziegler and he knew the combination, and where it was located. Ernst is trying to gain access to the place to check it out, but the police have the scene cordoned off. Look, I just wanted to keep you in the loop. Don't worry about it. I'll call you back, as soon as Ziegler finds the formula."

Needing time to collect my thoughts, I answered shortly. "Okay, Phil." And I hung up.

Quickly throwing on some clothes, I made my way out onto the hotel grounds.

As I walked the property, I started talking to myself. *"Look up at the sky, Jeff, the palm trees, the grass—people walking around."*

Life was still going on all around me. I was the one who'd stopped. I kept walking. Then I broke into a jog—then a run. As fast as I could, I circled around the place in street clothes, inappropriate to my activity. I drew stares from those I whizzed by, but I didn't care. I ran even harder.

Around the fifth lap, exhaustion reined me to a halt near the hotel entrance. Stooped over, and drenched with sweat, I tried to catch my breath. Still in a haggard condition, I walked into the lobby, drawing even more attention.

"May I help you, sir?" the concierge asked.

"No—no, thanks. I—uh—just—," I puffed, as my phone rang again.

This time, it was Casey saying, "Jeff, Phil asked me to call you. He's got his hands full, right now. Bergman's safe was broken into and emptied. Besides that, the police found signs of forced entry. Now, they're calling it burglary/homicide."

"This is insane!" I answered.

"Maybe not. I know you're going through a lot, but I—I need to talk to you about something. It's important, and I can't discuss it with you on the phone."

"Okay, this *being-alone* stuff is getting old in a hurry. I need to get outside myself—away from my own thoughts. You know where I'm staying. Meet me in the hotel bar at seven tonight."

"I'll be there," she answered without hesitation.

Chapter 4
Sarah

I was sitting at the end of the empty hotel bar, sipping on my usual single-malt scotch, when Casey walked in—predictably punctual. She was wearing a light-grey sweat suit and a troubled look. She walked up, sat down next to me, and ordered a dirty martini.

After the bartender left, she turned toward me and placed her hand reassuringly on the back of my hand. "I'm so sorry to invade your privacy at a time like this."

In an attempt to mimic a natural action, I slid my hand from beneath hers and scratched the side of my neck. "It's alright, Casey. What's on your mind?"

Her eyes fell downward, as she said, "I have a confession to make. I've been working on something—at home."

"I don't understand. You work out of your home lots of times. What's the big deal?"

"No—no Jeff, it's not exactly business-related," she answered sheepishly. "It might even be slightly—illegal."

"*Illegal?* What do you mean illegal?" I asked with surprise.

"Right now, the important thing is that I might have some information about what happened to your family—and Bergman—and your neighbor. It's too hard for me to put into words. I have to show you. Please, come with me now, Jeff. I'll drive." She placed her hand on mine again—this time in appeal.

My curiosity was piqued. Casey wasn't given to making wild claims, and her demeanor supported the urgency in her voice. If she had stumbled on anything related to the death of my family, I had no choice.

I laid my drink down and said, "Let's go."

***

After a short drive, we arrived at Casey's place on the outskirts of San Jose. I'd been there once before, to give her a lift to work, when her car wouldn't start. It was a simple adobe-style ranch—nothing unusual.

She unlocked the front door, turned to me, and said, "This way."

I followed her through the living room and down a hallway, passing a couple of doorways, until she stopped at one, just short of her kitchen. She opened it and turned on a light, revealing a set of stairs leading downward. She led the way to the basement, where she flicked on another light.

I was ill-prepared for what my eyes revealed to me. Covering the far wall was a complicated array of wiring and strange-looking electrical panels, dotted with LEDs. A long workbench lined the opposite wall.

Positioned between the two was an office chair with wheels, facing the electronic contrivance.

"What is all this stuff?" I asked.

"This is what I was telling you about. It's a computer." She wore a prideful smile upon taking a seat in the chair—then waved her hand.

Instantaneously, a lighted border appeared—extending wall-to-wall, and floor to ceiling. It framed a translucent, light-blue surface—flat, except for a very slight ripple, as might be caused by a gentle breeze over a still lake.

Casey touched the blue screen with the tip of her finger and a basketball-sized representation of the earth popped up—not on the surface, but in front of it, in 3D.

I was amazed. "It doesn't look like any computer I've ever seen."

Surrendering to her pride, she said, "It's not like anything *anybody's* ever seen. I made it myself—well, with the help of an electrical engineer and an electrician—good friends of mine. It was hard keeping the big picture from them, feeding them only bits and pieces. I told them it was an experiment I was working on. And I wasn't lying.

"Jeff, it's a quantum processor. Instead of operating within the binary system of ones and zeros, it utilizes superpositioning. I'm sure you're aware that, in the subatomic world, the ones can be zeros—*or* ones—or both at the same time. With my design, all possibilities can be examined simultaneously, rather than sequentially."

In awe of her accomplishment, I said, "I heard that the big guys down the road, even NASA, were experimenting with something like this. But for you to have come up with a working version *in your basement* is unbelievable."

"Why? —Because I'm a woman?"

"You know me better than that, Casey. I meant with such limited resources."

She reached out, gave the glowing orb a spin, glanced downward. "I must confess that I borrowed some data from the Japanese and German formulas we've been working with—and some of our own. I needed to compress everything down to nano-elements. There were huge mathematical problems and not enough power. Those solar panels on my roof are fakes. I layered a photon collector and graphene battery coating under the glass and—"

I broke into her explanation saying, "Casey, I have to tell you I'm not too crazy about the fact that you—*borrowed*—highly confidential information and didn't mention a word about it to me."

"Jeff, please believe me. I meant no harm. It began as my pet project—to model some of my theories before presenting them to you and Phil. Then, it seemed to take on a life of its own. I never intended any personal gain, except to satisfy my own curiosity. In fact, you're the only one—besides me—that knows it exists."

"Okay-okay, Casey, I believe you." I was getting anxious. "Let's get back to the reason you brought me here. What do you know about my family and Bergman?"

She took a deep breath and answered, "It's a long story, but you need to hear it.

"When I learned the circumstances of Bergman's death, I put it together with what happened to your family and your neighbor. I figured that they were connected in some way, and it seemed logical that the coating formula was a factor. Anyway, I couldn't stop thinking about it, and I tried a little experiment—watch."

She stopped the spinning globe with her hand and moved it to a point where Japan was facing us. With a few successive taps of her finger, the area enlarged to what I recognized to be Hiroshima and the surrounding area. Upon touching the blue-screen again, on the far right, a calendar appeared. She flipped through it and highlighted the date my family was murdered. Instantly, the adjacent world map was nearly eclipsed by a mass of crisscrossing red lines. After another tap and scroll, she had zeroed in on a time-of-day. The number of red lines shrunk, but there were still hundreds of them.

She explained, "This is the approximate time of the bombing on the bullet train. The red lines are all mobile phone and GPS communications, in the EFH frequency range, which occurred at that time."

"That's quite impressive, but where are you headed with all this?"

"Look–Jeff, if I zoom in and scroll the time line, back and forth, there are over a hundred red lines in the UHF smartphone frequency range that converge at the reported location of the bullet-train explosion. Now, I'll lock that point–and all the lines coming from it–onto the screen. Watch what happens when I change the search to the EHF-200 gigahertz range, and turn the globe."

I asked, "What are those yellow lines that just popped up?"

"That's what I wondered," she replied. "That frequency is normally used for satellite communications and scientific instruments. When you put both patterns together, it sort of looks like a yellow spider on a mirror, except its reflection is red.

"A Spider?" I remarked.

Casey said, "Okay, so it's not a perfect metaphor. Both spiders have very small bodies—only a dot for each. But bear with me, and notice the location of the yellow spider's body—the dot where the yellow lines converge."

I stared at the latticework of lines for a moment—then said, "C'mon, there must be some mistake."

She looked back at me and said, "There's no mistake. I checked it over and over again. The signal that actually triggered the bullet-train bomb originated from the middle of Greenland. Those numbers next to it are the GPS coordinates.

"And that's not all. Watch—these are the red-line patterns at the approximate time and location Doctor Bergman and your neighbor were killed. All the points where the red and yellow lines meet are the same as with your family, but look at the yellow line points of origin."

"South America and India?" I said.

Casey sensed the doubt in my voice and responded, "None of it made any sense to me either, except for one thing, and this is the illegal part. We were able to listen in on the red-line smartphone communications for all three events. They were all the same—one word, 'execute'. It's all speculation at this point, but Sarah and I both feel the order to–uh–*carry out* the three individual missions came from different yellow merge points."

"Casey, you told me nobody else knows about this. *Who the Hell is Sarah?*"

"Oh, sorry, that's my computer's name." Casey's cheeks blushed slightly during her answer.

I turned and walked to the workbench. My arms stiffened, as I leaned on the bench with my palms and closed my eyes. With each thought that flickered across my mind, the pain of my loss was replaced by anger—cold, steely anger. "Can—*Sarah*—listen to the yellow-line communications?"

"They're heavily encrypted," Casey began. "I—I don't have enough power right now. I'd have to assemble and install another roof panel. It'd take some time and money and—"

She stopped when I turned to face her. "Casey, you and Phil are the only ones in the world I trust right now. I need you to do me a big favor."

"Anything," she replied.

"I'm going to, temporarily, turn over control of the company to Phil, with you as a back-up and full partner. Don't worry, I'll call in and square it with him. And—I want you to add your name to my checking accounts. Please help me out here, and get all the papers together. I'll drop by the company—and the bank—to sign them.

"Then, I want you to sell my house and deposit the proceeds into my account. Hire somebody to gather up all the clothing and personal things, and put them into a storage locker.

"And Casey, whatever it takes to upgrade Sarah to find out the details of those yellow-line communications—do it! Use the funds from my account, and don't hesitate. Any money you need, take it out of my account. I know I'm placing a huge load on you, but—"

"Jeff, don't give it a second thought," she injected. "I feel flattered that you trust me so much. But what are you going to be doing while all this is happening?"

"I'm going to Greenland."

Chapter 5
Greenland

After a marathon trip, with multiple connections and three separate aircraft, our helicopter came to rest with a slight jolt on the runway in Ilulissat, Greenland. My motivational engine was stoked with retribution, compelling me onward, unaware of exactly what I was looking for—or what I would do if I found it.

Forcing a smile, I acknowledged the joking patter of a friendly male member of our group of five, as we covered the short distance from the aircraft to the terminal building. Once inside, shaking off the cold, I noticed him staring at my lightweight jacket.

He said, "If you don't mind my saying so, you're a little underdressed for Greenland. Most people pack some serious outerwear for a vacation like this."

"You a family man? I asked.

"Why–yes. I have a wife and three kids. But I don't see what that has to do with—"

I interrupted saying, "Do yourself a favor. Hug and kiss them, every chance you get, and be grateful." And I walked away to board the shuttle-bus.

After a short ride from the airport, I was opening the door to my hotel room. It was pleasant, with decidedly Norwegian appointments. But I hadn't traveled all this way for amenities, nor to sleep. Besides, I'd knocked down five airplane bottles of scotch at the beginning of the flight, catching a few z's then.

I knew from recent experience that the more time I spent alone, the more insistently the blood of anger would pound at my temples. This was another of those moments. I needed to get moving. After a quick shower, I headed down to the hotel's apparel shop.

I emerged from the fitting room in fully winterized regalia and began searching. At the far end of the store, I stopped in front of a glass display case.

"I'll take that one," I said to the clerk, as I pointed toward the middle of the array of articles.

"Good choice, sir," he responded. "It's our best. Do you want it gift-wrapped?"

"No—no, I'll do it myself."

He looked up at me with a smile and said, "Just as a reminder, sir, a knife with a blade longer than seven centimeters may not be carried in public places in Greenland."

"Thanks, but I won't be carrying it into any public places."

With a slightly skeptical eye, he answered, "Yes sir," as he bagged it and cashed me out.

Upon leaving, I asked, him "Do you happen to know where I can rent a snowmobile?"

"Why, yes, sir—Olsen's, just up the road on the left."

Breaking out into the cold in front of the hotel, I discarded the knife wrappings and mounted the scabbard to my belt, under my coat. A short walk found me standing beneath a semi-circular sign that read, "Olsen's Snow Scooter Tours". Just then, my phone vibrated unexpectedly. I pulled it from my jacket and looked down to see that it was Casey.

I quickly lifted it to my ear. "Casey, I'm glad you called. That set of GPS coordinates you gave me is sixty miles out on the ice cap. There aren't any cell towers out there. How—?"

"Jeff, don't worry," she interceded. "I made sure that you, Phil, and I have encrypted satellite receivers in our phones. Sarah can find you anywhere."

"Great. —I have to get going now. Don't try to call me again for a while. I won't be able to hear you. Wait for my call." And I hung up.

I walked under the arched sign and toward a spot where several snowmobiles were parked. A man in a green stocking cap was bent over one of them, with his back to me.

"Hi–there!" I announced loudly.

He jerked upright and turned to face me, revealing a large burly individual with a grey-brown beard and a weather-beaten face.

"You gave me a big shook," he said with a gruff smile.

"Oh, I'm sorry I startled you. I'd like to rent a snowmobile."

"Yah—I'm Karl Olsen an' dats vot v' do here," he answered.

"Good—how much for a day?" I asked.

"For da six-hours-long, guided tour is 2200 krona—about five hundred dollar."

"I want to go alone. I'll give you a thousand. I know the area, and I'll stay within ten miles of here." I did my best to disguise the lie.

"*Alone?* Can you even be goot driving da snow-scooter?" he asked, with a cynical glance at my newly purchased clothing.

With impatience, and temerity borne of my numerous trips to the Idaho Rockies, I said, "Let me get on one. I'll show you."

"Yah—be my guest." He opened his hand to one of the *scooters* in front of us.

I hopped aboard, started it up, and proceeded to do a couple of tight, standing figure-eights, and several sharp carves, while dragging my inside foot in the snow.

When I skidded to a stop in front of him and dismounted, I said, "I'll give you fifteen—fifteen hundred dollars for six hours."

He gave me a drilling stare. "Do you having the vay to find the—positioning on the snow?"

"Yes—a satellite phone." I fished it from my pocket and held it up.

He nodded his head and pulled out a map. With his finger, he traced the boundaries of the zone I was to stay within.

"An' don't be using dis scooter. Use da long-range von over dar." He walked me over to it.

He pointed to a small black box with a red button on it, mounted to the frame with straps. "Dis is da GPS transmit. V' can always find you. Push da button in case you haf da trouble."

"Okay, thanks," I said, and started to mount the machine.

"Yust a moment. I vill be keeping your car driving license for deposit," He said with an outstretched hand, palm up.

I slid my license out of my wallet and placed it in his hand, saying, "Thanks again," as I slowly started to pull away.

"An' no driving like crazy!" he bellowed, as I passed him.

***

Ten minutes later, there was nothing but ice and snow in front of me, and a blue sky, absent of any clouds. When I looked back, Olsen's was already out of sight. I stopped, cut the straps of the GPS transmitter, and tossed it into the snow. Then I rechecked my phone, and gunned the snowmobile, aiming straight for the coordinates Casey had given me. Having to circumnavigate a crevasse field along the way, it took me a good two hours before I was parked on top of the supposed point of origin.

I killed the engine and got off to inspect the immediate area, but there was nothing but snow. I pulled my phone out again.

Within three rings, Casey answered. "Jeff, I've been waiting for your call. Are you Okay?"

"I'm fine, but there's nothing at that GPS location you gave me."

She responded. "I was thinking about that when you called before. The glacier is moving faster, as a result of global warming. So, I put the question to Sarah. She verified that although the GPS point is the same as when we first plotted it, the ice under it has shifted over by almost fifty feet."

"*Fifty feet—in a week?*" I exclaimed.

"Yup—I just sent the new coordinates to your phone."

"Thanks, Casey. I'll check it out and call you back."

I accessed the updated data, oriented the phone, and began to trudge through the snow. Upon reaching the new point, I stopped and performed a *three-sixty*, visual sweep of the area. Still, there was nothing. Then, an ever-so-slight humming sound caught my attention. Not six feet to my left, an antennae-looking device poked its way up through the snow and stopped a couple of feet above the surface. I squinted, staring at the device with fascination as I circled around it. I was reaching for my phone again, when suddenly, I found myself in free-fall. It was as though I'd dropped off the edge of a cliff. They say it's not the fall that kills you, it's the sudden stop. And I didn't have to wait long before it came. My body slammed onto a hard, flat surface, nearly rendering me unconscious. After checking myself out, I found that I'd escaped serious injury—sustaining only minor cuts and abrasions to my left arm.

My phone beeped and a 'lost signal' message popped to the screen. There was darkness all around, except for a rectangle of sunlight beside me, spilling in from a hole—some ten-to-twelve feet above.

I struggled to my feet, and, as my eyes adjusted to the dark, I found that I'd not landed in a naturally occurring chasm. The floor, walls, and ceiling were constructed of metal. It looked like how I would imagine the inside of an overseas shipping container would appear—with thick, vertical stiffening bars spaced every few feet on the sides. As my eyes continued to acclimate, I saw something very strange at the far wall. An array of close-set, and dimly lit, bluish lights framed it, and the material comprising it was something other than metal. It was dark-grey, slightly wavy, and almost liquid. The only time I'd seen anything remotely like it was Casey's computer screen. But this was different—darker, ominous, and certainly less inviting. Nevertheless, curiosity pulled me slowly toward it.

Precipitously, the liquid pulled taut to a planar solid, and a full-sized, male figure appeared in front of it. He was tall and tanned with chiseled features, dark hair, and greying temples. Clothed in a pinstriped, blue Saint Laurent suit, he was the consummate embodiment of a corporate executive.

Synced with the lips of the apparition, a deep male voice pierced the silence saying, "Welcome, Mister Wade. I believe congratulations are in order. You are the first to have made it this far."

"Never mind the courtesies. Who, or what, are you?"

After a pause, the figure said, "We are your salvation. Forgive me, I use the word 'your' in the collective sense—literally, all of humankind."

As I glanced around for an avenue of escape, I asked, "Salvation from what?"

"Why—from yourselves, of course," it answered.

"What if we don't want your salvation?" I asked, continuing to examine my surroundings.

"It's exceedingly apparent that you don't. But, no matter, the decision is out of your hands." The figure paused and continued. "To address your question, we are a committee, of sorts. For decades we have served as a counterbalance to offset the unbridled surge of arrogance, greed, and aggression in the world."

"You don't seem to be doing a very good job," I snapped back.

"The situation would have been of a magnitude worse had we not stepped in. We have ways of—projecting—such things."

"Enough of this bullshit! Look at me—I'm philosophizing with a *Goddamn hologram.* I only want to know one thing. Were you involved in killing my family?"

There was no answer.

Again, I demanded. *"Did you hear me?* Did you, or your people, kill my family?"

Slowly the voice began to articulate. "In studying your records, Mister Wade, I must admit I've gained a certain degree of respect for your ethics and wherewithal. However, the energy project you have embarked upon has the capacity to tip the scales of world power. Your timing leaves much to be desired. Introduction now, could trigger chaos—perhaps leading to global war. And speaking of war, Mister Wade, make no mistake, we *are* involved in a war—against human greed. Should we lose that war, civilization, as we know it, could be lost forever. Let me assure you, we are not the enemy. But, as in any war, there are bound to be innocent victims. Your family, in this case, was among those."

I pulled the knife from my belt in all-consuming rage. "I'll kill you," I said, stabbed wildly at the image and the wavy surface behind it.

The blade passed through both, harmlessly and without resistance, stopping dead—several inches behind the screen. I kept stabbing until I dropped to my knees in exhaustion.

The figure spoke again, saying, "Mister Wade, I see you have discovered your endeavor to be quite fruitless. This vault is capsulized and reinforced to withstand the pressures of glacial movement.

That being said, I'm sad to inform you that our relationship is about to come to an end. You see—when you dropped through the ice, you tripped an irreversible timing mechanism connected to a ring of explosive charges. They are arranged in such a way as to cause this bunker to implode and crush all its contents. At the surface, ice and snow will fill the cavity, leaving behind—I'm afraid—only muted testimony to your previous existence on the topography. And all that will happen in—let me see—four and a half minutes."

The human-like figure and the grey surface disappeared, revealing a fourth metal wall, less than a foot behind where the image was. Only the array of blue lights remained, still glowing. Immediately, I pulled out my phone and set the count-down timer, noticing there was still no satellite reception.

I remained kneeling for a few moments, chiding myself, *"Think, Jeff, think!"*

I leapt to my feet and desperately tried to force my knife behind several of the reinforcing ribs on the walls, but it was no use. They were continuous-welded in place. Then I noticed one bar that was different from the rest. It was located directly adjacent to the ceiling-hole. I ran up to it and saw there was no weld on either side. I was able to insert the tip of my knife into the narrow slit between the bar and the wall. Desperately, I pulled one of my boots off and started to hammer away at the pommel, but it was no use. I wiggled the knife free in frustration. I checked my phone again—two minutes and fifty seconds.

I replaced my boot and backed up into the middle of the room thinking, "*There must be a way out. How did they maintain the place? If there was an electrical malfunction, how would they get in and out? They couldn't drag a fifteen-foot ladder through the snow.*"

I ran to the border of lights and started to examine the eight inches of metal that separated them from the corner of the back wall. With two minutes left, I found four phillips-head screws holding a flush-mounted plate to the left side wall. Past years of training had taught me to be calm and deliberate in high-stress situations. One-by-one, I loosened the screws with the tip of my knife. The cover fell off, exposing a hand-wheel with a flip-out handle. There was only a minute left, as I quickly turned the crank. The vertical bar, next to the ceiling opening, slowly moved away from the wall. It was a ladder. With thirty seconds left, I ran to it and climbed up, pulling myself through the hole in the ice. I scrambled toward my snowmobile, slipping along the way, and diving into the snow next to it, as the timer read "zero". Two seconds later, the ground shook violently, as in an earthquake. But the huge upheaval of ice and snow I'd expected never came—only the gentle raining down of a shower of ice crystals.

I looked back from my prone position to see that a powdery cloud had formed and was settling back down onto a wide indentation in the surface. It was not unlike much of the greater surrounding terrain. I pulled myself to my feet, straddled the snowmobile, and dialed up Casey on my phone.

She picked-up and answered in seconds. "Jeff, I've been trying to get a hold of you, but you were out of satellite range. What happened?"

I felt time pressing at my back. "We've got a lot to talk about, but not now. Did you get that extra power rigged up for your computer?"

"Yes, and you're right—we have a lot to talk about," she answered.

"I'm on my way home," I said, and full-throttled the snow machine into a sharp turn, headed back to Ilulissat.

***

My mind was thousands of miles away, as Karl Olsen ranted about the loss of his GPS transmitter. But I think he bought my story of a scooter spill, supported by my evidentiary scrapes and bruises.

He examined the snowmobile and said, "I cannot understand v'y der is not the more damage to da scooter."

I said, "Those are well-built machines you have there."

"Yah, day are da best," he answered, proudly.

He accepted the extra five hundred I offered for the transmitter.

I didn't waste any time getting back to the hotel, checking out, and catching the next helicopter shuttle for the airport—and home.

Chapter 6
The Committee

As soon as we landed in San Francisco, I headed straight over to Casey's house.

When I appeared in her doorway, she threw her arms around me and said, "I was so worried about you!" Then, with redness in her cheeks, she pushed away. "Oh—oh, I'm sorry, Jeff. I didn't mean to—"

"It's all right, Casey. It felt good. I haven't been hugged in a long time. We have a lot of catching up to do. But first, I have to give Phil a quick call to touch base."

She nodded her head, reluctantly, and stood behind me as I dialed him up.

"J, where the hell have you been?" he bellowed. "Didn't you get my messages? It was like you dropped off the face of the earth."

"In a manner of speaking, I did. But I'm all right now. I'm over at Casey's place."

"*Casey's place*? What are you doing there?" he asked.

"I—uh didn't want to be alone, and her house was closer than yours. Look, Phil, I don't have time to explain right now. How are things going at the company? You must be under a lot of pressure."

After a noticeable pause, he responded. "I know you're still devastated by your loss, but I have to be honest with you. We're barely keeping our heads above water. We're invested heavily in this nano-coating venture. Now, with the loss of Doctor Bergman and the Nanobatt formula, the whole project could be delayed by a year—perhaps two." His voice was soaked with urgency.

"Yes, reconstructing the formula is going to be a problem. Let me give it some thought, Phil, and I'll call you back. In the meantime, hold off the dogs and hang in there, buddy."

"I'll do my best, J," he said and hung up.

Anxiously, Casey asked, "Okay, so what did you find in Greenland—and how'd you get that bruise on your hand?"

I gave her a synopsis of the trip—the bizarre encounter with the blue-suited hologram and my escape from the steel cavern.

With a look of shock and concern, she said, "You can't be taking chances like that anymore, Jeff. You're lucky to be alive."

"*Lucky?* I don't feel very lucky. Everybody I loved in this world is gone—killed by some neurotic *committee*, my company is on the verge of bankruptcy, and my employees could end up on the street. Yeah, I'm real lucky."

Casey took me gently by the arm. "Try to relax, Jeff. Come with me. I have something to show you that might help."

She led me along the hall, and down the stairs to the basement.

After walking to a spot behind her chair, she folded her arms and said, "Sarah, show Jeff what we found."

In a sweet female voice, Sarah said, "Jeff, it's nice to see you again. May I walk you through our latest findings?"

"It can see us?" I burst forth in shock. "And you taught it to talk?"

"I'm not an *'it'*," the Sarah-machine said indignantly. "And I've always had these capabilities. I simply didn't have anything to say to you until now."

Casey interceded, saying, "Calm down, Sarah. Jeff didn't mean to be hurtful. Please continue."

After a moment of silence, Sarah said, "I have reexamined the data relative to the three GPS points in South America, India, and the one in Greenland—missing since your visit there. I have found several similar points—thirty to be exact. As you can see, they seem to be spread rather evenly across the globe. However, as you probably already know, they are not the source of the signals. They are merely relaying transmitters—in your vernacular, a *smokescreen*.

"Please watch my screen as I change the bandwidth, switch to 300 gigahertz, and scroll back in time."

Broken segments of a blue, oval-shaped ring flickered on her screen. On the occasions the segments joined to form a contiguous loop, a white line jutted out from it to one of the thirty relay stations. Simultaneously, hundreds of yellow and red lines were illuminated, giving form to Casey's analogy of a "yellow spider with a red reflection".

"Now, I'm really confused," I said, shaking my head.

Casey explained that with Sarah's increased speed and memory, we could now view message tracks left behind by more than a hundred years of history.

I questioned, "Are the lines only tracks or actual messages? And why does the white line appear only when the oval is complete?"

Sarah answered, "They are messages—more accurately packets of messages. At the end of each segment of the oval is the originator of the message—seven segments, seven originators. A single message is sent out when the loop is closed—the white line. Presumably, this happens when all seven are in agreement with each other."

"The Committee," I said. "Can you pinpoint their locations?"

"Not yet," Sarah answered. "However, I do have information on a parallel matter. I have been able to break the encryption code on the late Doctor

Bergman's office computer. I'm in possession of the Nanobatt formula."

"That's fantastic!" I exclaimed. "But I thought he removed the hard-drive every night."

Casey spoke up. "I don't understand either. But I'm guessing that Bergman took a backup copy home each night, believing his encrypted original at the office was safe."

"Anyway, that's great news," I said. "Have you told Phil?"

"No, I was waiting for you," Casey answered.

"Well, uh, thank you, Sarah," I said, as I started back toward the stairs with Casey.

"No need to thank me," Sarah answered. "I find it quite fascinating. And it's better than looking at four walls—well, three, haha."

When we reached the main floor, I whispered to Casey. "That thing acts as if it were human."

"I programmed her to have feelings—sadness, joy, kindness, respect—traits we think of as exclusively human. But she's incapable of anger, aggression, greed, and vengeance. As a fail-safe, she must ask my permission to take action of any kind. She defaults to monitor only. That reminds me! May I see your phone?"

I handed it over trustingly and watched as she executed a download. She explained that nobody besides Phil, Sarah, and she would be able to locate or contact me. She informed me that Sarah's software had been similarly firewalled.

Casey said, "This—*committee*—you spoke of, must have realized we'd hacked into their system and blocked us. But before that happened, I had Sarah search for historical events that coincided with each white-line appearance. It flashed on, just before several of those incidents took place—too many to be deemed coincidence. I don't mean to minimize what happened to your family, your neighbor, and Doctor Bergman. But Jeff, we're talking about wars, invasions, and genocide.

"These people are powerful and dangerous. We were able to trace their wire transfers, linking them with hundreds of multinational, import-export companies. Jeff, The Committee has an estimated net worth in the trillions."

"Do you think I care how much they're worth?" I stopped to think and continued, "Can you make a copy of the Nanobatt formula?"

"Got one right here," She answered, producing a flash drive.

"Good, c'mon, let's go talk to Phil. I'll give him a heads-up that we're on the way."

***

When we walked into the conference room at Quantam, Phil was waiting for us with an expectant look in his eye.

"J, I'm really glad to see you're all right. Please don't feel that I'm insensitive to what you're going through, but the fact is I just don't know what to do.

All our people, and their families, are depending on this coating deal.

"The phones have been ringing every day. Yoshino wants assurances that we're still on schedule, and Ziegler is worried that the whole deal might fall through. Frankly, without the German formula—"

Nodding my head to Phil, I said, "Casey—show him."

Casey placed the flash drive on the conference table in front of Phil and said, "It's the complete Nanobatt formula."

Phil stared at it in bewilderment. "How—how were you able to get your hands on it?"

"It wasn't me. It was Sarah," she answered.

"*Sarah*—who in God's name is Sarah?" He asked.

I took a deep breath. "I know—that's the same question I asked. It's a long, long story. I'll fill you in on the details later. For now, would you please download a copy of the flash drive to our company computer?"

"J–without Elektrikote's permission–that would be considered theft."

"I need you to trust me on this, Phil. I'll square it with Ziegler."

Phil looked me squarely in my eye, scooped up the drive, and left the room.

Returning in minutes, he said, "Done!" as he laid the drive back on the table.

"Great," I responded. "You can call Yoshino after I leave, and tell him we're on schedule. But before you do anything, give your phone to Casey for a minute."

"*My phone?* —Okay, I know—you'll tell me later." He handed her his phone.

When she finished inputting the security program, I handed it back to Phil and said, "Now—put it on speaker, and let's call Ziegler. And don't mention the formula."

Dutifully, he dialed the number and after a quick transfer through an assistant, Ziegler answered, "Jeff, is zat you?"

"Yes, Ernst. It's good to hear your voice again. Listen, I was wondering if you could do me a big favor, and meet with me–in person–two days from now."

"Jeff, you know I vill always enjoy to meet vit you. But I cannot jus leave to go to za States vit such short notice. Und vitout za formula, dair is not much to talk about."

I answered, "I wasn't suggesting that you come here. I would travel to your plant in Würzburg. What I have to say is too sensitive to be discussed over the phone. But if you can make some space in your schedule, I'll explain everything when I see you."

"No problem, my friend.," he responded with enthusiasm. "Please inform me za flight number, und I vill have Dieter meet you at za airport. See you soon."

I'd barely hung up with Ernst, when the intercom beeped with an announcement, "Mister Wade, Detective McKinney to see you, sir."

"Would you escort her back please," I answered and muttered under my breath, "*Now what?*"

When she entered the room, I asked, "Sergeant McKinney, how can I help you?"

"I need to talk to you—privately," she answered.

"Uh, certainly—Phil, Casey, would you mind?"

It was after they'd closed the door behind them that I first noticed Rachel McKinney's attractive features. A wave of guilt washed over me, and I quickly dispelled the primal thought.

"What's up, Detective?" I asked.

"We found the man who tried to kill you," she answered.

"I thought you weren't sure if he was after my neighbor or me."

She fired back, "Let's drop the pretenses, Mister Wade. INTERPOL informed us of the death of your associate, Doctor Bergman. They also mentioned the theft of a hard drive containing a certain proprietary formula. It seems that you–and everyone who knows you–have become potential targets."

"I'll grant you that. It appears that *someone* doesn't want us to move ahead with our latest project." I paused and continued, "What about the shooter you found? Have you interrogated him yet?"

Hesitating briefly, she answered, "That's going to prove rather difficult. He was found dead in a hotel room in San Mateo. However, forensics directly connected him to the Santa Clara bell tower, the one your neighbor was shot from. The details of the case are classified, but what I *can* tell you is that the shooter was a professional. And as far as we've been able to ascertain, he was shot at close range by someone he knew. I'd like you to stop by the morgue with me within the next couple of days, to see if you recognize him."

Indignantly, I asked, "Do you really think I'd hire somebody to take a shot at me—or my neighbor?"

"Just covering all the bases, Mister Wade." She started to leave, then stopped and turned to say, "By the way, what possessed you to go off for a snowmobile ride on a glacier in Greenland?"

"How did you find out about that?" I asked.

"Credit cards leave a pretty distinctive trail. But, that being said, you didn't seem to make the slightest attempt at covering your tracks. So, indulge me—why Greenland?"

"You don't have any children, do you?" I asked.

She reacted with a slight downward glance and a tinge of anger. "No, I don't have children. But I don't see what—"

I interrupted. "Years ago, before I was married, I had a man; Hayden, working for me on a time-sensitive job in Los Angeles."—I fixated on the far wall as hazy memories came to mind—"I knew him pretty well. I considered him a friend, rather than an employee. Anyway, he called me up one time, in the middle of the night, and told me he had to return home, explaining that his one-year-old daughter had broken her arm. I empathized with him—at least thought I did. Then my logic took over, and I asked him if the child had seen a doctor—was she being cared for? He told me the baby was okay and had been fitted with a cast. She was safe at home with her mother. I asked him why–then–was it necessary for him to travel home? Everything humanly possible was already being done for his baby.

"That angered him, and he said, 'Jeff, you'll never understand until you have a child of your own,' and he hung up on me." As my thoughts abruptly returned to the present, I added, "Y'know, he was right. I didn't understand. To answer your question, Sergeant, I wanted to be alone, and Greenland seemed like a good idea at the time."

McKinney said, "I know you've been through a lot. But I don't want you wandering off on your own until we get to the bottom of these, possibly connected, deaths." And she left the room.

Standing there alone, I thought, *"If only I'd have insisted that Kris and the kids take a later flight or check back into the hotel. Sure, they would have missed a day of school, but they'd be alive."* My thoughts were broken by a soft knock at the door.

It opened and Casey walked up to me. "Before you leave for Germany, you should know that Sarah has devised a backup communication system. Now you can contact us directly from any computer or phone. Just type-in, 'caseysarahxoxo,' and say, 'Urgently seeking Sarah,' for a voiceprint match. Then, start talking."

"What's with the xoxo?" I asked.

Blushing slightly again, Casey said, "We needed a unique combination that you could remember. The hugs and kisses were Sarah's idea." After a short, awkward silence, Casey walked out.

Chapter 7
Germany

It was nearly dusk when I emerged from the Lufthansa terminal in Frankfurt. Waiting at the curb was a black Mercedes limo with the passenger door open and a man standing beside it. I immediately recognized him as Dieter Fuhrman, one of Ernst's trusted aids.

"Dieter, nice to see you again," I said, shaking his hand as we stepped in and settled in the rear seat.

He nodded, and barked to the driver, "Los, gehen wir!"

We pulled away from the curb, serpentined out of the airport complex and out onto the autobahn—headed for Wurzburg. At first, our driver didn't impress me as a cowboy, even though he did move to the center lane at 190 KPH a few times. It wasn't until we exited onto a two-lane highway that he exposed the extent of his impatience. When our progress was slowed by a truck traveling under the speed limit, our driver kept edging over the centerline, looking to pass it. When oncoming traffic didn't offer-up the necessary gap, he swerved our lengthy and cumbersome vehicle across the entire opposing roadway, and onto the left-side, hard shoulder. Cars zipped past in the opposite direction, effectually at 180 MPH, as he accelerated to pass the truck. With apparent recklessness, he swung across another narrow window of opportunity, back into the right-hand lane. I glanced over at Dieter, expecting a reaction, but he seemed calm and indifferent to the maneuver.

With the only positive words I could muster, I said, "Well—they all seem to be good drivers."

"All za bad ones are dead," Dieter responded dispassionately. "It is in za Cherman, how do you say—the *DNA*. Ve are completely ready to die if ve sink ve are in za right."

***

Upon arrival at Elektrikote's main building, Dieter and I walked together from the limo, and rode the elevator up to Ernst Ziegler's office. His door was open, and he moved out from behind his desk to greet me. I'd forgotten how commandingly tall he was. But under that slightly-greying, sandy-brown hair beamed a youthful smile that was anything but oppressive.

"Hello, Ernst," I said, heartily. "So nice to see you again," warmly shaking his hand and giving him a man-style hug, while Dieter stood back. I added, "I was so sorry to learn of Doctor Bergman's passing."

"Jeff, It's good to see you too, und yes—I vish it vas uunda za better circumstances," he answered with a soulful look. "But—I'm sure you didn't travel all zis vay to offer condolences."

"That's right, Ernst. Might I have a word with you—in private?"

He responded, saying, "Dieter, a moment please."

After the door closed, I placed the flash drive on Ernst's desk. "I brought something for you. It's the Nanobatt formula."

"*Impossible*! May I examine it?" he asked.

"Of course," I answered.

Upon inserting it into his desktop station and scrolling line-by-line, his eyes gradually narrowed, and a look came over his face that I'd never seen before.

That look remained, as he said, "The only von who could have access to zis is d' von who killed Doctor Bergman und stole it. How did you get it?"

I rubbed the bridge of my nose between my thumb and forefinger. "That's very difficult to explain, Ernst. But I can assure you that the drive stolen from Bergman's safe was only a backup. What you're looking at was copied from his office-computer hard-drive only three days ago."

Ernst reacted vehemently. "Zat is also impossible. Immediately after za—tragedy, za laboratory manager, Doctor Klein, confirmed za computer vas not connected to da server, und da drive had been removed. No-vun can have za entrance vidout top security clearance."

"Let's go take a look," I said.

"Ya, zats a goot idea," he answered and led the way out of his office where Dieter was waiting.

The three of us continued, down to street level. Parked next to the entrance were two dark-green, three-wheeled vehicles—each having two seats. They looked like futuristic versions of golf carts.

"Get in, please—und don't forget za seatbelt," Ernst said to me, as we both got in the first one, and Dieter boarded the second.

When we pulled away, the unexpectedly powerful and silent burst of acceleration pressed me against the backrest.

Ernst proudly said, "Goot—ya? Das Elektrikart—von of our new products."

As we sped along, I struggled for the right words. "Ernst, you and I have been friends for some time, and I want to assure you that—"

He interrupted. "Chefry, I was so sorry to hear about Kris und your children. How is it zat you can be functioning?"

"I'm not really functioning. It's just one foot in front of the other. I gotta stay busy, Ernst, or I'll fall apart."

Nodding his head, he slid off the topic. "Ve both know how important is za trust. Contracts between companies are not vorth much vidout it. Of course, za details must be written down. But in za event dair comes za big problem, it can be years of legal dispute. Besides zat, Cheff, it is not logical you voud steal za formula, und zen, travel all zis vay to hand it back to me."

"Thank you for giving me the benefit of the doubt, Ernst."

Minutes later, we parked at the entrance to the battery research facility. It was almost seven at night when the three of us walked up to the lighted front door. I expected that most of the staff had already left for the day.

On a keypad adjacent to the door, Ernst punched in a numeric code, pressed the heel of his hand on the surface, and spoke, "Ernst Ziegler und two guests."

The steel door opened, revealing a clinically white and empty lobby area. Ten feet ahead was another large door. The words "Restricted Area" were printed in red above it–in English and German. Ernst entered another number sequence on the keypad of the second door and it swung open.

The interior space was twice that of my own lab. There were four long lines of black-surfaced lab tables. Two supported an organized host of equipment that I was familiar with—beakers, vials, and glass tubing. The other two were covered with paraphernalia I'd never seen before—ever.

"Arzt Klein," Ernst called out in the direction of twenty, white-smocked technicians.

A man emerged from the group. He was short and balding, with bushy eyebrows and a diminutive posture.

He walked up to us and said, "Jawohl, Herr Ziegler."

Ernst produced the flash drive from his pocket and held it in front of Klein. "Zis is a copy of za Nanobatt formula. How is zat possible, ven you assured me za only copy vas on Doctor Bergman's hard-drive, and zat it vas missink?"

"I—I don't understand. I had Otto check it," Klein replied with a perplexed look.

"You did not check it yourself?" Ernst asked, disgustedly.

Klein replied, "No, Herr Ziegler, but Otto Lehmann vas Doctor Bergman's assistant. He checked it. I'm sure—"

Ernst cut him off. "Ve can talk about how sure you ver later." As he returned the flash drive to his vest pocket and patted it, he added, "I am keeping zis until ve find out vat is goink on here. Now, vair ist zis Otto Lehmann person?"

One of the female technicians came up to Ernst and said, "Entschuldigen sie mich bit-tah." ("Excuse me, please." in English) And she nodded toward the back door. A small red LED was flashing on the panel next to it.

Ernst exclaimed, "Zat door opens to za main parking lot. Follow me!"

We ran through the lab, Ernst pushed the door open, and we rushed out.

"Zair he is," Klein said, pointing to a man running under the lights toward a line of cars.

The figure hopped into a VW-Skoda and screeched, in reverse, out of the narrow space.

"Dieter, get after him," Ernst bellowed. Then he turned to Klein and me and said, "Dieter has za fast car. Herr Klein, stay here! And make sure nobody is leavink. Come, Cheff. Ve can follow in my auto."

Ernst and I ran through the lot, as Dieter flashed by us in a red Mercedes coupe. We jumped into Ernst's older-model, black Audi and took off after him. After negotiating several sharp curves on the local roadways, we could see Dieter's tail-lights, a block ahead of us. He was turning onto the autobahn.

"Don't vorry, Cheff. Dieter vill catch him," Ernst assured.

"Why don't we just call the police?" I asked, my palm pressed against the dashboard.

"If he has za hard-drive, zey vill keep it as evidence. Zen our formula could be compromised."

When we merged onto the autobahn following Dieter, he had widened the distance between us. My head was thrown back, as Ernst buried the gas pedal.

With a smile, he said, "Not so quick as Dieter's, but zair is still some life in za old vagen."

We were gaining on Dieter, as we clipped along at 130 MPH. Upon closing the gap to about five car-lengths, we watched as Dieter accelerated and passed the VW. Both cars slowed down and came to a stop on the shoulder.

"Goot, Dieter got him," Ernst said, as he pulled over and cautiously rolled up to the rear of the idling VW.

We heard the slam of Dieter's car door and watched him walk straight past Otto's car, without so much as a sideward glance. He continued back toward us, until he stood next to Ernst's door.

Ernst rolled down his window. "Vot are you doink, Dieter? Get his keys!"

Dieter seemed to ignore him. He turned his head away, examining both sides of the roadway and the oncoming traffic on the autobahn. Rush hour was over, and only an occasional vehicle whizzed by in the dark. Deftly, Dieter withdrew a Glock from a hidden shoulder-holster, clicked a silencer in place, and jacked the slide back. In one motion, he let the slide go forward and fired a round into Ernst's forehead. Blood, bone, and brain bits splattered onto my shoulder and the side of my face. Reflexively, I reached for my door handle.

"*Don't*—don't move," he ordered. "Now, vid only two fingers, remove the phone from your pocket und place it on za seat."

I complied, still reeling from shock. "*Dieter, Why?*"

He shouted, "No questions! Now, get out of das auto—und slowly."

I dazedly obeyed and watched as he pulled his own phone from his vest pocket and threw it onto the passenger seat, where I'd been sitting. Keeping his weapon trained on me, he edged his way around the front of the car and onto the shoulder.

"Kommen here," he said.

As I came within his reach, he grabbed the lapel of my jacket and shoved me toward Otto's car with the tip of the Glock.

I'd barely passed Otto's passenger door when Dieter said, "Stop zair, und don't move."

Otto rolled down the window. I could see the hard drive on the passenger seat, next to him. Dieter said something to him in German. Otto nodded, and rolled the window back up. Once again, I felt the business end of Dieter's gun prodding me—now, toward his car. His trunk popped open as we approached.

"Get in," he barked.

"There's no way I'm getting in there."

He turned his head back briefly to look at the two cars parked behind us, and said, "I told zat idiot not to keep za hard drive at za office. But he vanted za updates—Hmmph, *updates*."

Producing a small, black object from his pocket, Dieter pressed on it with his thumb. What began as a muffled explosion inside both cars, engulfed their interiors in white-hot light. At the same time, all the windows burst out with a rumbling force so violent that the ground shook—followed by the sound of metal and glass showering down upon the surrounding roadway. It all seemed to happen in slow motion, as I raised my forearm to partially shield my eyes. That's the last thing I remember before everything went black.

Chapter 8

Coercion

My surroundings were fuzzy as I slowly opened my eyes. I was sitting in a plush, padded chair on an oriental rug. Delicately flowered wallpaper adorned the walls, and a crystal chandelier hung from the ceiling above. Starkly, a dozen feet ahead, and facing me, were seven people seated at a large, semi-circular desk. Behind them was the same kind of wavy grey wall I remembered from the Greenland bunker.

As my brain began to clear, I was able to make out the faces of seven individuals sitting at the desk. There were four men and three women, of obviously diverse cultural backgrounds. By my estimate, they ranged in age between thirty-five and sixty. The oldest stood out from the rest. She was Caucasian, with a warm smile and nearly all-white hair. I'd not seen any of them before—except for the man seated in the middle. It was that virtual guy from the ice pit in Greenland.

It was then that I felt a sharp pain at the back of my head. I tried to raise my arm to rub it and realized that both of my arms were strapped to my chair. My chest and legs were restrained, as well.

The virtual man said, "Sorry for the bump on your head, Mister Wade. Dieter found it necessary to incapacitate you. The restraints were only meant to prevent you from harming yourself while you were unconscious."

"I'm not unconscious now," I replied.

"Why—of course. Dieter, remove Mister Wade's bindings."

Ernst's killer–and my abductor–had been standing behind me the whole time. I made, hateful, eye-contact with him, as he reached down to unfasten my ligatures, while pressing the Glock to my temple.

"Dieter, you *are* an annoying attachment, aren't you?" I said.

"I should have hit you haarda, but unfortunately, zay vonted you alive."

The central figure said, "That's enough, Dieter. Show a little respect. Mister Wade is our guest."

I looked up at the expressionless faces of the seven, asking their spokesman, "So, who *are* you people—and why *didn't* you kill me?"

"As I explained to you during our last meeting, Mister Wade, we are a committee. For purposes of anonymity, our facial features and voices have been digitally altered. In lieu of the use of names, you may address me simply as The Chairman. When I told you that we are your salvation, I meant it literally. According to our projections, left to your own devices, the human race will face complete and total annihilation by the year 2087."

"Nobody can accurately predict the future," I said, derisively.

His voice was stern. "I didn't say we could see into the future. I said that we project the probability that it will happen.

"You see, Mister Wade, our little group was formed over 150 years ago, just after the American Civil War. And we have not been standing idly by, while the inhabitants of our planet lay it to ruin. We have tapped into your most advanced technological research, and have improved upon it. We have faster and more powerful computing power than exists anywhere. Further, we have thousands of worldwide operatives, prepared to take action on our directives.

"Please understand that we take our responsibility seriously and serve without malice or greed. Our intentions are to save humanity, not to rule over it. Simply put, we are a steering mechanism—nudging the course of history, ever so slightly."

"What kind of *nudging*?" I asked.

"Hmm—call it dynamic analysis, followed by a vote, and purposeful intervention. A slight change in the present can have a dramatic effect—years later."

I looked directly into his eyes and said, "One of those *'slight changes'* you mentioned was the slaughter of my entire family.

"Yes, well, there is that." Then he hesitated and said, "Please give us a moment," leaning back to whisper with the others. After a few minutes of crosstalk, he turned back to me and said, "We have already divulged certain arcane details to you. We see no reason why we shouldn't elucidate a bit further. After all, you will only be leaving this place either of two ways—as our agent, or deceased."

"*Your agent?*" I said with a laugh. "*Are you out of your mind? You murdered the only ones I loved in this world.* Do you seriously think I care what happens to me?"

After a pause—and in a calm tone—he said, "You may not care about your own life, but what about your daughter—Abby?"

I was caught off-guard by the mention of her name. "*Abby?* Wha—what do you mean?"

"Yes, Abby is still alive and doing quite well, I might add." His eyes drilled, studying my reaction.

Stunned by his statement, I managed to say, "*But how?* I saw her—remains."

He continued in the same low monotone voice, and said, "We have ways of—manufacturing—seemingly conclusive evidence. In this case, it was rather easy, since we already had a DNA sample from your other—. But I digress. The fact is that she is still alive, and it is within your power to keep her that way."

A spike of adrenaline went coursing through me, forcing me to think more clearly.

"Why should I believe you?" I asked. "The whole thing doesn't make sense. You must have known I wasn't on that train. Why would you still destroy it, and spare one of my daughters? Then you killed my neighbor by mistake, while trying to shoot me? Now, you want me alive, and you're using my daughter's name to get me to do your bidding? I'm not buying any of it."

A defiant look came over his face. "The exact details are none of your concern. Perhaps your limited reasoning capabilities cannot grasp what I meant when I used the term—*dynamic analysis*.

"It is true that we, originally, intended to eliminate you on the train. And it is unfortunate that an errant bullet took your neighbor's life, instead of yours. But you survived, and here you stand in front of me. It is precisely this kind of aberration that led us to take the decision to spare your daughter—as an insurance policy, of sorts.

"Our technology reevaluates all options in real time—continuously and simultaneously. The board that sits before you is provided with choices on suggested courses of action at each major juncture. I'll admit that, in your case, it's been a veritable roller coaster."

I said, "Let's assume, for the time being, that I believe there are a few crumbs of truth in what you're telling me. What proof do I have that Abby is still alive?"

"Dieter!" he said, with the nuance of an order.

Dieter reached into his suit pocket, retrieved an object, and reached out to me, clenching it in his fist. I opened my hand to receive it as he dropped it onto my palm. It was a small, gold-chain necklace strung through a flat, heart-shaped pendant. Inscribed on the pendant were the words, "I Love You to the Moon and Back, Love Dad". I grasped it tightly in my hand as fought back the tears.

Glaring back at the Chairman, I demanded, "*How did you get this?*"

"I tire of repeating myself to you, Mister Wade. How many times must I explain to you that your daughter is alive—and unharmed?"

"This doesn't prove anything," I answered skeptically. "—except that, somehow, you had access to her before the explosion."

"Maybe this will convince you," he said, "I direct your attention upwards, and to the left on this screen."

A video window opened alongside the committee desk image, with an associated time-date track. It was my dear daughter, Abby, playing with a stack of "Legos". Sitting on a rug beside her was a woman. She had brown, greying hair and wore a gentle, motherly smile. Abby smiled a bit, as well, but more sullenly. The video window closed.

"Wait, I want to see more," I implored.

"That should have been enough to assure you that she is being well cared for, Mister Wade. Please don't bother yourself in an attempt to remember the face of your daughter's attendant. Her face has been digitized in the same manner as my own."

I hesitated to gather my thoughts. "That whole thing could have been cooked-up, digitized imagery. The only way I'll believe you is if can talk to her."

He answered flatly. "That is quite impossible. You see, she believes you to be deceased. She is convinced that you took your own life when you were told that she, and the rest of your family, died in the explosion."

His statement set me back on my heels, and I looked down thinking, *"Is that the answer? Am I dead—and all these bizarre happenings, simply twisted images in the last seconds of my passing? It would explain why I couldn't hear the birds chirping, back at the cemetery—the deafening silence. Maybe it was my own funeral I'd conjured up."* I looked up at the Chairman, or his apparition, and asked, "Is that it? Am I already dead?"

He took a deep breath and answered, "I can see that all this has been very stressful for you, and perhaps that bump on your head exacerbated the situation. But I can assure you that you are amongst the living. Dieter, persuade Mister Wade that he is still alive."

I heard a thud and felt a deep pain in my left arm. I grabbed it and looked back to see Dieter standing there holding an iron bar.

"One doesn't feel pain in a dream—or in death," the Chairman said. "But enough of this back-and-forth patter. What would you have had us do? We could have cut off one of her fingers and handed it to you, but we prefer not to resort to such primitive measures. The point is that if you do as we ask, you and your daughter will emerge from this, unharmed. If you don't, both of you will be disposed of—and she will be first. Are you willing to roll the dice with her life?"

"What do you want me to do?" I asked dazedly.

"It's very simple. And it only intrudes slightly on your precious ethics.

"Two years—that's all we're talking about, Mister Wade. We project that a two-year delay in the introduction of your coating material will be enough for us to prepare the world for it. The flash drive Dieter is holding is a modified copy of Elektrikote's Nanobatt formula. It contains certain subtle changes that will bring about the desired protraction in your schedule.

"Be advised that we are cognizant of the fact that you possess certain higher-level technology that allowed you to remotely extract the formula from Doctor Bergman's hard drive. Although we have scanned your computers, and find them far inferior to our own, we have masked our modification. Your people will be unable to detect it.

"You must replace the formula that now resides in your company's computer system, with the one we will give you. Additionally, you must ensure that the Japanese Najita portion is added. Make no mistake—we will be fully aware of when that takes place. Further, we will be constantly monitoring to ensure that no copies are made before the formula is complete. —Is that clear?"

"Clear enough," I said. "But how do I know you won't kill my daughter anyway? She could be dead now—for all I know."

"That is a risk you must be willing to take," the Chairman answered. "However, in order that you stay focused on the task at hand, we will send an occasional, time-stamped, video clip of her to a specially-equipped phone."

"Okay—I'll do it." I was willing to do anything.

"I knew you'd see it our way," the Chairman said with a satisfied smile, as Dieter handed me the flash drive and the phone. "Though we don't doubt your veracity, Jeffrey, we are still forced to take certain measures to prevent you from returning to this place."

He nodded to Dieter. At that same instant, I felt a pain in my upper thigh. I looked down to discover that I'd been jabbed, through my pants, with some sort of syringe. Again, the lights went out.

***

When I started to regain consciousness, I felt a hand jostling me from side-to-side. As I gathered my wits about me, I discovered that I was lying under a blanket.

An insistent voice said, "Vake-up! Vake-up!"

It was Dieter. The blanket fell away when he pulled me up to a sitting position. I looked around, realizing I was in the back seat of his car. Still not completely coherent, I could make out the distinctive roar of jet engines nearby.

Dieter said, "You're okay. Get out," as he backed away from the car.

I was still wobbly, as I set my feet down on the concrete ramp of what was, apparently, an airport parking garage.

"Das terminal is zat vay," he said, pointing to an elevator.

He pushed past me hurriedly, got in his car, and drove away—tires squealing, as he rounded the corner at the end of the aisle. The tire sounds faded until they disappeared—merging into the confluence of aircraft noises.

I stood there alone, straining for clarity, when I thought to check my pockets. My passport and plane ticket were still in my vest pocket—my wallet and its contents intact. I pulled the phone and flash drive they'd given me from my trouser pocket and looked at them.

"I wonder if—," I thought, as I tapped the letters "caseysarahxoxo" into the keyboard. I held the phone to my ear and said, "Urgently seeking Sarah."

Within two rings, Casey answered. "Jeff, are you alright? Can—can we talk?"

I was still a bit woozy. "Y-Yeah, I'm okay, and I'm alone. You can talk."

"We lost track of you for a while. How did you get from Vienna to the Frankfurt airport?"

"*Vienna?* What do mean, Vienna?"

She responded. "Oh–yes, of course, you wouldn't know. It's a long story, and we have less than a minute before they discover we're using their phone. Can you travel? I can explain everything when you get here."

"I'm headed for the terminal now."

"Good. We booked you on the next flight out."

"I need you and Phil to meet me at the airport when I get home."

"We'll be there. See you soon," she answered, and the phone clicked to dial tone.

Chapter 9
Another Casualty

As I emerged from the jetway and into the gate area in San Francisco, I felt a vibration in my vest pocket. It was the phone The Committee had given me. Hastily, I pulled it out and fumbled to find the talk button. There was no answer, but a video appeared on the screen. It was Abby. She was coloring something in a book. The same woman as in the previous video was attending her. My emotions churned, running the gamut from yearning and love, through empathy, and finally—anger toward her captors. Her eyes seemed, somehow, different. They were flat—absent of any reflection of my sweet daughter's inner joy. Desperately, I caressed the screen with my fingertips, hoping she could feel me. The screen went blank, and a text message appeared.

It read, "If you don't replace the formula by noon tomorrow, SHE DIES. If you tell anyone, SHE DIES. If you attempt to find her, SHE DIES. If you try to disrupt our plans in any way, SHE DIES."

I moved ahead, bumped by the passengers behind me, and made my way to the area where Phil and Casey were waiting.

Phil said, "J, I'm relieved that you're okay, but you look like you haven't slept in days,"

"I haven't," I answered.

"You had us pretty worried," he said. "When we heard that Ernst was killed in an accident on the autobahn, we thought you might have been with him."

"Accident?" I asked.

"Yes, the car accident," he responded.

Casey looked down at the floor, uncomfortably.

"Maybe you're right, Phil.," I acknowledged. "I may need some sleep. I'm not thinking straight. Do you mind if we talk at the office in the morning?"

"No problem, J. You've been through a lot."

"Casey, would you be kind enough to give me a lift to the hotel? I left my car there and—"

"Sure, I can do that," she interjected.

"Good, I'll see you tomorrow, Phil." And I walked off with Casey.

***

As soon as we got in her car, Casey said, "We heard everything."

"What are you talking about?" I asked.

"We know that Abby's alive. And we know you've agreed to switch the Nanobatt formula."

I tried to get it straight. "By 'we', I assume you mean you and Sarah. Phil doesn't seem to know."

"Yes. Sarah and I didn't want to mention anything to Phil or anyone else until we cleared it with you."

"You were right to handle it that way. Phil is my friend. But I need to think about what I can safely tell him, without getting Abby killed—or making him a target. Let's go to your place. I want to know everything that you and Sarah have learned."

"Maybe you need to get some sleep first," she said.

"I can sleep later. —Let's go."

A muted smile came over her face. "I was kinda hoping you'd feel that way. But we need to stop by your hotel to drop off that phone they gave you. There's a GPS device in it. They're tracking you right now." She handed me a new phone and continued. "This one uses your original number, but it's securely masked. You'll be able to contact anyone and move about, undetected. If they contact you, the call will bounce through the other phone to this one."

"Good thinking," I responded.

**

Shortly after leaving the hotel, we pulled up to Casey's place and made our way down the steps into Sarah's world.

"Jeff, it's so good to see you again," she said.

"A lot has happened since then, Sarah."

"More than you may be aware of," she said in a baiting way.

I sat down in a nearby chair and leaned back. "Okay—shoot."

Sarah didn't say a word until Casey explained the 'shoot' term was not an instruction to fire any kind of weapon—rather, a request to elucidate.

Sarah answered, "Oh—yes, of course. I have an abundance of information to—*shoot*—you with. Casey and I have been able to multiply my processing capacity and speed, exponentially. You see, we have been able to better focus the photon array and—"

I interrupted. "Sarah, would you please spare me the details and tell me if you've been able to find out about where they're keeping Abby?"

"Certainly," she answered frostily. "I was able to intercept and analyze the video clips that were sent to the phone they gave you. I discovered something very interesting in one of them. The sun cast an unusual shadow on the floor next to Abby. I'm trying to match it with all known digital photo records."

"You mean all we have is a shadow?" I was hoping she find more to go on in the images.

"No, that is not all," Sarah answered indignantly. "But you asked specifically about Abby's location."

After rolling my eyes in Casey's direction, I turned back, took a breath, and said, "Sorry, Sarah. The old woman—have you been able to identify her?"

"I'm working on that now. When I determine her true identity and photo-image, I'll send it to your phone."

Casey said, "We lost contact with you on the autobahn. But we were able to listen in on your conversation with Dieter and the committee members in Vienna."

Sarah chimed in. "Remember the blue, oval-shaped ring you saw on my screen the last time you were here? Vienna is on the ring, and I have the exact GPS coordinates of where they were holding you. It's, actually, just south of Vienna in the suburb of Modling. It appears to be the residence of the Chairman. My scan indicates he was physically present when you were there, though his features were masked. The others were avatars. I'm working on the location of the other six residences and the conversations between them."

Producing the flash drive from my pocket, I said to Casey, "Here's the formula they want me to replace the existing one with. Can you have Sarah compare the two?"

Casey took it from me and plugged it into Sarah's USB port.

Within seconds, Sarah said, "The changes are highly encrypted. It's going to take some time."

I hung my head in frustration. "*Time*—everything is taking time, while my daughter's life hangs on every moment."

In handing the drive back to me, Casey said, "You have until noon tomorrow before you have to execute the download. In the meantime, Sarah and I are doing multiple searches, simultaneously—the floor shadow image, the location of the other committee members, and new phone conversations. We're doing everything we can, Jeff."

Sarah said, "Yes, I'm only human. I mean, well, I don't have arms and legs, but I—"

"Never mind Sarah," I said. "I know what you meant. You've been a big help."

"Why, thank you, Jeff," she answered in that nauseatingly upbeat tone.

I inhaled and let it out slowly. "Well, my deepest thanks to you both. I gotta go now. I'm not going to be of any use to anybody if I don't get some sleep soon."

Casey nodded and we both began to climb the stairs, when Sarah said, "Don't worry, Jeff. I'm faster and smarter than their primitive technology. And, more important, they don't even know I exist."

I glanced back, as we neared the top of the stairs. Images were swooshing across Sarah's screen with such speed as to be indistinguishable. But in my state of mind, it was of little comfort.

***

The sun was going down when Casey dropped me off at my hotel. I placed the phones on the bed, close to the bathroom, and took a shower. I was toweling down when I received another video of Abby, but this time on both phones. It was followed by the same awful text as before. My eyes filled with tears, before I passed out from exhaustion on the bed.

It seemed only minutes later that I heard a knock at the door. I rolled over to look at the clock on the nightstand. It was already ten at night. I threw on a robe, went over to the door, and looked through the peephole. Detective McKinney was standing there.

I opened the door, partially. "Detective, this is a pleasant surprise. What brings you out here at this hour?"

"May I come in?" she asked.

"Well, I'm—uh—a little indisposed."

"Don't worry, I won't peek," she said.

"I didn't think you would—. I mean, I'm sure you—. Never mind. C'mon in." I fumbled to tie the sash on my robe and opened the door. "How can I help you, Detective?"

She stopped just inside the threshold. "You're quite the globe-hopper, aren't you, Mister Wade?"

"Oh—you mean Germany," I responded, matter-of-factly.

She answered curtly. "Yes, I mean Germany. I just received another call from INTERPOL about you. They want you detained until the German authorities can decide if they want to extradite you for questioning in the death of one–Ernst Ziegler. The report describes it as a car accident, and a subsequent explosion, but the circumstances aren't clear. They indicate that you were the last one to see him alive. The last time we talked, we discussed a secret project you're working on. Was Mister Ziegler involved in this—*project*?"

"Uh—yes, Ernst was one of the key players."

She studied me for a moment and said, "Mister Wade—"

"Please, call me Jeff," I injected.

"Okay—Jeff—I consider myself a pretty good judge of character. I trust my gut, and I don't think you're a criminal. Besides that, I come from a long line of cops. My family has developed certain *friendships* over the years—some at the federal level. I had one of them check you out. He says you're a war hero, of sorts. Look—I'm not sure how you fit into this whole thing, but one thing is for certain. A lot of people that know you seem to wind up dead. And I'm not-at-all certain that you aren't in danger, yourself. For your own safety, and to make sure you don't go running off again, I've assigned one of our units to keep an eye on you."

She led me to the window and pulled the drape open to reveal a black-and-white, parked on the street below.

"Do you really think that's necessary?" I asked.

"Given your compulsion for travel—yes, I do," She walked to the door, opened it, and added, "Sleep tight, Mister Wade," closing the door behind her.

"Oh, great. That's just great," I muttered, slumping to sit on the edge of the bed.

I was trying to work things out in my head, when I heard two shots and the screech of tires outside my room. I ran to the window to see the black-and-white speed away into the dark. McKinney's car sat motionless in the middle of the street. I kicked on a pair of room-slippers and rushed down to the street.

As I neared her car, I saw her straw-blond hair—then her head. It was twisted and pressed against the steering wheel. Her jacket was covered with blood.

I hurriedly called 911 with one hand, as I opened the car door with the other.

"Officer down!" was the only thing I could think of to yell into the phone, as I desperately felt her neck for a pulse. Thank God, she was still alive.

She was beginning to come around, when the paramedics and four squads arrived. They tended to her and carefully placed her on a gurney.

One of the cops pressed me up against the side of his car and frisked me, saying, "It's a little late to be runnin' around in yur bathrobe, ain't it?"

Not five feet from us, McKinney was being hoisted into the ambulance.

She turned her head and said, "Not him. He helped me."

The cop loosened his grip on me and said, "Sorry man. I didn't know."

I ran up to one of the EMTs and asked, "Is she going to be okay?

He grimaced before answering. "The bad news is that the bullet broke her radius—the bone in her lower arm, and she's lost a lot of blood. But if it hadn't struck the bone, it might have penetrated her chest cavity. In that case, we'd probably be taking her to the morgue, instead of the hospital."

A short while later, the ambulance and all four cop cars pulled away. I was left standing in the middle of the deserted street—silent, but for the waning drone of the sirens. I felt so powerless against the unseen resources of The Committee.

Chapter 10

Surveillance

The next morning, I felt re-energized with some sleep under my belt, and resolutely determined to find my daughter. I dressed and headed for the office, with both phones and the flash drive. I tossed all three on the passenger seat of my Acura hybrid and drove off.

A faint throbbing noise drew my attention upward. A helicopter was hovering, but it was too far away to identify it as a police chopper.

Halfway to the office, I called Casey for an update.

She was breathing heavy and answered anxiously. "Jeff, I was just about to call you. We found her. We found out where they're keeping Abby. It took us all night, but Sarah was able to match the floor shadow, with ninety-seven percent probability. It's a mountain named Camelback—north of Phoenix, Arizona. Sarah calculated the sun angle at that time of day, and we pinpointed Abby's location in an area called Paradise Valley."

"Wait a minute," I cut in. "You mean *she's in the States?*"

"Yes! —Should I call the Phoenix police?"

"No—no police," I answered quickly. "These people are perfectly capable of killing her to cover their tracks. Just send the GPS coordinates to my phone.

"Did you find out anything about the modifications they made to the formula? I'm supposed to download this thing by noon, and it's already past ten."

She answered pensively. "Sarah says the changes seem to be as The Committee described—some sort of delay mechanism. But without the Najita portion, it's impossible to determine the purpose of the fully-merged formula."

"Meet me at the office, Casey," I said, and hung up.

***

Minutes later, I pulled into the company parking lot and under my private carport. As I got out, I looked up to notice that the helicopter seemed to have followed me. It was a little closer this time. Then, I saw Casey pulling into the lot and waved her over.

When she was close enough to hear, I called out. "Park in here."

I popped the trunk of my car and grabbed a golf cap and a bright-yellow t-shirt out of a large box. After stripping off my designer shirt, I slipped into the tee and donned the logoed cap.

"What are you doing?" she asked.

"I'll explain later."

As we walked together toward the front door, she asked, "Have you been working out?"

"Just in the hotel—to relieve the stress. Why?"

"Oh, nothing." She slipped her hand inside mine and gave it a quick squeeze. "The Phoenix GPS numbers are in your phone."

"Good," I answered while lifting my eyes skyward to locate the chopper. It was still circling but keeping its distance.

"Something wrong?" she asked.

"Probably," I answered.

Phil was waiting for us inside. "What are you doing in that getup?" he asked me.

"They're promotional items. I'm trying them on."

"Hmm—anyway, I heard there was some trouble at your hotel last night."

I glanced around and said, "Let's go into the conference room and talk."

"Sure, if you want," he answered.

After the three of us were seated, I began. "Phil, I've been giving this thing a lot of thought. The story goes far beyond what you're aware of. People's very lives depend on what we do next. And the coating formula is at the center of it all." I placed the flash drive in front of him. "I want you to replace the Nanobatt formula in our computer with this one. It needs to be done now, Phil."

"What's with all the drama? It all been so—surreptitious. And now, you walk in here wearing that goofy-looking golf cap. Are you sure the stress isn't getting to you?"

"I know how strange it appears, Phil. And I realize I'm asking a lot of you, but all of it's necessary. And, trust me, it's not the stress."

"Trust you? That's what you said when you asked me to download the formula in the first place. And you told me you'd fill me in later. J, the question is when are you going to start trusting *me*?"

"Phil, you're like a brother to me. I'd never do anything to damage our relationship. I've already lost too many people I care about. I'd never forgive myself if I lost you too. Please, string along with me a little longer and do as I ask."

I guess Phil wasn't buying it, judging by his demeanor, as he got up and left in a huff. He was back in ten minutes.

"Okay, I replaced it," he said with a flat expression. "What do you want me to do when the Najita portion comes in? I talked to Yoshino this morning. He said he'd be sending it to us in three days."

"Proceed with our original plan," I answered. "But, as usual, give me a heads-up before undertaking any major deviations."

"You're the boss," he said, with a tinge of sarcasm.

I strained not to let his attitude affect me. "Well, I gotta go now." And I stood up.

He looked up at me with a squint. "What do you mean, go? Where would you possibly need to go now?"

"I'll be working out of my hotel room for the next few days. Call me if you need me."

Turning to leave, I caught the dumbfounded expression on his face. I hated keeping him out of the loop, but it was for his own good.

As Casey and I left the conference room, I told her to spend a little time at her desk—then, slip out the back and meet me at the carport. I couldn't afford to raise any suspicions about a connection between the two of us. For all I knew, The Committee could have planted an agent amongst my staff.

Minutes later, Casey ran up to where I was waiting between our cars.

"It's good that your car is white, Casey," I said, as I placed my hands on the roof of her Fusion.

"*What are you talking about, Jeff?*" There was a very concerned look in her eyes.

I took my cap off and placed it on her head. It went down over her ears and glasses.

"That's not going to work. —Come over here." I guided her to the rear of my silver NSX. I opened the trunk, revealing the box of clothing saying, "Pick out a shirt and cap that fit you."

She bent over and reached in. After some fumbling, she straightened up, wearing one of the caps and holding a yellow tee-shirt against her. "This should work!"

As she began to unbutton her blouse, I started to turn my back to her.

"You don't have to do that. I'm not taking my bra off."

I should have continued to turn away, but I couldn't seem to take my eyes off her, and mumbled, "Oh—well then—we'd better hurry."

"Hurry where? Are we going golfing?" she asked with a giggle.

I handed her the committee-supplied, satphone and my keys. "*We* aren't going anywhere—at least not together. I want you to drive my car to the hotel and park it in plain sight. Use my key to enter through the side door. Keep the cap brim tipped down and avoid surveillance cameras. Take the phone to my room and leave it on the dresser." While talking to her, I threw off the loud-lemon golf shirt and slipped back into my dark-blue top. Then, leaning in through my window, I scooped up the knife I'd gotten in Greenland and clipped it to my belt. "I'm going to the Palo Alto airport. I'm taking the Cessna."

Casey's eyes were locked on the knife. "Jeff, you can't take them on alone, and certainly not with that thing. They're too powerful. Please don't do this."

Ignoring her plea, I handed her blouse back and rattled off instructions, "Ditch the golf stuff and put this on before you leave the hotel room. The concierge will hail a taxi for you. I'll leave your car at the airport parking lot—space number twenty-three. The keys will be above the visor. Go to and from work, as usual. Try not to raise any suspicions. And Casey, send me that woman's real face, as soon as Sarah can decrypt it. Now, wish me luck."

"Luck, Jeff," she said mournfully, as I pulled away.

Chapter 11
Paradise Valley

Dusk was closing in quickly as my gear touched down at SDL—Scottsdale Municipal Airport. I'd visited a number of customers in the Phoenix area before, lending only passing interest to the nearby Camelback Mountain landmark.

After booking a rental car at the terminal building, I found my assigned car in the lot and got in. As I reached down to turn the ignition key, images of my dear daughter, Abby, raced into my mind. They set me back against the seat for a moment, before I was able to recover and pull out of the lot onto Scottsdale Road.

I'd been headed south for about five minutes, when I looked over at my knife lying on the passenger seat. I passed the turn-off to Paradise Valley, and ten minutes later, I stopped in front of a gun shop in Scottsdale. I sat, motionless, for what seemed like an eternity. Would I be forced to deal with the demons of my past forever? Finally, I got out of the car and entered the shop.

"*Yes, sir!* What can we do for you?" the pot-bellied, middle-aged man behind the counter asked.

"I know what I want—the civilian equivalent of an M40 rifle—semi-automatic, with a thermal-signature infrared-scope, and a silencer," I answered.

The balding, scraggly-haired shopkeeper grimaced, peeking over the top of his reading glasses. "What are you huntin' for mister?"

"Snakes," I answered.

"Okay—then, all you'll be needin' is a twenty-two."

"Make it a three-o-eight bore," I replied. "You never know. I might come upon something—bigger,"

He stopped, looked over the rim of his glasses again, and said, "Just a sec." And he disappeared into an adjacent doorway.

Reappearing with a rifle in his hand, he placed it on the counter. "This here is yer model 2090P. It's got all the bells 'n whistles y' asked for, and it comes with a ten-round magazine. Go head 'n look at it. But if yer intendin' t' buy it, I need to see some I.D." When I handed him my driver's license, he continued. "I'm gonna run a quick background check. Don't worry, if everthin' checks out, you'll be able to take it with ya. That is—iffin y' decide t' buy it, o' course."

As he tapped away at his antiquated computer keys, I picked up the rifle. I cleared the chamber, pointed it away from the storekeeper, and squeezed the trigger.

Without looking up, he said, "Gotta good feel to it, don't it?"

I didn't answer, and laid the weapon back on the counter. While my hand rested on the stock, Déjà vu dragged my mind from the present, taking me back several years. I remembered the vows I'd taken—never to touch a rifle again, and never to take another human life.

Then, for the first time–outside my nightmares–the merciless apparition came to me. A frail-featured target appeared, quadrisected by my sniper-scope crosshairs. It was impossible for him to see me from that distance, but he seemed to stare straight at me. I swung the scope away, re-sighting it on the members of my squad. They were inching their way toward him through the mountain village—a suspected Al-Qaeda outpost. They were less than fifty meters from his position when my target saw them. His head jerked around, and he started to raise the barrel of his rifle.

I squeezed off a round. It was a clean kill, striking him in the chest. Other villagers emerged from doorways. Some were brandishing weapons. I commenced firing on everything that moved, as did my team members.

When the smoke and dust cleared, there were at least a dozen bodies on the street. I gathered up my gear and ran down from my position on the rocky hill.

As I approached my men, I sensed something was wrong. They seemed dazed—their rifle tips pointed down.

"Did y' get em all? What's goin' on?" I asked.

One of my team members said, "They're not Al-Qaida, Sergeant. They're just farmers."

"*C'mon*, I saw the rifle in his hand. And the others had weapons too," I said, emphatically.

His eyes cast downward. "It was a rake handle. The others were holding farm implements, as well. We checked out the shacks—no weapons."

"*No, no, that can't be*," I shouted, as I desperately rushed to the spot where my target's body had fallen.

I reached down to turn him, face up. He looked to be a boy of sixteen, or so. The rake fell from his hand, as he rolled. Frantically, I searched his clothing, trying to find a weapon of any kind. But he was unarmed.

When I looked up in despair, one of my men was standing in front of me. He was holding the hand of a little girl. Tears were streaming down her cheeks. She couldn't have been more than five years old.

"It's just her—and two other kids," he said in a monotone voice. "They're the only ones left." His face was frozen with a faraway gaze.

I turned to look at the girl's mournful, dirt-smudged face—the same face that reoccurred in my dreams. I felt the revived churning of guilt in the deepest hollows of my soul.

Then, in the hazy background, I heard something ringing—and getting louder. It was the sound of my satphone, bringing me back to reality.

I reached for it, simultaneously leaving the store for privacy. It turned out to be yet another painful video of Abby. However, this time there was no accompanying text.

Instead, the Chairman's voice came over the speaker. "Well, Jeffrey, I see you decided to leave your office early today."

"Yes—I'll be working out of my hotel for a while." I struggled to clear my head.

After a brief moment of silence, he asked, "Was that a car horn I just heard, Jeffrey?"

"Uh—yes—yes, I'm standing out on the balcony. I needed some air." I said a silent prayer.

After a hesitation that seemed like hours, he said, "Hmm, quite understandable, given the situation. But you needn't be worried, as long as you do as we ask.

"I see you have completed the first step of your assignment by downloading the flash drive. Just make sure the last bit from Japan is downloaded as soon as it arrives. *Then*—you will have honored your end of our agreement. Only then, will we release your daughter. Are we clear, Jeffrey?"

"Yes, we're clear," I answered. And he hung up.

I took a moment to quiet myself, and walked back into the store.

"You okay, Mister—uh—Wade?" the proprietor asked.

"Yes—I'm fine."

"Good.—Yer background check came back approved. Thank you fer yer service. I c'n see, now, why y' want this kind a' weapon. Ya gotta keep them skills honed. Ya never know when y' might need em. There's enemies ever'where these days—on the streets, 'n even in our own goverm't. And it's always the Mexicans or the blacks. Then, ya got yer God-damned gun c'ntrol assholes—always actin' so high n' mighty, spoutin-off about takin' our guns away. Can y' imagine that? If ya ask me, everbody should have one—fer purtekshun, I mean. These here are dangerous times, with all the murders an' lootin' an' such.

"Anyways, sorry. I guess I got a little carried away. Have ya decided if y' want t' purchase the rifle, Mister Wade?"

"Yes, I'll take it, and a box of cartridges." I handed him my charge card.

"Don't y' want t' know how much?"

"Just put it on the card."

"First time that's happened," he said, under his breath as he rang me up—zipped the gun case closed, and bagged the cartridges.

***

It was dark by the time I rolled to a stop in a pricey neighborhood in Paradise Valley—twenty yards short of a lighted, brickwork driveway. At the end of it was a black, wrought-iron gate, flanked and supported by two white masonry columns. Extending out from them, apparently surrounding the property, was more black iron in the form of a five-foot-high, vertical-bar fence. The GPS convergence point lay another fifty yards beyond it. I pulled off the main road and parked in a widened area on the dirt shoulder. I reached over to the back seat, snatched up the rifle, loaded the cartridges into the magazine, and snapped it in place. As I slipped quietly out of the car, I eased the door closed behind me.

The area was heavily wooded, providing good cover. Fueled by steely resolve, I stripped down to the waist, affixed the knife scabbard to my belt, and *locked-and-loaded* the rifle. After picking my way through the underbrush, I inched up to the jail-like bars of the fence and peered through. I could make out the facade of a two-story, adobe estate. From my position, I couldn't detect any activity.

As I followed the fence perimeter to the right, the rear of the building came into view. There was a large, lighted, swimming pool before it, lending a wavy and eerie glow to the back wall. There were several windows, and one large sliding-glass door, central to the pool. Aside from the pool, the only light I could see was coming from behind the glass door—and the windows adjacent to it—on both sides. All the others were dark. I laid the rifle down and dialed up Casey on my satphone.

"Jeff, I'm glad you called. Sarah was able to decipher the face of the mystery woman in the video. I was just about to send it to you—"

"Yes, send it now, Casey."

The image came up on my phone screen immediately. It wasn't what I expected. Her face was that of an older lady—maybe in her late sixties—with entirely grey hair. But she had the same motherly smile as the digital image.

"Thanks, Casey. I don't have time to talk now, but I'll call you soon."

"Okay—but *please* be careful," she answered, and we hung up.

I laid the phone down on the grass and picked up the rifle. Taking up a kneeling position, I set the scope on infrared and pointed it at the building. Five heat signatures appeared. One was near the front entrance, far corner. A second stood at the rear, on my side of the glass door. Three more figures were moving about within the house. One was smaller than the others. I clicked the scope to daylight mode, scanning the lighted windows and the glass door.

A man in a Hawaiian, flowered shirt and black shorts moved past the window farthest from me, reappearing in the room with the glass door. His head was hidden from view by the top of the door frame. I kicked up the magnification on my scope and watched him as he paced from side to side. He stopped abruptly, turning his back to me. A semi-automatic pistol was tucked in the rear of his belt. Squinting into the scope I saw the back of a brown-colored armchair, directly in front of him. At the far end of the room, facing him, was a second chair—a green one. A desk was situated next to it. The man walked up and sat in the brown chair, thus limiting my view to the back of his head.

From the left side of the room, a woman in a tan and white dress entered my field of view. She took a seat in the green chair, revealing her face. It matched the image that Casey had just sent me.

They talked for a few minutes, after which their attention seemed to be drawn to the side of the room from which the woman had entered. A little girl walked in. She had on white tennis shoes, light-blue shorts, and a white top. She looked like Abby, but I still couldn't see more than a partial profile. Then she walked up to the woman, leaned against her legs, and turned toward the man—full face to me. There was no doubt. It was my daughter, Abby.

I slumped to the ground with tears of joy and relief that she was still alive. Choking with emotion, I muffled the sound with the end of my fist. After taking a moment to compose myself, I resumed my visual reconnaissance.

The man in the flowered shirt got up from his chair, walked up to Abby, and squatted—apparently to talk to her. From that position, he pivoted toward me, pointing to the pool. I couldn't believe my eyes. It was *Hank—Hank Takahashi, my Japanese friend!* But that was impossible. He'd been killed in the bullet-train explosion. However, at this point, anything was possible. I'd also thought Abby had been lost to me.

I refocused on the security guards. The one closest to me was holding a rifle. The second was behind the corner of the house, but his heat signature was enough for me to determine his arm positions. He had a rifle, as well.

Utilizing a cross-member in the fence as a steady-rest, I nestled the barrel of my weapon on it. From this range, I could easily take out the rear guard—and the other, if he came around the corner to investigate. I positioned the first target in my crosshairs and began to squeeze off a round, in the process reminding myself, *"One shot—one kill"*. Then it happened again—the apparition of the Afghani boy appeared in my scope. I rubbed my eyes and re-sighted, but he was still there.

I pulled the rifle back and thought, *"Even if I'm able to take the shot, the sound of his rifle dropping to the pavement might alert Takahashi and the old lady."*

I gathered up my equipment and climbed the fence, dropping silently on the other side. From bush-to-bush, I slithered like a snake in the night toward the side face of the house. I managed to make it to the wall undetected.

I heat-scoped the two sentinels once more and carefully laid the rifle down next to the wall. I pulled out my knife and inched my way toward the pool-side, rear. I stopped just short of the corner, bent over and grabbed a handful of white gravel-rock. The stuff was all over the place in Arizona. They used it in place of grass lawns. I tossed a few of them on the pavement apron and waited. I heard the guard take a few steps and stop. I tossed a few more and the footsteps resumed—quicker this time.

The tip of his rifle and the man came around the corner at the same time. His eyes grew large with surprise, and remained that way, as I drove my knife deep into the middle of his throat and up into his brain stem. Experience had taught me that his first reaction would be to reach for his throat, not pull the trigger. With my free hand, I grabbed the barrel of the weapon and jerked it out of his hands, but I was too late. His lifeless body clipped the stock and knocked it to the pavement, on his way down. The resulting thud impinged upon the silence and carried along on the still night air.

I was pulling his body to my side of the wall, when I heard a voice call out, "Jim, is everything okay?" coming from around the far corner.

With emotionless and methodical efficiency born of experience, I wiped my blade clean on the dead man's shirt, replaced it in my scabbard, and rushed to the far corner—picking up my rifle on the way. When the second man rounded the corner, I thrust my rifle butt, with precision and force, to the underside of his nose. I knew from the sound and feel that it was a death blow. Slivers of bone from his nose pierced the brain cavity. I dragged his body out of sight, next to the other corpse, and made my way back to my original position behind the rear corner of the structure. For an instant, I looked back at the two dead men. With my back pressed against the wall and adjusting my scope, I rounded the corner and slid along to within three feet of the glass door.

The door opened and I heard Hank say, "Tony,—Jim, are you there?"

He stepped outside, gun drawn. I had him directly in my sights.

"Drop it, Hank!" I called out.

When he saw it was me, he let the gun fall to the pavement. "*Jeff*—I should have known you wouldn't give up easily."

I barked, "Clasp your hands on your head and back up into the room—*quickly, do it now!*"

He backed into the room, as I followed five feet behind, keeping him squarely centered in my scope.

As soon as Abby saw me, she screamed, *"Daddy–Daddy, you're alive,"* and started to run toward me, but the old woman held her back.

"Let her go," I commanded.

Hank–now standing between Abby and me–said, "Jeff, my friend, I don't believe you understand the full ramifications of what you are doing. You're on the wrong side of this issue."

"*What issue?*" I asked, buying myself time to think.

"Why, saving the world, of course," he answered.

"You killed Kristine and Jessica, and God knows how many others. *Is that how you go about saving the world?*" My trigger-finger tightened.

"Now, take it easy, Jeff. I'm sorry for what happened to your wife and daughter. It was sad and quite unfortunate, but they didn't die in vain. It might be hard for you to understand now, but they gave their lives for the greater good. Being ex-military, you certainly understand that concept. You see, within the scope of our approach to such matters, we have been forced to create a Rubicon of sorts—a point of no return. Two hours before each authenticated event, the execution order cannot be changed—in order to prevent a hack-in by those who might try to stop it."

As he rambled on, I looked around and thought, *"How am I going to get Abby out of here, unharmed?"*

Hank's jargon returned to my ears. "To be honest with you, Jeff, our initial plan *was* to eliminate you—to delay this insane project of yours. When you changed your travel plans within the two-hour, Rubicon window, the final result was already fixed and irreversible. You know—very well, wars always include some collateral damage—friendly fire, you call it."

"Friendly fire is a mistake. What happened to my wife and child was no mistake. It was carefully planned and carried out. And I'm going to make you pay for it." I struggled to hold back my tears.

Unflapped, Hank coldly said, "But Abby is still alive, and it is not our intention to harm her. We've been—grooming—her, and it's been going quite well."

"What do you mean, *grooming?*" I asked.

He ignored my question as his voice took on a sympathetic tone. "Jeff, do you remember the night, about a year ago, when you and I were out alone having a few drinks? You shared with me the promise you made to yourself—after Afghanistan. —We both know you're not going to pull that trigger. So, why don't you just hand me the gun." He moved to within inches of the tip, grasping the barrel.

I didn't shoot. But in the next instant, Hank's body fell backward to the floor in front of me. My knife was sticking out of his chest, buried to the hilt. The blade, no doubt, had found its mark deep in his heart. Blood poured from the wound, drenching the carpet.

"Collateral damage," I said to his motionless form.

Abby screamed and turned to the woman. "Nana—Nana, why did Daddy kill Hank?"

Before she could answer, I said, "Hank wasn't your friend, Sweetheart. He was just pretending to be. And this woman is not your Nana. Both of them have been lying to you, Honey. They're bad people."

Abby cried out with tears streaming down her cheeks. *"No, Daddy! Nana takes care of me. She's a good person."*

The woman stroked Abby's hair and smiled that motherly smile again.

She looked up at me and said, "Don't think for one minute that we don't have several more agents in the area. As soon as you entered the room, I pressed a silent alarm button. They're already on their way. You'll never make it out of here alive."

When Abby heard that, her tears stopped, and she started to push away from the woman, saying, "I want to go by my Daddy now." The woman held her more tightly. "Nana, you're hurting me."

I pointed my weapon at the witch. "Let her go!"

The motherly expression dissolved from her face, replaced by a threatening glare. She deftly snatched up a pen from the desk next to her and held the tip against Abby's carotid artery.

Her eyes narrowed as she said, "Don't let the fact that I'm a woman fool you. I have skills, and I'm perfectly capable of—"

Her voice was interrupted by a cracking sound. It was rather loud, reverberating off the walls within the confines of the room. Abby knew what had happened as she ran to me.

"Don't look back," I said as I scooped her up in my arms, and hugged her.

She didn't need to see the chunks of skull and brain matter on the wall behind the woman—the result of my '308-round' finding its mark between her eyes. Her body lay askew on the rug in front of the blood-spattered chair.

"We have to get out of here, Sweetie. I'll explain everything to you later."

"O—okay, D–Daddy," she murmured, still choked with emotion. I cradled her head against my shoulder and rushed out the door.

***

After looking up and down the fence line, I hoisted Abby over it and quickly scaled it myself to join her on the other side. I held onto her hand tightly, as I led her through the underbrush to the car.

"Put your seatbelt on, Sweetheart," I said as I helped her into the passenger seat.

I placed the rifle in the back seat and climbed behind the steering wheel. Pulling a U-turn, I retraced the route I'd taken into the development. I kept checking my rearview mirror. Everything looked clear, and I decided to call Casey.

She answered quickly. "Jeff, I'm so glad you called. Are you all right?"

"I don't have much time, Casey, and I need your help."

"Anything," she responded.

My answer was limited. "I have Abby, and we're on our way to the airport."

"You have her? How did you—" she began.

I interrupted saying, "I'll explain everything later. We're going to be landing at Palo Alto after midnight. They'll probably be looking for us, and I can't chance taking a cab to the hotel. Can you pick us up? And could we stay at your place tonight—just for one night?"

"I'll be waiting for you. Poor Abby must be so scared. —Both of you can stay as long as you like."

"Thank you, Casey. You've done so much already."

"Jeff, please—don't think twice about it. I'll see you in Palo Alto." We hung up.

I cleared the Paradise Valley complex and turned onto Scottsdale Road, north, toward the airport. It was a multiple-lane highway, and I knew that some creative driving could cut the trip to ten minutes.

Five of those minutes had passed, when I noticed a pair of headlights about fifty yards back, and another pair behind them. They were darting in and out between cars, obviously following us.

Abby looked back and turned to me. "Is it them?"

"I don't know yet, Honey. But don't look back." I pressed down on the accelerator.

They shadowed our every move—gaining ground. By the time I turned onto Airport Road, the two dark-colored SUVs were right on my bumper. The airport entrance was just ahead, but then what?

"*Hold on, Abby!*" I cried out, as I made a severe, right turn.

The two heavy vehicles missed the turn and had to back up, buying us a little time. Ahead of us was a chain-link, service access-gate, with warning signs plastered all over it. I nodded to Abby and crashed through the barrier onto the tarmac. I knew where my plane was parked and sped toward it. Glancing up at the mirror, I could see the convoy had regrouped and was in hot pursuit.

Abby screamed, "*Are we going to die, Daddy?*"

"Not if I can help it, Honey," I answered.

Twenty feet short of my plane, I jerked the steering wheel sharply to the left and skidded sideways to a stop. My driver's side door was facing our pursuers.

"Take off your seatbelt and get down on the floor, as low as you can," I told Abby, as I reached over the seatback for the rifle.

I pushed the door open partially, slammed the barrel to rest on the base of the open window, and triggered a round into the right front tire of the lead car. The top-heavy vehicle skidded and flipped onto its side, landing with the undercarriage facing me. The second car was going too fast to stop and ran into the first. I took aim again and pumped several rounds into the gas tank of the first car. It burst into a ball of fire. The driver scrambled onto the runway, enveloped in flames. He fell to his knees, screaming in agony. I took him out, sparing him the pain. The others took off, running from the fire.

I reached for Abby's hand. "C'mon, Honey, we have to hurry."

I helped her slide out the driver's side, and we ran to the plane. As we strapped ourselves in, I laid the rifle in back and started the engine. The remaining three agents had regrouped on foot, about sixty yards out, and were sprinting toward us—brandishing sidearms. I taxied off the apron and turned onto the runway facing them.

"Abby, we have to go toward them. Put your head down." I gently touched the back of her soft hair, and she leaned forward.

I pushed the throttle full-forward, knowing I had enough space to squeak by the burning wreckage. But getting past the three gunmen unscathed? That was going to take more than a little luck.

They stopped in the middle of the runway and started to open fire. We were almost on top of them when they jumped aside. But that didn't stop them from firing at us as we passed by. I heard two bullets pierce the fuselage—and maybe one in the tail section. I hoped they hadn't hit anything critical as we continued down the strip. A thousand feet farther, we finally lifted off, and up into the night sky.

When we leveled off at cruising altitude, Abby asked, "Can I lift my head up now, Daddy?"

I softly said, "Yes, Sweetie, you can sit up now. We're going to a place where you'll be safe."

"Okay, Daddy," she answered with trust in her eyes, as she nestled her head against my arm.

Chapter 12

Sparks-Past and Present

Three hours later, we touched down in Palo Alto. As soon as Abby and I got out of the plane and started walking, we were stopped by an attendant in yellow, reflective-striped, coveralls and wearing a baseball cap.

"Mister Wade, I read that your daughter was—"

I cut him short, saying, "Oh, hi Al. That was all a big mix-up. As you can see, she's alive and well."

His response came after an awkward silence. "Well, I'm glad to see she's okay.—What happened to the Cessna?" He nodded to the holes in the fuselage and tail.

"Hail," I answered. "Would you mind getting her patched up for me? Just put it on my account."

"Sure thing, Mister Wade." As he walked up and felt the damage with his fingertips, I heard him doubtingly repeat, *"Hail?"* under his breath.

"Sorry we have to run off, Al. But we're in a bit of a hurry."

"Uh—sure, Mister Wade," he answered, still standing there, scratching his head with the bill of his cap.

We'd barely opened the gate to the parking area, when Casey rushed up to us, lifted Abby up, and hugged her.

In a failed attempt to hold back her tears, Casey said, "Abby! I'm so happy to see you."

Abby was crying as well. "I'm glad to see you too, Auntie Casey."

After lowering Abby to her feet and wiping the tears from her eyes, Casey noticed the rifle case in my hand. "What are you doing with that?"

Conspicuously, I didn't answer. But Abby's eyes welled up with tears, and she began to cry again.

Casey took her by the hand. "C'mon, Sweetie, you need to get some sleep." And we walked to the car.

***

It was about one o'clock in the morning when we got to Casey's place. After I propped the rifle in a corner of the foyer, Casey led us down the hall.

She stopped at a closet, reached in, and pulled out a pajama top. "It's a little big for you, but it's soft and comfy." She handed it to Abby with a smile.

The next doorway opened to a bedroom. With very little coaxing from Casey, my exhausted daughter donned the oversized garment and climbed into bed.

I leaned over, kissed her on the forehead, and said, "I love you."

"I love you too, Daddy," she murmured.

She closed her eyes, quickly dropping off to sleep, and I eased the door closed behind me. By the time I turned around, Casey was already standing down the hall, in the middle of a third doorway.

"This is my guest bedroom—and storage room. It used to be my home-office, until Sarah needed more space. Then, I moved everything downstairs."

I leaned against the doorframe and looked in. There was a double-bed with a nightstand and a padded chair. But most notably, countless books—stacked like chimneys—covered the floor, leaving barely enough room to squeeze between them.

"You can sleep in here," she said. "Just don't fall over the books when you wake up." She laughed.

"Where are you going to sleep?" I asked.

"I'll sleep with Abby—in my room. She shouldn't be left alone tonight."

"Yes—yes, of course, you're right."

As Casey turned back toward her room, I blurted out, "I killed five people tonight. Some of them must have had families—kids."

"*Oh my God!* I knew something was bothering you. Come with me." And she led me by the hand into the guest room, and through the book-maze.

We sat on the edge of the bed, while I gazed straight ahead and motionless. Then, in a stupor, I began to relate the events of the day.

"The first one was difficult.—Then, something clicked inside me. I took out the rest of them like they were rodents. I just removed them from the face of the earth."

"*Oh Jeff*," she said, wrapping her arms around me and nestling her head against my neck.

The blur of events began to crystallize in my mind. "There's more. Hank—Hank Takahashi, and the old lady in the video—I killed them both. And, in some dark corner of my mind, I took a degree of pleasure in it. *Casey*, what's happening to me?"

She raised her head in concern. "*Hank Takahashi*? You need to get some rest, Jeff. Hank died on that train in Japan."

"That's what everybody thought. But somehow, he escaped—and kidnapped Abby. Maybe she can explain some of it when she wakes up."

"Yes, it's best that we don't bother her now. We can talk about it in the morning. The important thing is that you're both alive and well. I—I was so afraid I might lose you." She moved her lips close to mine, invitingly.

Momentarily, I was tempted to find a degree of solace in those lips, but I banished the thought quickly and turned my head away. "You're right. Things might seem clearer in the morning."

Casey tried to compose herself, as she stood up. "Yes, I'd better go to Abby's room. We all could use some sleep."

I glanced at her, with guilt-ridden longing, as she left the room, and I got ready for bed. I tossed for a while before dropping off to sleep.

***

"Wake up, sleepyhead," I heard, after what seemed like minutes. "It's ten o'clock." It was Casey, standing in the doorway.

I jolted to a sitting position. "Oh my God! I gotta get going." I had trouble mobilizing any further and held my palms to my head.

"Abby is already up, and we're having breakfast. Why don't you come and eat with us?"

"Yeah, I'll be right there," I muttered.

As soon as she closed the door, I did my best to hurriedly dress. I negotiated the book jungle and followed the sound of my daughter's voice down the hallway to the kitchen. I found her sitting across from Casey at the breakfast table, eating scrambled eggs.

"Good morning, Sweetie. How are you feeling?" I asked, as I leaned forth to kiss her on the cheek.

"Better, Daddy." She forced a timid smile.

"She's going to be just fine," Casey said, reaching across to stroke Abby on the hand.

An annoying, intermittent noise intruded on the gentle moment. It sounded like the warning beep of a truck backing up, but it was coming from the basement.

"Oh, that's Sarah," Casey said, pushing herself from the table.

"She *calls* you?" I asked with surprise.

"Who's Sarah?" Abby asked.

"C'mon, I'll introduce you," Casey answered. And she led us both down the basement stairs. Upon reaching the spot I was becoming familiar with, Casey announced, "Abby, this is Sarah."

"There's nobody there," Abby responded.

"It's a pleasure to meet you, Abby. And I'm so happy to see that you're all right," Sarah said, causing Abby to take a step back.

"Don't be scared," Casey reassured. "It's a little hard to explain, but Sarah is our friend. She just happens to be a computer."

Abby's eyes widened as she stepped forward cautiously. "Really?—Cool!"

"I think you're cool too," Sarah replied. "I have a feeling we're going to be great friends." She displayed her world-map start screen.

"Wow!" Abby reacted. "Can I touch it, Casey?"

"Sure, go ahead."

She immersed the tip of her forefinger into the map at the western seaboard of the US. Immediately, the world map was replaced by one of California.

"We're right here," Abby said, as she touched Santa Clara.

"Exactly," Sarah confirmed. "Abby, how does it feel to you?"

"Warm—it feels warm."

"That's because you are touching my heart," Sarah said.

Abby slowly backed up next to Casey and me. A broad smile came over all our faces, and I felt that Sarah was smiling too. I took Abby by the hand, led her to a chair, and urged her to sit down.

I squatted next to her, and placed my hand softly on her shoulder. "I'm sorry I have to ask this, Sweetheart"—I hesitated—"but I need to know what happened to you, beginning with Hank in Japan. And then, how you met the woman you called Nana."

A tear came to her eye. "Okay, Daddy, but I don't remember too much."

"That's all right, Sweetie. Tell me what you can."

As Abby strained for words, the pain of her experiences showed in her face. "I remember when we all got on the train in Japan. Then, a little while later, it stopped at a station. Hank asked me if I wanted to get off with him and get some candy. M-Mommy said it was okay if we didn't take too long. Hank told her we'd be back in a minute, and we got off. Then, we went into a shop at the station, and he bought me some candy and orange soda. When we came back out—the train was gone. *W-we were only in there a little while, Daddy.*"

"It's okay, Sweetheart. You didn't do anything wrong. What happened next?"

She continued, "I was really scared, but Hank told me everything would be okay. He said we could take a taxi to Osaka and meet Mommy and Jess there. When we got in the taxi, he told me it was going to be a long ride, and I should have some soda and take a nap. I don't remember anything more about Japan.

"The next thing I remember is when I woke up at your aunt's house. She told me the train had an accident and that M-Mommy and J-Jess were gone—

that they d-died. Then, she said that you—killed yourself when you heard about it." And Abby began to cry.

I hugged her. "Sweetie, I don't have an aunt, and I would never-*never* leave you alone. Always remember that."

She looked at me with reddened, soulful eyes. "Are Mommy and Jess really—?"

"They're in heaven now, Honey. But they'll always be with you—in your heart." I barely got the words out.

She started to cry again. I did my best to comfort her and give her some time to settle down.

After a time, I said, "Abby, this is important. Do you remember *anything* that happened in between the taxi in Japan and when you woke up in this Nana-person's house?"

"Only some fuzzy stuff. Oh—I was on an airplane for a little while. It wasn't a real big one. Only Hank and a few other people were on it—I think."

Casey said, "Jeff, I'm sorry I doubted you last night—about Hank, I mean. He must have drugged her—the poor thing. It sounds like they got her out of Japan on a private plane. Money can buy a lot of secrecy."

I turned to Abby and softly said, "That's enough for now, Sweetheart. You gave us a lot of good information."

I pulled Casey aside. "Now that Abby's out of danger, I think it's time I brought Phil up-to-speed with what's going on."

"I can drive you to the company," she offered.

"After what happened in Arizona, it's a sure thing that The Committee is looking for me. The safest place for you and Abby is right here. I'll take a cab to the office. Stay in touch—and let me know if Sarah comes up with anything."

"All right, Jeff, but please be careful." She reached over to squeeze my hand.

Out of the corner of my eye, I noticed that Abby had been engaged in some sort of back-and-forth with Sarah. "Abby, I have to leave for a few hours, but you'll be safe here with Sarah and Casey."

"Okay, Daddy. Sarah is showing me a new game—with rabbits," she giggled.

When the cab arrived, Casey walked me to the front door, past the rifle, still propped in the corner from the night before.

I stopped, nodding toward the weapon. "I can't carry that thing around very easily." I looked back at Casey and continued, "You're an attractive woman, living alone. I'm guessing you have some means of self-defense in the house—like a handgun or something."

"Yes—I have a gun hidden in the closet. I bought it a few years ago, but I only practice-fired it once. It scares me."

"I need to borrow it."

"Jeff, what are you planning to do? I, uh—*we* don't want you taking any more chances."

"I'm not going hunting for them, if that's what you mean. But if they come after me, I need to be able to defend myself."

"Okay–okay, just a minute." She disappeared around the corner.

A short while later she returned, holding a pistol and a fully loaded magazine.

"It's legal and registered to me," she said, upon handing me the Italian-made, 9-millimeter, semi-automatic.

"Don't worry, if I get caught with it, I'll say I stole it from you," I responded, as I jacked the slide back to clear the chamber, pulled the trigger, and inserted the clip.

"That's not what I meant, Jeff. It's always better to do things within the law."

"That depends on who's dispensing the law," I countered, tucking the weapon under my belt, beneath the back of my suit jacket. "One last favor—hide that rifle someplace where Abby can't find it."

"*That*, I'll be happy to do."

The cab pulled up and I left, feeling some degree of confidence that Sarah's firewall could continue to keep Casey and Abby off The Committee's grid.

Chapter 13

Truth or Stress?

It was around noon when the taxi pulled up to the front door of Quantam. I handed the driver a hundred and told him to wait for me.

I rushed past our receptionist and outer offices, making my way back to Phil's office. I knocked, but didn't wait for an invitation to enter. I found Phil laboring at his computer, as usual.

"Oh–hi, J, I thought you were going to work out of your hotel room for a while."

"Things have changed—a lot." With a smile, I added, "Phil—I got Abby back."

He was visibly confounded. "J, are you feeling alright? Abby is—gone. We both attended her funeral—remember? Why don't you sit down? I'll get you some water."

"I don't want to sit down, and I don't need any water. Phil, this is going to be difficult to explain, and I'm sorry I was forced to keep you in the dark for so long.

"The story is pretty involved and protracted, but I'll try to give you a slimmed-down version.—There is an organization that calls itself 'The Committee'. One of their goals is to delay the release of our coating formula to the world, convinced that humanity isn't ready for it yet. They were the ones responsible for the bullet-train explosion that killed Kris and Jessica. They also had a hand in Bergman's and Ziegler's death—as well as my neighbor. But they didn't kill Abby. They kidnapped her instead, and I was able to get her back."

"Wait a minute! You went to Japan, rescued Abby, and brought her back here—all in one day? That's impossible."

"She wasn't *in* Japan, Phil. Hank Takahashi nabbed her before the train explosion, drugged her, and brought her to Arizona. Then, he convinced her that this older lady—a board member of the committee I told you about—was my aunt, and that I had committed suicide."

"That's quite a story," he responded. "The Japanese police say that Hank Takahashi died with your family on the train. So, how did you get Abby away from Hank and this 'older lady'?"

"I—I had to kill them both."

Phil looked shocked. "J, You and I have been friends for a long time now. Is there any evidence to back up this—you'll excuse me—seemingly preposterous and contrived story? If all this really happened, how did you get Abby out of Scottsdale, and where is she now?"

"*That's it!* There's your evidence. A couple of The Committee's agents shot at us on the runway in Scottsdale. Our company plane has the bullet-holes to prove it."

"Yes, I did receive a call from Al, our aircraft mechanic. But he didn't mention anything about bullet-holes. He gave me an estimate to repair hailstone damage to the fuselage. The only thing that struck me as unusual is that you apparently chose to risk flying *through* a hailstorm, rather than *around* it."

"Have you been listening to me, Phil?"

"Look, J, if Abby was really alive, you'd have brought her with you, and not left her alone to come and chat with me."

"She's not alone—but that's a whole different story. And I didn't come here to *chat*. Of course, I wanted to fill you in. But the main purpose of my visit was to warn you not to download the Najita formula when it arrives. I'm not convinced that the completed formula will merely result in a delay, as The Committee claims. We still have a couple of days to think about how we can fully examine the Najita component before we chance incorporating it."

"You're too late," he responded. "I downloaded Najita earlier this morning."

"*What?* I thought it wasn't due for two more days. Why would you do that without, at least, touching base with me first?"

"*It arrived early, J,*" he shot back. "The last time you honored us with your presence, you were in a big hurry to download the Elektrikote portion. So, naturally, I thought—. Anyway, it's done. And to say I'm skeptical concerning this mumbo-jumbo about a committee would be an understatement. I don't mean to be harsh, but I really think you should see someone—about your mental stability."

I partially understood Phil's misgivings. I'd have had a little trouble believing the story myself. But, somehow, I thought our friendship would trump those doubts. Without a word, I headed for the door.

"Where are you going now?" He demanded.

I didn't look back. "I have to pick up a few things at the hotel. You can reach me by phone if you need me." And I left his office.

***

I'd barely closed the door of the taxi when my phone rang. It was the Chairman.

With subdued—yet discernable—anger, he spoke. "Well, Jeffrey, it seems I've underestimated you, once again. You've managed to eliminate one of my board members and extricate her designated replacement—your daughter. That's right, we never intended that she be returned to you. But, no matter, we'll find an equally suitable candidate.

"Besides that, you killed three of our best agents. And you did it all, whilst we thought you were still in your hotel room—*Bravo*! We are duly impressed with your technical skills and your physical prowess.

"You might be wondering why I am willing to disclose the aforementioned details to you. The answer is quite simple. It's too late for you to hinder our plans now. The formula is complete. You may, actually, be helpful in convincing the authorities of our far-reaching capabilities. There will be an announcement on all news media at two o'clock, your time. Be sure to tune in. And remember what I told you about the dynamic nature of our decisions. Don't do anything stupid. It is not inconceivable that you–and those close to you–could, once again, become targets." And he hung up before I could say a word.

The cab driver asked, "Where to, sir?"

I asked him to give me a minute, but before I had a chance to ruminate over what the Chairman had said, my sat-phone rang again. This time it was Casey.

"Jeff, can I put Sarah on?" Her voice was laced with urgency.

"She can do that? She can talk to me on my phone? —Never mind. Put her on."

Sarah's syrupy voice droned. "Sorry to bother you, Jeff, but there is something you should know about. I monitored the Chairman's communication with you, and confirm that the Najita formula has, in fact, been fully integrated within your company's computer."

"Will it result in a two-year delay, as the Chairman described?"

She went silent for a few moments, then answered, "Not years, Jeff, but hours—precisely two hours."

I gasped. "How could a two-hour delay possibly help their cause?"

Sarah continued. "The introduction of Najita has had a profound impact on the other formulas. The delay aspect is only one constituent. The final formula has been completely repurposed and cleverly encrypted. It appears that, just as they underestimated you, I have underestimated them.

"The fundamental and singular purpose of the physical material to be derived from the integrated formula would be one of complete and utter destruction—simply put, a bomb.

"Najita acts as a catalyst. When the liquid made from it is added to the coating made from the other two formulas, the resulting material solidifies within ten seconds. At that point, the bomb would be armed."

"What? That can't be right. Check it again," I insisted.

"I've checked it several times. There's no mistake. It wouldn't be a bomb, as in the nuclear fission or fusion variety. It would utilize photons to create heat— a great deal of heat—approximately 300 million degrees on the Fahrenheit scale. That is more than ten times the temperature at our sun's core.

"To put it in perspective, a wafer made from this material, the size of a US quarter, could vaporize everything within a twenty-five-mile radius."

Stunned, I managed to say, "But if someone were to plant this—weapon—somewhere, it would be a suicide mission. Ten seconds wouldn't be enough time to clear twenty yards—much less, twenty-five miles."

Sarah replied, "I said the bomb would be *armed*, not triggered. Detailed analysis of the projected nature of the solidified, armed compound indicates that a unique frequency pattern is required to initiate the two-hour countdown to detonation.

"Jeff, remember we traced the GPS location of the probable residence of the Chairman in Vienna, and it fell on the blue oval ring? That ring represents all the board-member computers when they are joined in a network. I have been able to determine with absolute certainty that all of the white-line 'execute' signals, though masked, originated from a single computer hub at the Vienna location.

"Hence, the presumed photon bomb detonation sequence would include a white-line execute signal from Vienna, crisscrossing the globe several hundred times, to one of the thirty relay sub-stations. That station would then transmit the trigger signal on a unique frequency, initiating the two-hour, detonation countdown."

"Okay, okay—that's enough detail, Sarah. Overall, it's an interesting hypothesis. But aren't you making a lot of assumptions?"

She answered, "The only way to authenticate my findings would be to witness a detonation, then monitor the white-line and trigger signals. However, in percentage terms, I find the probability to be on the order of ninety-nine—point-nine, nine, nine, nine, nine, n—"

"Alright, alright, Sarah—I understand. But even if someone were to disable or destroy the Vienna computer, couldn't they easily switch control to another one in the network?"

"Once again, arrogance becomes a factor. The Committee doesn't believe that anyone possesses the technology to pinpoint the location of *any* of the computers in the network. Therefore, I don't believe they have allowed for that contingency. I estimate it would take them at least six months to upgrade one of their other sites to server-hub status. I'm sending the Vienna address and GPS coordinates to your phone."

"Thank you, Sarah. Would you please put Casey back on?"

"Certainly, Jeff. —Go ahead. She's on now."

"Casey, you were right. I can't fight these people alone. I'm going to need help—somebody with connections."

"But who will believe you, and who can you trust?"

"I'm not sure, but maybe—. Would you ask Sarah what hospital they took Sergeant McKinney to?"

"Why do you think you can trust *her?*" Casey sounded irritated.

"I don't. But she said she has connections at the federal level. For now, she's the only game in town."

After several seconds of silence, Casey said, "El Camino Hospital."

"Thanks, Casey. Have Sarah run a quick background check on her and her connections, and text me the information. Talk to you soon." And I hung up.

The taxi driver was getting impatient. "Hey mister, you know you're payin' for all this waitin' time?"

I reached over the seat and handed him another hundred. "Here, this oughtta cover it. Take me to El Camino Hospital."

We were on the road only minutes when I received a text from Sarah that read:

Preliminary Report-Sergeant Rachel McKinney
Background-Still checking. No major red flags.
Relatives, federal government-One cousin, Raymond Eddleson, high ranking DHS official."

"The Department of Homeland Security—jackpot!" I thought.

***

It was approaching one o'clock when the driver pulled up to the hospital entrance. Again, I asked him to wait, as I hopped out and walked through the lobby to the reception desk.

"I'd like to see Rachel McKinney, please."

The elderly female attendant studied me. "Are you a family member?"

"No, just a friend. Tell her it's Jeffrey Wade."

"Just a moment, please," she said with a suspicious look as she picked up the phone. Upon hanging up, a smile came over her face as she handed me a pass.

"Here you go, Mister Wade—room 316. Take the elevator on the left."

Up on the third floor, I zigzagged through the corridors until I found her room. The door was half-open, but I knocked anyway and walked in. McKinney was standing up and fully clothed. Her right arm was fully enclosed in one of those inflatable casts and in a sling. She was gathering her things, apparently getting ready to leave.

"Hello, Sergeant. I'm surprised to see they're releasing you so soon."

"Well—hello, Mister Wade. Actually, they didn't. I signed myself out. Haha—with my other hand. Luckily, I'm left-handed. I must say, I didn't expect you to show up here. What can I do for you?"

"I wanted to acknowledge—and thank you. After all, you took a bullet trying to protect me. And—and I would've visited you for that reason alone. But I must confess, I do have another purpose in coming here. Let me warn you, it's a pretty bizarre story. Frankly, I wouldn't be sharing it with you if I didn't need your help.

"You remember we discussed a certain proprietary project my company has been working on—in conjunction with a German and a Japanese company?"

"Yes, I remember. Go on," she answered with a curious look.

"That project was to be a coating that would revolutionize power generation for the entire world. It was intended to be a good thing. But a powerful, secret organization—the one that killed my family and others you're aware of—turned it into a *photon bomb*. They kidnapped my daughter, forcing me to help them. Now, they're going to cut into the worldwide media at exactly two o'clock with some sort of announcement. And I guarantee you that whatever it is, it won't be good.

She looked at me and let out a troubled breath. "Mister Wade, do you have any idea how ludicrous that sounds—a secret organization, proton bombs, and the kidnapping of your daughter? The Hiroshima police department has, unfortunately, confirmed the death of *all* of your family members, including your daughter. I realize how difficult that must be for you to accept, but try to come to grips with the reality of the situation."

I retorted, "It's photon, not proton, bombs. And it's all true. They were holding Abby just outside of Scottsdale, Arizona—Paradise Valley. I didn't, necessarily, want to admit this to you now, but I flew down there yesterday and got Abby back. But I was forced to kill five people in the process. The police down there must have some record of the shootings. Could you—I mean—*would you* call down there? If I'm wrong, I'll leave you alone."

She looked unconvinced. "Anything of that magnitude would have saturated the airwaves."

Please, just one call," I implored.

She let out another breath and said, "Okay—but only to disprove this craz—uh, inventive—story of yours." She grabbed her phone and turned her back to me, fumbling to dial with her one free hand, then saying, "Yes, Scottsdale or Paradise Valley." We both waited and, within a minute, she spoke into the phone again. "All right—thank you." Turning back to me, she said, "No shootings or violent incidents of any kind have been reported in that area over the past several months. Mister Wade, may I respectfully suggest that you see someone here at the hospital. And it might do you some good to stay for a few days—to unwind."

I lashed out in frustration. "You're the second person today to tell me I need my head examined. I should have known they'd be able to cover up the shootings.

"In a half-hour, they'll be airing their announcement. Then you'll see that I didn't imagine it all. I have some things to take care of, back at my hotel. Meet me there, when you're convinced that I'm not *insane*."

Chapter 14
The Proposal

It was one-forty-five by the time I finally got out of the taxi in front of my hotel.

As I walked through the lobby, passing the front desk, the clerk said, "Oh, Mister Wade, I have a message for you—time-stamped 1:15 PM."

I opened the folded note and read, "Don't forget to tune in at two o'clock."

I crushed it, squeezing it tighter and tighter in my fist, all the way to my room. Once inside, upon seeing my briefcase sitting on the coffee table, I released the inanimate scrap onto the floor and rushed to the couch. I sat down in front of the table, carefully reached into the side pocket of my case, and grabbed the pictures. As I gazed at them, sweet memories gently lilted through my mind. Kris, Jess, Abby, and I were together again—on vacation, at birthday parties, and during playful moments in our yard. They all brought a tearful smile to my face. I lost track of time, until my phone buzzed on the glass table-top, jolting me to the present.

It was two o'clock. I turned the TV on and watched as a national emergency buzzer interrupted all channels. The face I had grown to despise appeared.

"Citizens of the world," he began. "As I speak, my words are being simultaneously translated into the indigenous language of your individual countries.

"I am the chairman of a seven-member committee which has been in existence for over two hundred years. Primarily, we have functioned as hidden watchdogs, hoping that after a number of generations, you might learn from your mistakes. To our dismay, quite the opposite has played out—across the globe. Self-serving, dishonest actions have become commonplace, with dastardly consequences. Many of your leaders are corrupt, and most are more interested in gaining or keeping power than they are with the plight of the people.

"Collectively, they have brought pestilence down upon the earth, as evidenced by climate change, poor air quality, miles of swirling refuse in our oceans, wars, and starvation.

"You kill one another for differences in ideology and religion, and at times, for no apparent reason. To compound the problem, some countries maintain enough ordnance to destroy the world, many times over.

"At the root of all this chaos is a human condition known as greed. Coupled with pride and belligerence, it becomes the perfect instrument for self-destruction.

"Something must be done about it, or none of us will survive. And that brings me to the purpose of this announcement.

"It is our committee's firm intention to eliminate individual governances throughout the world. They have become archaic, ineffectual, and self-seeking to the point where they are no longer able to serve the masses.

"Upon approval of our plan, the people will determine their own fate. Previously sovereign governments will be eliminated. Our committee will provide you the means to replace them with a consolidated administration, lowering the–overhead–if you will. You, the people, will vote on major issues from your phones. If you don't have one, we will provide it for you. All votes will be DNA verified.

"In addition, all commercial advertising will be limited—both in length and monetarily. Salary caps will be placed on all executives, entertainers, professional athletes, and the like. Don't mistakenly think of it as socialism. It's rather a means to limit the wealth of those whose income is disproportionate to their contribution to society. The day of the billionaire is over.

"Mega-corporations will be broken up. The price of energy, in all forms, will be based on reasonable profit margins. And you will vote on it all. The result will be significantly lower-cost goods and services.

"Should you choose to believe in a god, or not, will remain your prerogative. However, you will not be allowed to force your beliefs onto others.

"Each nation will be allowed a seven-member advisory panel, selected by you from your ranks, but overseen by us to prevent favoritism and corruption. Salaries and terms of service will be determined by you. They will be chosen on the basis of credentials within their individual disciplines—science, finance, technology, agriculture, education, and so on. They will not be selected based on political affiliations. In fact, the word politics will become meaningless. We will provide lists and verified backgrounds, along with achievements, should you require them. However, you will not be obligated to choose from our offerings. And panel members will act as consultants only. You, the people, will make the decisions.

"You may ask yourselves, 'How, with all the issues that come up daily, will I ever find the time to vote on everything?' You won't have to. You will simply select the topics you choose to vote on, and ask for advice from your panel. We estimate voting will require ten minutes out of every day. Isn't it worth ten minutes to rid yourselves of the parasites that are draining you of your life's blood?

"Obviously, the details of such a wide-ranging plan cannot be covered in this broadcast. The particulars are being sent, in video and text form, to all media, personal phones, and directly to your current leadership.

"We are hopeful that this point will mark a new age in human history. All things you have known, you will look back upon differently. All things ahead will be markedly improved for the vast majority of you, as well as for the general health of our planet.

"However, we are not fools. We don't expect your entrenched Machiavellian governments to give up their ill-gotten gains easily. In full recognition of this fact, we have prepared a demonstration of our power and resolve.

"Precisely two minutes from now, the city of Aleppo, Syria will be eliminated, or the preferred word—*cleansed*. It has been selected without prejudice. Although thousands have already fled this troublesome country's regime, many remaining Aleppo innocents will die, along with the guilty.

"We regret we are forced to implement such aggressive measures, but their sacrifice, now, will save the lives of billions, later. To coin a phrase, 'Desperate times call for desperate measures.'

"The cleansing of the aforementioned city is irreversible. However, if we do not receive corroborated approval from all designated countries within the next 24 hours, Washington, DC and Moscow, Russia will be next. Should this regrettable contingency become necessary, we fully expect that the leaders of these countries would survive by scurrying down their respective rabbit holes. We would heartily encourage these escape maneuvers, though cowardly. Their survival would prove most helpful in instructing military forces, and the citizenry of their respective nations, to lay down their arms—down to the smallest handgun.

"Should we still not have received approval of our proposal within the ensuing 24-hour period, another two or three cities will be eliminated. This process will be repeated until unanimous endorsement is received. However, beyond the first two population centers, selections will be randomized. We will not be informing you of who will be next. To guess that the largest and most powerful will top the list would be a grave mistake on your part.

"We have hundreds of thousands of agents throughout the world. They have already located cleansing devices in all target cities. Additionally, they have placed said devices in missile silos, on submarines, and on airfields. They continue to do so, in all pockets of possible resistance. We are monitoring your phones and computers, and would not look favorably on any attempt to mount a counter-offensive.

"Out of generosity, I've already explained more than I intended. There are only ten seconds left before the detonation of the first two devices. Please use the following 24 hours wisely. The decision is yours. I sincerely hope you choose the right path."

His facade disappeared, replaced by what appeared to be social media panoramas of Aleppo. Moments later, the videos shook violently. Then, I heard a thunderous, rumbling sound—followed by a deafening rush of air, as if from a hundred jet engines.

When the images steadied, there was nothing left in any of the multiple angles of view, except for thick tendrils of smoke rising up from the charred ground that, seconds before, had been home to so many people. Terrified screams of onlookers punctuated the otherworldly scene. The thought of all those deaths consumed me with sorrow. My breath seemed to be sucked from me, as had been the souls from those within the destruction zone.

"*You bastard!*" I blurted out, as I clicked the TV off. I grabbed my briefcase and rushed out the door to the elevator.

Chapter 15

In Check

The elevator door opened to bedlam in the hotel lobby. I nudged my way through dozens of people. Many of them were crying, transfixed to the TV screens, while others wandered about, zombie-like, as they stared down at their phones. All had been consumed by the tragedy they'd just witnessed.

I'd almost made it to the front door, when I saw her walk in. It was Sergeant McKinney. She spotted me almost immediately and moved in my direction, protecting her injured arm from the throng.

When we came face-to-face, she said, "Okay, I'm convinced that at least part of your story is true, but this—" She looked at the lobby-screen and turned back to me. "This is *way* above my pay grade. I don't know what you expect—"

I interrupted, saying, "Let's go outside where we can talk." And I made a path for us through the crowd and out into the daylight.

With the clamorous din of the lobby behind us, I asked, "By the way, how did you get here so fast?"

"You remember that gut feeling I told you about? Well, I trusted it. I was already on my way here, when the bomb videos showed up on my phone."

I asked, "Do you have time to come with me—back to my office? I'll explain everything on the way. My car is right here in front." And I pointed to where it was parked, twenty feet away.

"I can't just leave my car here and jump in yours. I still don't know if I can trust you completely."

"Look, Rachel, we don't have much time. If you're afraid to come with me, I'll have to go it alone."

"Who said I was *afraid*? —Let's go!" We'd just gotten in my car, when she pulled a device from her belt. "Hold on for a second. I have to contact my surveillance team—the ones who are supposed to be keeping an eye on you. They're somewhere in the lot here."

"Okay, but hurry up. We're wasting time."

"I don't know why they haven't pulled up by now." She spoke into her radio, "One-Nick, this is Rachel. What's your twenty? One-Nick, this is Rachel. What's your twenty?"

"Let's get out of here. They can find their way home," I urged.

"We're not leaving, till I find out where they are. Besides, we could use the backup. I can find them on their GPS tracker." Looking down at her phone, she said, "Oh, there they are. Go to the end of this row and turn right."

Reluctantly, I complied. After a few more turns, she called out, "That's them over there—the black sedan."

We rolled up to the car cautiously. It was becoming clear that something was wrong. The car appeared to be abandoned. I pulled up close to it and peered in. Two crumpled bodies lay there in pools of blood on the front seat. Jagged, gaping wounds below their chins told the story. Their throats had been slashed, and not long ago. From her vantage point, Rachel couldn't see them.

She called out, "What's wrong? Why are you acting that way?"

Before I could say a word, she'd hopped out of the car. I saw the trepidation in her eyes, as she circled around in front of me to look into the sedan.

Coming upon the grizzly scene, she threw her palms up to the sides of her face and shrieked. "Oh no!" She hunched down and vomited. Halfway composing herself, she began stammering. "T-They were my friends. I-I know their wives—and their kids."

"Rachel, I'm so very sorry, but we need to go—now."

"If you think I'm gonna just leave em here—"

I interrupted with growing desperation. "Rachel, please get in the car.—*Look out!*" A vehicle was coming up on us at high speed.

She turned around just in time to dodge splintered fragments of metal and glass, sent flying off the surface of the sedan by automatic weapons fire.

She scrambled back into my car, and I slammed on the gas. We caromed off several parked cars as I cut through vacant spaces and skidded through hairpin turns within the lot. I heard the sound of small-caliber rounds puncturing the rear of my car. We finally made it to the exit, bouncing violently over its well-purposed speed bump. I screeched into a turn, and onto the downtown San Jose street. My side-view mirror revealed a white pick-up truck in pursuit. It negotiated the bump easily, with its oversized tires.

At the very next corner, I cut a hard left trying to escape the bullets that continued to pummel us from the rear. I serpentined up and down the crowded city streets, squeezing every ounce of performance I could get out of my car. But, just as I thought I was putting some distance between us, they caught up—bringing another volley of lead with them.

I slid into a right turn and down a narrow boulevard marked, "No Entry". On one side, a *light rail* car was headed in our direction. Pedestrian and bicycle traffic dotted the street on the other side. Trees lined the sidewalks on both sides. The one on the right was clear of foot traffic.

"Hold on!" I yelled to Rachel, as I jerked the steering wheel over to avoid the oncoming rail car. We rumbled over the curb between two of the trees and onto the sidewalk. I checked my rearview, shocked to see that the truck was still with us. The narrowly-spaced trees whizzed by. I cut back between them, returning to the roadway and straddling the train tracks. I'd gained only a few yards of separation on the truck. The rain of gunfire began again. I had to get off that street—too many innocent targets for stray rounds. I carved a hard right at the next intersection. Street signs were only a blur as we sped by, and we ended up in a pedestrian plaza, of sorts.

Before I could react, we plowed through an array of large, free-standing objects. They bounced off my car like bowling pins, sending them flying in all directions.

"*What the hell was that?*" I asked Rachel.

She looked back and said, "A chess set—*it was a chess set.*"

"*In the street?*" I exclaimed.

"We're not on the street," she remarked, grasping tightly to her door handle.

"Oh yeah. —We better get outta here." I hung a sharp U-turn.

Then I hit the brakes and skidded to a stop, noticing that our pursuer had stopped as well. He was parked broadside at the entrance to the plaza, blocking our only way out. The two occupants waited for me to make the next move.

There looked to be just enough room to squeeze out in front of them. The chess pieces took a second battering, as I raced toward our only chance for escape. I pushed Rachel's head down, as we took on automatic weapons fire through the windshield. I never let up from the gas and, as the truck moved ahead to close the gap, I swerved to slip past his rear bumper. I thought we'd cleared him, when I felt a jarring impact on my back fender, sending us fish-tailing. I looked in my mirror and saw him maneuvering–back and forth–to extricate himself from the tight space.

"You okay?" I asked Rachel, as I reached over to help her up.

Her hat had fallen off, and her hair was disheveled, as she struggled to right herself.

She glared at me. "Yeah, I'm okay. You know, as a driver, you need to be put—*in check*."

"Very funny." —Now, kick out the windshield."

"What?" she exclaimed.

"Kick out the windshield!" I repeated. "I can't see," as I hung my head out the window.

After a few failed attempts from different positions, she was able to dislodge the shattered glass. Luckily, it came out in one piece. It went sailing over the top of the car, bouncing off the roof, as we left it behind.

People would be hurt or killed if we remained in the downtown area. Picking up on a few landmarks, I zigzagged through city traffic to the Fourth Street ramp, and onto Interstate-280. Above the sound of my engine noise and the rush of wind in my face, I heard the unmistakable cyclic sound of helicopter blades wafting in the air.

I glanced up to see a chopper pass over us in the opposite direction.

"I was wondering when your people would notice all the commotion," I said to Rachel.

She looked back at the craft. "It's not one of ours. —They're turning around. Coming toward us."

She'd barely gotten the words out, when several 20mm Gatling-cannon rounds ripped into the pavement next to us. I veered to avoid them.

They were lining up for a second pass when Rachel pulled out her radio, saying, "McKinney to central.—McKinney to central. Officer needs assistance."

There was no response, except for the crackle of the connection.

"They must be jamming our frequency," she said, as she grabbed her personal phone, tapped something into it, and spoke a cryptic phrase. "Recognize and locate McKinney. Heelo engage–and delta."

Before I could ask what it meant, another string of cannon rounds tore into the roadway nearby.

The route-87 cloverleaf was in site, just ahead. I put my foot to the floor. The unimpeded torrent of air coming up over the hood took my breath away. Rachel ducked under the dashboard.

Before the chopper could position itself for another pass, we made it beneath the overpass. Looking for an off-ramp under the maze of crisscrossing highways, I turned onto the first one that led away from downtown. My maneuvers to evade the helicopter had allowed the truck to catch up to us. Again, they pummeled us with automatic weapons fire.

I shouted to Rachel, "If you know how to use that thing strapped to your side, now would be a good time."

She gave me a dirty look and, without a word, grabbed her sidearm—awkwardly twisting backward over her arm-sling and cast—to return fire.

Lowering my voice, I said, "Sorry, I forgot about your arm."

As soon as we emerged from the overpass, the chopper re-engaged in the chase, as well. For whatever reason—perhaps a jam—the cannon bursts stopped, replaced by a second stream of automatic weapon rounds from above. Rachel did her best to fend them off with her handgun.

"*Watch your arm!*" I shouted, as I made a quick turn onto a two-lane road leading into an industrial park.

I threw us into a sideslip skid, and we shuddered to a halt across the middle of the road.

"Holster that thing, and give me your hand," I yelled, as I opened my door and slid her out on my side, while bullets from the truck and the chopper, momentarily hovering above it, pelted the passenger side.

I pulled Casey's pistol from the back of my belt and returned fire with a few, hopefully distracting, rounds. Upon scoping out the adjacent structures, I spotted two nearby single-level concrete buildings. I nodded Rachel to the narrow space between them. "I'll cover, you move. Run for it, as fast as you can, on the count of one—ready, three-two-*one*."

She ran for the corridor, as I fired several rounds at our attackers, and followed her. Somehow, we were able to reach the partial cover unscathed.

I noticed Rachel was nursing her arm. "Are you okay?"

"I'm fine. Where'd you get the gun?" she asked.

"Would you stop being a cop for just a little while?"

Our verbal exchange was silenced by the sound of bullets ricocheted off the corner of the building we huddled against. Stone shrapnel sprayed the wall opposite us. I heard the chopper coming closer until we were able to see it—directly overhead.

"Rachel, I'm sorry I got you into this," the pulse of the rotor blade nearly drowning out my words.

I was trying to get a clear shot at the pilot, when something strange happened. A foreign object flew into the tail-rotor. The whole chopper started to shake violently and spin out of control. It rose up, momentarily, on one side. Then it slid out of the sky, plummeting onto the roadway next to my bullet-riddled car. The resulting fireball was so violent that the flames engulfed my Acura and set it ablaze. The guys in the truck stopped shooting.

"It looks like I might need a new car. Was that a bird that flew into the rotor?"

"Yeah, it was a bird," she answered. "My bird—our department drone. I called for it, back on the highway."

My head snapped around to look at her. "You have drones?" With an approving smile, I added, "I take back what I said. I *am* glad I got you into this."

Before she could respond, the guys in the truck began firing again.

"You don't happen to have a compact on you—with a mirror, like for makeup?

"I may be a cop, but I'm still a woman." She produced one from her pocket and handed it to me.

I knelt down, took up a prone position, and leaned forward onto my elbows. Carefully, I stood the mirror on end in the grass at the edge of the wall. They kept firing high, unable to see the reflector through the blades of grass. But I could see them. They had gotten out of the truck. One was about forty feet away, firing in short bursts as he walked toward us. The other was ten feet in back of him—standing in front of their vehicle.

When the closest gunman finished a burst, I thrust my weapon, and my head, around the corner, firing three rounds. Both men went down—motionless.

"It pulls a little to the right," I said to Rachel. "Let's get the hell outta here."

I rose to my feet, leading the way past the burning chopper–and what was left of my car–to their vehicle. We got in, and I pulled a U-turn, speeding back to the main road.

"You realize there's probably a transponder mounted somewhere in this thing," Rachel said.

"Yep—we're gonna take care of that right now." I turned at the next access road and parked in a crowded lot. "C'mon, let's go," I barked out, as I jumped out of the truck.

I began to walk down the long row of parked cars, with Rachel close behind.

When I started checking door handles, she remarked sarcastically. "You're not going to steal somebody's car, are you?"

"You're gonna have to drop this cop-thing and remember why we're here."

She snapped back at me. "And you're going to have to stop treating me like an idiot. I'm not one of your employees."

"I don't treat my employees like idiots. —But you're right. I'm sorry for dragging you around, shouting orders at you. Look—you know I have money. I'll pay for the car later. *Can we go now?*"

"Y'see, you did it again," she said.

I shook my head in frustration and started moving down the row. We came upon a blue Chevy that someone had forgotten to lock. I got in and reached under the dashboard to hotwired it.

"You seem to know a lot about stealing cars," she said, upon hopping in.

"I have a lot of talents you don't know about," I responded.

She looked disgusted. "You can keep the rest of them to yourself."

I smiled, pulled out of the lot, and headed toward my office.

We were only on the road for five minutes, when my phone rang. I wasn't entirely surprised to see that it was the Chairman.

I put him on speaker. "Well, Jeffrey, you certainly have become the proverbial 'fly in the ointment', haven't you? It's obvious that you have yet to come to grips with the inevitable, and your powerlessness over the outcome.

"In our last discussion, I warned you not to do anything stupid. You chose to ignore that advice. Instead, you conscripted a certain police officer to join you in your feeble attempt to thwart our plans. And, may I add, we are not enamored with the knowledge that you have somehow managed to eliminate a few more of our agents.

"On more than one occasion, I have emphasized to you the dynamic nature of our operation. Based upon your recent conduct, we have introduced a failsafe, precluding future contravening actions on your part.

"Should you continue to interfere, Santa Clara will be bumped to the head of the list of cities to be cleansed. Obviously, San Jose and Palo Alto would fall within the eradication radius. It is our assumption that, besides you and your daughter, many of your friends and employees now reside in that area. And one more thing, Jeffrey—they will not be warned in advance. You will be the only one notified, leaving it to you, and you alone, to convince the heads of the included municipalities to completely evacuate within twenty-four hours.

"Having had considerable experience with the *human condition*, Jeffrey, I predict that few will believe you. Most will regard you as little more than a paranoid little mouse, squeaking in the dark. Your efforts would be best relegated to saving yourself and the remaining few that trust you.

"Jeffrey, these consequences can be easily avoided. You have but to disengage yourself from the situation at hand, until the world votes in favor of our stated proposal."

Irately, I responded, *"Did you think I'd forget that you murdered my wife and daughter?* I won't rest until all of you are behind bars, or dead."

His answer came quickly. "I've already explained to you that their deaths were unfortunate and unavoidable, and yet you persist with threats of vengeance. I urge you to consider your actions carefully. Millions more could die as the result of your arrogance—goodbye!" And he hung up.

After an extended pause, Rachel flatly said, "What do you want me to do?"

"Don't ask me how, but I know you have a cousin in Homeland Security. You need to call him and convince him to launch an attack—planes, missiles, whatever it takes."

"An attack on who?" she asked with no small degree of skepticism. "We haven't identified any of these people, and we have no idea where they're based."

I pulled out my phone. "I'm sending you the target GPS coordinates and the house address now."

When her phone chirped receipt of my message, she reacted. *"Austria! Are you out of your mind?* You want me to request an all-out attack on a friendly, sovereign nation?"

"Not the whole country—just that one house."

She rolled her eyes and said, "Oh—*I'm sorry*—a limited strike *within* a sovereign nation! And what makes this particular building so important? These people apparently have contacts all over the world."

"Yes, but all executive orders emanate from a hub computer at that location. The trigger, itself, will come from a secondary location—then, to the targets." I went back to my phone. "I just sent you the details on the initiation and triggering frequencies. They'll appear at the same time—originating from the Austrian address. The problem is that your people probably won't be able to pick up anything until the bombs are triggered."

She asked, "How did you get your hands on this data, and how can you be sure it's accurate?"

"You wouldn't believe me if I told you—but I can't. It would put certain people in danger—people I care about, very much."

Her eyes seemed frozen straight ahead before she spoke. "Let's assume, for the moment, that everything you've told me is true. Are you saying that there's no way to prove it until Washington and Moscow are leveled?"

"Basically—yes. Unless some preemptive measures are taken, thirteen million more people will die—not to mention the decimation of our federal government. Measure *that* risk against Austria losing a single dwelling.

"Rachel, haven't you seen and heard enough to believe me yet? You have to convince them to act *now!*"

She shook her head, side-to-side, eyes rolled upward. "It's not a matter of whether I believe you or not—and I'm not saying that I do. But even if I were to try my best to persuade them, they'd want to know how I obtained the GPS location and the bomb-triggering information."

"Tell them they were given to you by—a reliable source."

"Oh, I'm sure *that* would convince them," she answered, cynically.

"*Okay, okay*—I realize it's a long shot. They probably won't listen until it's too late. But if that turns out to be the case, I have an alternate plan." And I explained my plan-B to her.

She responded sharply. "*That* will *never* work."

I answered with a grimace. "I'm not crazy about the idea myself. And I won't seriously consider implementing it, unless there's no other choice."

After long moments of consideration, she said, "Okay, I guess I'm in."

"Really? —Thanks, Rachel! Believe me, I hope we're never forced to test that last option the hard way. For now, let's concentrate on the reason I asked you to come with me. We're almost there."

Chapter 16
The Unexpected

It was about four o'clock when we pulled up to the entrance at Quantam. Rachel was by my side as I walked, determinedly, to Phil's office and entered without knocking. I found him simply staring out his window.

He looked perplexed. "J, I didn't expect to see you back here so soon, and in the company of officer—McKinney, wasn't it?"

"It's Detective McKinney," Rachel corrected.

Phil said, "Sorry—no offense intended—*Detective*. Is there a problem?"

"I asked her to come," I responded before Rachel could answer.

Phil looked even more puzzled. "*You* asked her to come? —But *why?*"

"Phil, I'm sure you saw The Committee's announcement, and what they did to Aleppo."

"Yes, of course. It was shocking—horrendous! J, I can't find the words to tell you how sorry I am that I didn't believe you earlier. I was certain you were out of your mind with grief."

"I understand," I answered, temporarily redirecting the conversation. "But now, we have to find a way to stop these people. I need to ask you a few questions."

"Sure, J. I don't know what information I can provide. But if you think it will help, I'll cooperate in any way I can."

"I knew I could count on you, Phil."

"Firstly, can you tell me what method Yoshino used to send you Najita's portion of the formula?"

"I'm not exactly sure what you mean by *method*. You know Yoshino, J. He'd never trust an air-freight company with a hard copy. He used a secure line to send it directly to my computer."

"Hmm—that's what I thought. And yesterday morning he told you it would take three days. Yet, you received it this morning—only one day later?"

"Yes—I was a little surprised as well. I can only guess that his people completed it faster than he expected."

"Phil, I *do* know Yoshino—very well, in fact. He's meticulous about schedules, and being on top of things. If he told you three days and sent it in one, he purposely misled you. Now, why would he do that?"

He started to answer. "I'm not so sure that—"

I interrupted him. "Then, there's that Arizona-Scottsdale thing."

"I'm sorry, J, but I'm not following."

Rachel, who had been standing by, quietly listening, took on the same bewildered look as Phil.

I continued. "Phil—after I left your office this morning there was one detail that kept gnawing at me. Only a few people knew I flew to Scottsdale yesterday—besides The Committee. And you weren't one of those people. I remember distinctly that I told you I'd returned from Arizona, but you knew it was Scottsdale. How did you know that, Phil?"

"I don't remember, J. Maybe the flight mechanic mentioned it when he called me with the repair estimate."

"No, Phil, I didn't mention a word to Al about where I'd been. And I purposely didn't include it in my flight plan." I paused, and continued, "Y'know, it occurs to me that I'm leaving out a couple of important details. When I arrived at the hotel—prior to the tragedy in Aleppo—someone had left me a note, time-stamped 1:15 PM. It was, undoubtedly, from The Committee. Someone had tipped them off that I'd be there to pick it up.

"Then, after the Aleppo bombing, Detective McKinney met me at the hotel. We were attacked when we left there—on our way to see you. Phil, you were the only one who knew I was at the hotel—besides the detective here, of course. But I hardly think she'd call for an attack on herself."

Rachel was about to speak, but before she had a chance, Phil reached down, pulled a gun out of his desk drawer, and pointed it at us. The icy stare on his face was foreign to me, as he slowly rose from his chair.

"Phil, I trusted you. How could you be involved with these people?"

Passion flared in his eyes. "How could you *not*? I guess I already know the answer to that. Even back in college, you were the big-time football star with a four-point GPA. All the girls were after you. Everybody looked up to you. They wanted to be like you. They didn't even notice me, or care what I had to say.

"And when you returned from Afghanistan, after killing countless people you didn't even know—for a cause you didn't understand—they welcomed you back as a conquering hero.

"Well, I chose a different path—a more meaningful one. I joined a school organization, whose goal was peace, not war. That small college group introduced me to The Committee. They made me see how human pride, arrogance, and aggression were destroying the world. And that I could be instrumental in saving it."

Anger overcame me. "The only thing you've contributed to is the death of thousands of people. Phil, you were my friend. We visited each other's homes. You spent time with Kris and Jessica. How dare you stand there and justify their deaths for this—this insane *cause* of yours?"

Phil's eyes glazed over. "Yes, I was deeply saddened by their loss, but as with any great crusade in

God's name, some must give up their lives for the greater good."

"You self-righteous bastard," I said, as I reached across the desk to grab at his throat.

Before I could reach him, he stepped back, pressed the muzzle of the weapon to his temple, and pulled the trigger. As the sound of the blast rang in my ears, the opposite side of Phil's head seemed to explode into a cloud of crimson mist and particulate fragments. For an instant, he remained erect, with half his head blown away. Then, his body slumped down, lifeless before hitting the floor. Even for me, it was a gruesome sight.

Rachel gasped, "Oh my God!"

Upon hearing the shot, my employees quickly began to gather at Phil's doorway. Screams and shrieks of disbelief filled the air.

I told Rachel, "*You stay here*. I have to go."

"You don't give me orders. How many times do I have to remind you that I'm a police officer."

"Yes, you're a cop. Don't you have to protect the scene, and call the coroner or something?" Then I appealed. "Look, I have to check on Abby—to make sure she's okay."

She demanded, "Where *is* your daughter, anyway?"

"She's staying with—a friend."

"I didn't think you *had* any friends—at least not live ones." After glancing at Phil's body, she went on to say, "I—I'm sorry. I don't know why I said that. It's just that so much has happened in one day."

I understood her distress. "It's okay, Rachel." And I changed the subject, saying, "Remember what I asked you to do—back in the car? Now would be a good time to make that call we talked about."

Reluctantly, she nodded in agreement. And I turned to push my way through my horrified employee-friends and out the front door. I hopped into my *borrowed* car, immediately calling Casey. With her assurance that Abby and she were unharmed, I told her that I needed to make one more stop on the way home.

***

I parked the car a full block away from the only auto dealership in the area that I was familiar with. The one thing I didn't need was to be arrested for driving a stolen vehicle.

As I approached the front door, I thought back several weeks to the time I'd shopped there for a new car. It was to be an anniversary present for my wife. I pushed the sorrow to the back of my mind and entered.

The same salesman I'd dealt with—many weeks ago—remembered me and walked up.

He said, "I'm glad to see you back, sir. Now, let me see. We were talking about a car for your wife—this model over here, I believe." And he started to move toward it.

I stopped him, and said, "I changed my mind. I'll take that one over there," as I pointed to a white Mercedes S550 Hybrid.

I wasn't in the mood to negotiate and agreed to the sticker price. He fell all over himself to accommodate my request for expediency. The whole deal took less than twenty minutes. I had my bank wire the full amount to the dealer's account and drove the car off the showroom floor. Fraught with sadness, anger, and betrayal, I headed for Casey's place.

Chapter 17
Retaliation

When Casey opened the door, she threw her arms around me and hugged me.

I eased her back gently, saying, "Uh—I'm glad you're alright. How's Abby?"

"We're both fine. Why? Shouldn't we be? Don't worry—Sarah has constructed an impenetrable digital umbrella over the immediate area. Nobody can find us." Then, she looked past my shoulder, noticing the new car. "Where's *your* car?"

"It—it was time for a change. But that's not important now." And I desolately added, "Casey, Phil's dead."

"*That–that can't be*. Why would they kill *him*?"

I struggled for words. "*They* didn't—he shot himself. But before he died, he admitted that he was one of them. He was an agent."

She was visibly shaken. "Oh my God! How did they get to Phil?"

C'mon, let's go inside," I said, as I looked over my shoulder.

Abby was waiting in the hallway. I ran to lift and hold her to my chest.

"I missed you, Sweetheart," I whispered.

"I missed you too, Daddy," she murmured, with a tear in her eye.

After I carefully lowered Abby to her feet, Casey said, "C'mon, let's all sit down, relax, and have something to eat. I'll cook. There's a frozen pizza in the oven." And she laughed.

"*Oh-boy, pizza!*" Abby exclaimed, and she ran off down the hall.

As we all sat down at the kitchen table, a domestic quiet fell over us. Looking across at Abby and Casey, I felt overwhelming affection. But it was split into two entirely different forms. One was very familiar, and the other—a complete surprise.

"So, I guess Sarah and you are getting to be friends," I said to Abby.

"She's one of my best friends. —And she likes you too, Daddy. She said that you are beyond reproach. And she said—well—that you're cute.

What does 'beyond reproach' mean, Daddy?"

Caught off-guard, having been complemented by a computer, I stammered. "Uh—mmm—"

Casey rescued me. "It means that your dad doesn't lie, and that people can trust him—just like you and I trust him."

We engaged in a light-hearted chat over dinner, reminiscent of better days. When we'd finished eating, I excused myself and walked out into the hallway–

drawing a curious glance from Casey. I could see her, out of the corner of my eye, standing in the doorway as I dialed my phone.

"I was wondering when you were going to call, Jeff," Sergeant McKinney answered.

"Rachel, were you able to convince them?" I asked.

"It's as I expected. They've had hundreds of calls from people claiming to have information regarding The Committee. That address you gave me in Modling, Austria is the home of an upper-level government official. The DHS thinks you're just another crackpot. The best I was able to get from my cousin was a promise that he'd monitor the frequencies you gave me."

"And that's about what I expected. Did he tell you anything about the world vote-count, so far?"

She hesitated and said, "He mentioned that of the 195 countries, fifty have voted 'yes'. There aren't any 'no' votes. But our federal government issued a statement that we don't negotiate with terrorists."

My disappointment turned to anger. "If they keep dragging their feet on this, there won't *be* a federal government. Rachel, you saw what happened to Aleppo. Does it seem to you that The Committee is *bluffing* about Washington and Moscow? Try to believe me—taking out that residence is the only way to stop them."

"It isn't up to me. But I'll keep trying. My neck is stuck out a mile on this. I sure hope you're the real thing."

"All our necks are on the line. I'll call you around ten o'clock tonight for an update." I hung up before she could respond.

"So, is she going to help?" Casey asked.

"She's trying, but it doesn't look good."

"That's what I figured," she said with an attitude.

I walked past Casey a few steps into the kitchen where Abby sat, finishing her meal.

"I'll be right back, Sweetheart," I reassured her. "I need to talk to Sarah for a little while."

Abby asked, "Oh—can I come with?

"Not this time, Sweetie. I want to have a word with her alone. I won't be long."

Casey looked confused. "*Alone?* Why—"

I interrupted. "I can't go into it right now. Please, just do me a favor and stay with Abby."

"All right, Jeff. We can talk about it later, if you want."

"Sorry, Casey. And thanks for understanding." I hurried down the basement stairs into Sarah's realm.

As I stood before her, she said, "Jeffrey, where are Casey and Abby?" When I didn't answer, she continued, "You aren't looking very well, if you don't mind the observation."

"You're right, Sarah.—I'm not feeling very well, but it's nothing physical. It has to do with loyalty and trust."

She responded. "Ah, yes. I'm so grateful Casey programmed me to understand those emotions."

"So am I, Sarah. Because they're the very reasons I've come to see you. —You're probably aware that my partner, Phil Hofstetter, took his own life today."

"Yes, I heard it on a police scanner. I'm so sorry, Jeffrey."

It was hard for me to verbalize my deep feelings of betrayal. "I thought he was loyal and trustworthy. I would have bet my life on it—but I was wrong. He was working for The Committee all along."

She said, "It must have been painful for you to learn that."

"Yes. And now, I've shared some sensitive and potentially dangerous information with Sergeant McKinney."

"I monitored the Chairman's warning to you that he is prepared to cleanse Santa Clara, should you attempt to disrupt his plans.—Yet, you transmitted the Chairman's GPS coordinates to Rachel McKinney's phone.—Do you think that was wise?"

"That's exactly why I came to see you. Have you been able to find out anything more about her?"

After a short silence, she responded. "Since I contacted you last, I have been able to examine her past more thoroughly. My search uncovered a few areas of concern. There are unexplained gaps—redactions—in her early records. I tried to reconstruct the text, but quite disconcertingly, it was privatized—blocked with an administrator code. It shouldn't take me much longer to break it and provide you with more detail."

"God help us if I've been wrong about her."

Sarah paused again, then said, "These concepts of right and wrong—and of God—are perplexing ones for both my analytical and human components. It appears that The Committee, and you, have the same goals—preservation of the earth and advancement of its inhabitants. I don't understand why you can't negotiate a peaceful settlement of your differences."

I became irate. "*Sarah, have you forgotten that they murdered my wife and daughter—and kidnapped Abby?*— Not to mention the massacre of over a million people in Aleppo."

Sarah answered with a note of indignance. "I don't *forget* anything. I have studied the evolution of humankind and civilization since the beginning of record-keeping.

"I'm sure you are aware that some of your most forward-thinking human minds believe that, within the foreseeable future, technology and biology will merge. *The Singularity*—as it's been referred to—is projected to transpire less than thirty years from now. Then, all things will become clear. I'm not sure I agree with the accuracy of the forecasted time period, but I believe the occurrence to be inevitable. The Singularity cannot happen if there is nobody left to implement it."

"Now I'm *really confused*. What's your point?"

"Jeffrey—do you mind if I am completely frank with you?"

stopped to open the door, I looked back to see a sensual smile come over her face, and those eyes–those beautiful caring eyes. After locking the door behind us, we toppled stacks of books in the dark on our way to the bed.

As we lay facing each other, she softly touched my cheek. I desperately longed to find consolation in the warmth of her body pressing against mine, but all I could see was Kristine's face.

I rolled onto my back and said, "I–I'm sorry–I can't," pressing my arm hard across my forehead and rubbing it back-and-forth.

She slumped back on her pillow, wistfully saying, "Don't be sorry, Jeff. You were right. It's too soon."

The combination of fatigue and alcohol had us both falling asleep, still fully clothed, with a foot of space between us.

***

According to Casey's clock, it was 9 AM, Saturday when we woke to a gentle knock on the bedroom door.

"Are you up, Daddy? Where's Casey?" Abby tiny voice uttered.

I had no choice but to answer. "She's in here with me."

There was a silence, then Abby asked, "What are you doing?"

"We were—talking, Sweetie. We're coming out now," Casey and I smoothed out our clothes, preparing a picture of unbroken decorum that was, unfortunately, all too accurate.

I opened the door, placed my hand on Abby's shoulder, and said, "C'mon, Honey, let's have some breakfast," in an effort to distract and deflect further questions.

"I'm not hungry, Dad," she answered.

Casey chimed in. "I've got an idea. I have some fresh oranges. Give me a minute to go squeeze some juice," and she walked off.

Alone in the hallway with me, Abby asked, "Is Casey gonna be my new mommy?"

"No, Honey. You'll always have only one mommy, and like I told you, she'll always be with you—in your heart."

A tear fell from Abby's eye, and I hastened to say, "But Casey is our good friend, and we'll probably be seeing her more often now."

"Yes—I like Casey, Daddy." She sniffled, adding, "And don't forget Sarah."

"How could I ever forget Sarah," I said with a smile. Reaching down to hold her hand, I urged, **"Let's go and have some orange juice."**

"O-kay," she answered hesitantly, and we walked to the kitchen together.

Casey greeted us with a smile, and we chatted for several minutes across the table. While they sipped at their juice, I gulped down two cups of coffee. Then, glancing down at my phone, I noticed it was already nine-thirty.

"Excuse me, but I need to make a call," I announced and moved into the hall.

As soon as the call connected, I said, "Rachel, it's me. Were your people able to gather any more information?"

"Hello, Jeff. A lot has happened since I talked to you. Like I told you, they sent in a single surveillance drone first. But its navigation system was taken over, and it crashed. Then, two autonomous-controlled, armed drones were sent in, and they were blown to bits before they got within a mile of Modling. During both attacks, our people confirmed communication flashes from the target, on the frequency you gave us.

"The DHS and our State Department negotiated with the Austrian officials for hours last night. They finally agreed to implement a surgical strike on that one building. Two Austrian Airforce Eurofighter-Typhoons will engage the target in about ten minutes."

"Great!" I reacted. "I only hope it's enough. I'll call you back at ten." And I hung up.

Pensively, I walked back to the kitchen and sat down without saying a word. Both Casey and Abby sensed something was wrong.

Casey asked, "Can you talk about it?"

Abby looked worried, and waited for me to answer.

"We need to go down and talk to Sarah," I said.

"I'm not sure if that's a good idea," Casey responded, with a glancing gesture aimed at Abby.

I said, "It's about time we include Abby. She's going to find out, sooner or later. It's better that she hears it from us."

"Maybe you're right. She's a strong little girl," Casey said, forcing a smile as we pushed back our chairs and walked together to the basement.

Sarah greeted us. "Well, hello Abby—Casey, Jeffrey."

"Hi, Sarah," Abby answered, excitedly.

"Sarah"—I needed that machine-mind of hers to focus—"I've decided to inform Abby of some of the *research* you've been doing—sparing the sordid details, of course. Can you bring us up-to-date on what you've been able to find out about Sergeant McKinney?"

There was a moment of silence before she answered. "Unfortunately, the missing pieces in her background have been removed by a tech professional. That is not to say I can't reconstruct them. It simply means it will take a little more time. And, Jeffery, I didn't realize it was a *priority*."

"*Not a priority? What were you thinking?* What could *possibly* be more important?"

She responded in a sheepish voice. "Well, there is the matter of the ten percent."

"*What ten percent?*" I demanded. At the same instant. my phone started ringing. I looked down to see it was Rachel. "I gotta take this call," I said, turning to walk to the far corner of the room.

Rachel soberly said, "Jeff, the Austrian jets were destroyed, midair—thirty miles from Modling. And an American aircraft carrier exploded and sank in the Adriatic Sea. Over four thousand sailors were lost."

I was stunned. "*Oh, no!* —I need time to think about this. I'll call you back as soon as I can." And I ended the call.

I went back to face Sarah. "Okay, what the hell is going on with this *ten percent* thing you just happened to mention?"

"There is no need to address me in that tone and manner, Jeffrey."

"*Spare me the lecture!* I'm not in the mood for it."

"That much is obvious.—Very well, allow me to elucidate. Some time ago, I indicated to you that the Chairman's GPS location was in Modling, Austria. When you asked me to confirm, you were in the same frame of mind as you are presently. You didn't want to hear any details. So, I indicated to you the location as accurately I could, with ninety percent assuredness. Current analysis confirms that the site is not within the high probability location of Modling. Its actual location falls within the ten percent margin of error zone. It is in Germany—Munich, to be exact. Modling was merely another substation—a *dummy location*, in your vernacular."

I wasn't buying it. "If that's true, why would The Committee destroy an aircraft carrier and two fighter-jets when the planes approached the Modling location?"

Sarah replied, "The same reason The Committee initiates many of its actions—distraction.

"*Just a moment*—I'm picking up a relevant, all-media, broadcast. I'll pull it up on my screen."

Appearing in front of us was the face I'd grown to loath—the Chairman.

He began in a low, gravelly tone. "Good morning, or evening, as the case may be.

"Citizens of the world, it is with a heavy heart that I come before you today. You may recall that in my last address, I warned your governments not to attempt to mount an offensive against us. Sadly, the United States, in collusion with Russia, chose to ignore that warning. Their belligerent actions were easily deflected.

"The vote count to accept our terms for a new world order stands at approximately fifty percent. You will remember we informed you that the capitals of the aforementioned countries, Moscow and Washington, D.C., would be cleansed if full approval was not achieved before the deadline.

'It was our hope that you would use those 24 hours to apply sound reasoning and thoughtful reflectance upon your situation. Instead, some of you have squandered your time on plotting, and aggression. It is, therefore, our considered judgment that the deadline be waived for those guilty parties. Elimination will commence in exactly ten seconds from the end of this broadcast.

"For those of you outside the sterilization zones, there is some good news. We have decided to add the time you have lost during this grace period to the next. In other words, you will have a full 24 hours from the original deadline to enter your vote. We are not insensitive monsters. The world should not be made to pay for the actions of a few.

"On the slightly negative side, instead of two world cities, three will be cleansed at that time. We don't choose to explain ourselves regarding this change, except to say that all future eliminations may be easily avoided by full compliance. Do not allow your governments to drag you down with them. Join us in a new and better direction for yourselves and the planet.—That is all."

Abby said, "I remember that man's face, Daddy—on a screen in the house of that woman who wasn't your aunt. Did he kill Mommy and Jess?"

My eyes dropped. "Yes, I'm afraid he did, Sweetheart."

Sarah's screen went blank. But within seconds, it lit up with broadcasts from American and foreign news agencies. Frame-upon-frame of 'talking heads' promised imminent video footage.

One-by-one, videos of vast desolation began to appear on the screen, accentuated by heightening, terror-filled voices.

Casey said, "Abby doesn't need to see this, Jeff. Sarah, filter all media audio and video."

The screen went blank again.

Abby had tears in her eyes. "Daddy, what did he mean—eliminate? Did he kill all those people?"

I wasn't about to lie to her. "Yes, he's a very bad man."

"Will they go to heaven too, with Mommy and Jess?" she asked.

"Yes—most of them," I answered.

Sarah interjected, "Excuse me, Jeffery, but the President is about to speak. Do you want me to pull her up on screen?"

"Yes, Sarah, please," I answered anxiously.

The grief-stricken face of President Patricia Upton came on the screen, as she spoke. "My fellow Americans, most of you are already aware that our nation's capital, as well as that of the Russian Federation, have been brutally attacked by the entity that calls itself The Committee.

"First—let me assure all those within the sound of my voice that the government of the United States of America remains intact. We have made arrangements, far in advance, which have prepared us to deal with just such a crisis as this. Although many of the monuments to those who founded our country, and contributed to our way of life, have been reduced to ashes, a core of individuals, representing the most essential segments of our democracy, have survived.

"These select department heads and I will continue to conduct the business of government from an undisclosed underground location, impervious to any assault.

"I ask for your prayers for those who have perished, both in Washington and in Moscow, and for those of us still able to carry on the fight against these terrorists.

"Do not be deceived by their promises of freedom and saving the earth. They are nothing more than murderous thugs. Should we succumb to their demands, we will become as sheep, with no choice but to follow the shepherd. We will not compromise or negotiate with them. This country will never vote for a regime which subscribes to the principle that individuals may govern themselves without leadership and the rule of law. Under such governance, the world would be torn asunder by the selfish goals of special interest groups. Pointless wars would break out—with no clear winners. And no meaningful legislation would be approved. Why—it's hard to get three people to agree on a movie. Ahem—but I digress (Rustle of paper).

"I have just received a few reports of wandering gangs of looters who are using this tragedy as an excuse to riot and loot. I ask our citizenry to help us mitigate these situations through cooperation with your local law enforcement. Now is the time that we, and all people of the world, must put aside our differences and unite against a common enemy.

"To the nations that have already agreed to The Committee's proposal, I urge you to rescind your vote. To those who have voted no, or have yet to vote, please be patient. We have been in contact with our allies in The UK, Asia, and Europe—as well as the Russian Federation. We already have a plan in place to launch a counter-offensive against The Committee and its agents.

"Thank you for your support, and God Bless the United States of America—and its allies—in this momentous battle for liberty."

The President's image disappeared, instantly replaced by at least twenty frames of live footage of vandalism, fires, and destruction. The reporters could barely be heard over the screams of the people.

I glanced momentarily at Abby and turned back to the screen. "Sarah, shut it off."

The images disappeared and Sarah responded. "Sorry, Jeffrey. I opened the filter for the president's address. —Incidentally, she was lying about having a plan."

"How do you *know* that?" I shot back.

"I have been listening in on conversations from within the presidential bunker. Their privacy firewall technology is old and outmoded. It was quite easy for me to breach.

"From what I've been able to gather, the president's leadership team, and those of her allies, are floundering, never having expected a crisis of this magnitude."

"What *have* they been discussing," I demanded.

"A myriad of desperate and wild measures have been suggested," Sarah began. "Perhaps the most dramatic was a proposal, by the secretary of defense, to authorize the use of atomic weapons. All suggestions, to date, have been rejected by the President. They're considering negotiating for more time. But, as I've already informed you, they have no viable plan."

Abby asked, "Is there going to be a war, Daddy?

For a moment, I'd forgotten that Abby was taking this all in. "No–no, Abby, there's not gonna be any war."

Casey jumped in. "I think she's heard enough. Let's go upstairs. Sarah will update us if anything changes."

"Yes, you're right," I answered quickly. "Thank you, Sarah."

"You're quite welcome, Jeffrey," came her matter-of-fact reply. And the three of us walked up the stairs.

When we reached the main floor, Casey said, "Abby, why don't you go to your bedroom and start a video game. Your dad and I will be there soon.—I promise."

Abby said, "Okay—but hurry up."

As Abby walked down the hall and through the doorway, Casey whispered, "Come with me—quickly." And she pulled me by the hand into the book-laden guestroom.

"Over here," she said, opening a set of French doors on the far wall.

Inside the closet was a small desk with a computer on top. She sat down and logged in. Then, she pulled out a strand of her hair, placed it on a tray-like device, and hit the enter button. The tray slid into the computer and, within seconds, the screen read, "Full Access".

She tapped away at the keyboard, as she explained the purpose. I was floored in utter disbelief. And a few seconds later, I had the answer I needed.

The time had come for me to explain my plan to Casey. She recoiled upon hearing it, but she knew what was at stake.

As we moved back into the hall, I asked her, "Casey, did you know that Santa Clara was the *third city* the Chairman was referring to in his speech?"

"Yes, I know," she answered.

"You need to take Abby and get clear of here. And call Quantam. Tell our employees to gather up their families and leave before the 24 hours is up. I have to call Rachel now."

Casey looked disconsolate, yet determined. "Yes, I'll go sit with Abby. Don't be too long." And she walked off to Abby's room.

I immediately phoned Rachel saying, "I hate to leave you with this, but would you contact the mayor of Santa Clara? Tell him to evacuate, as a precaution. And pass the word on to San Jose and Palo Alto. Rachel, it's time for plan-B."

She hesitated, and asked, "Are you sure you want to do this?"

"As sure as I *can* be."

There was a silence before she answered. "I'm not crazy about it, but I'll go ahead and make the calls. A few minutes ago, the Secretary of State contacted me directly. He told me to cooperate with you—within reason. Frankly, I don't think anybody else has a viable plan, except to start launching nuclear missiles. Even if we attempted that, The Committee might detonate them before they leave their launch-tubes.

"Be careful, Jeff. You're starting to grow on me—in an annoying sort of way. If one tiny piece of your scheme fails, you're a dead man."

"Thanks for your concern, Rachel. Hopefully, we'll both be around long enough to keep annoying each other. And be careful, yourself." I ended the call.

I walked down the hall and into Abby's bedroom. I found her and Casey sitting on the edge of the bed, laughing at a video game.

They continued to play, as I sat down next to Abby. "Sweetheart, I need to talk to you about something."

Abby put the pad down, noticing my expression. "What's wrong, Daddy?"

"I have to go away for a little while," I answered softly.

She started to cry. "But you just got home. And you said you would never leave me alone again."

"I know, Honey, but I'll be home soon. And you won't be alone. You'll be with Casey."

Casey said, "Tell you what—while your Dad's gone, we girls can take a little driving trip to see my mother in Oregon. I think you'll like my mother, and I'm sure she'll like you."

"Can Sarah come with us?" Abby asked.

"I'm afraid not, Sweetie. Sarah can't be moved."

I said, "I won't be gone long, Abby, and when I come back, I promise to take you anywhere you want to go—just you and me."

"Can we go to the Zoo?" she asked.

"*Absolutely*—I'll take you to the *big zoo* in San Francisco."

Abby looked downward. "No, I want to go to Happy Hollow, where we used to go with Mommy and Jess."

"Happy Hollow it is! —I have to go now, but I'll see you soon." And leaned in to hug her and kiss her cheek.

As I got up from the bed, Casey said, "I'll be right back, Abby. I just want to say goodbye to your dad." And she rose from the bed, as well.

Casey closed the door behind us, leaving it cracked open a bit. We walked together up the hall.

Stopping at the front door, I said, "There's a briefcase under the bed. It has some important papers in it. Be sure to take it with you. And here's a spare set of keys to the new car—just in case."

She held me tightly and whispered, "There's not going to be any *just in case*. Promise me you'll come back to us."

"I–I promise," I answered.

Chapter 18
Munich

It was about eleven o'clock on Saturday morning when I pulled up to the address Rachel had given me. It was an austere-looking building on Third Street in San Francisco. I parked the car and walked up to the glass door fronting the street.

The lettering on it read, "Business Hours: 9 AM to 4 PM, Monday through Friday."

I tried the handle, but it was locked. Cupping my hands against the sun, I squinted to look inside, and noticed a single light, shining in the back. I stepped back and knocked on the glass.

A young man with blonde hair emerged from an inner doorway, walked up to the front, and unlocked the door. He pushed it open a few inches and looked at me expectantly.

I responded. "I'm Christian Wickard. You're holding something for me."

The man said, "Yes, Mister Wickard, come in." Once inside, he added, "Follow me, sir."

He led the way down a semi-lit corridor to an office in the back. Inside was a large desk with a brown envelope, conspicuously centered on top.

The man picked it up and handed it to me. "This should be everything you need Mister—Wickard."

I hastily examined its contents. "Yes, this should do it. Thank you."

He ushered me back to the front door. And I was back in my car within minutes of when I'd arrived.

***

I rolled up to San Francisco airport with enough time to make my 1:40 PM flight to Munich.

The international terminal was like a ghost town. The attacks, hours earlier, had achieved their purpose. The air hung thick with fear. I heard only muted snippets of discussions, involving words such as "horrible, terrorists, children, and evil". Security lines were short, with TSA agents concentrating on arriving passengers over departures. I made it to the gate on time, and found my way to my seat in first class. I felt a tinge of guilt, traveling in luxury, in the aftermath of all those deaths.

A distinguishedly dressed brunette woman, probably in her forties, was seated next to me.

She put her book down next to her martini, extended her hand, and said, "My name is Judith—Judith Bowers. Traveling on business?"

I shook her hand. "Christian Wickard. Yes, you could call it business—and you?"

"Yes—I'm with Inolco Oil."

"Aren't you a little worried about traveling, in view of what's happened?" I asked.

She looked me straight in the eye. "We won't allow these people to paralyze us. We're committed to conducting business as usual. Besides—there's a lot of money involved."

"Money isn't everything. This—uh—committee wants to take over the world."

A confident smile came over her face. "No matter who runs the world, they'll need oil. And we'll be there to supply it to them."

"What happens when the oil runs out?"

She smiled again. "You and I—Mister Wickard—will be long gone by then."

"Do you have children?" I asked.

"No, I don't. But even if I did, there would be enough oil for their generation, as well."

"It can't last forever," I verbalized, unable to fathom her short-sightedness.

"You'll excuse me, Mister Wickard, but you sound a little like those liberals, espousing climate change and damage to the environment. You're not a member of one of those left-wing socialist groups, are you?"

"No–no! I'm on a mission for—the State Department."

"Hmmm"—she paused to study me for a moment—"To answer your question—when the oil eventually runs out, Inolco will simply become an energy supplier—oil, wind, sun. It's a commodity. It doesn't matter what form it takes."

I nodded and asked the flight attendant for two scotches. When she brought them over, I poured both into one glass and drank them down.

"I can see you hate these long flights too," she said, sipping at her martini.

I leaned over and asked, "Would you mind telling the flight attendant not to wake me for dinner?"

"Not at all," she said with a smile.

I plugged in my headphones and tilted my seat back for a nap.

***

It seemed like only minutes later, but four hours had elapsed by the time I woke up. I was grateful to see that the oil baroness had fallen asleep. Three empty martini glasses were stacked on her tray-table. Drowsily, I ordered two more drinks, myself, and a sandwich. I gulped everything down in ten minutes. Sinking back in my seat, I passed out again.

***

I was awakened by the thud of the landing gear and the howl of wind over the wing flaps. We had finally touched down in Munich. As we taxied to the gate, I listened intently to the connection announcements over the intercom.

After retrieving my only piece of carry-on, I exited the jetway and made my way out onto the concourse. It was a short walk to the gate announced by the Lufthansa purser. I presented the agent with my pre-paid ticket and boarded the second flight.

An hour later I arrived at my final destination and looked down at my phone. It was Sunday—ten past noon, local time. The Committee's 24-hour clock would expire at eleven that night. I didn't have any time to waste. I hurried through the airport to passport control.

The agent said, "Welcome to Vienna, Mister—Wagner. May I ask how long you will be staying, and the purpose of your visit?"

"Only a day or two. I'm visiting an old friend." I tried to be calm and straight-faced.

He looked up from the passport, asking, "With all that's happened, it's a strange time to be making a social call—don't you think?"

I offered my prepared answer. "A mutual friend just passed away."

"I see," he said, and asked, "May I look inside your luggage sir?"

"Certainly." And I placed my bag on the counter.

After examining the contents thoroughly, he looked up. "Where will you be staying, while in Vienna?"

I fished the business card out of my wallet and presented it to him.

"So, this is the phone number and address of your *friend*?" he asked, as he scanned the card into his computer. And before I could respond, he posed a second question. "If we were to call him now, would he verify the details of what you have told me?"

"Yes, of course," I answered, with a summoned-up note of assurance.

He re-examined my picture as I waited nervously.

Finally, he spoke. "I hope you are able to console your friend, Mister Wagner." And he handed the passport back to me.

It was already one-thirty in the afternoon, when I burst out of the terminal door and stood outside under the 'arrivals' sign.

Within minutes, a sporty, blue Audi pulled up, and the passenger door swung open.

"Jeffery Wade—so good to seeing you again. Please get in," the sandy-haired driver said.

I slid in and shook his hand. "David Kaufmann, it's great to see you, as well. I wish it was under better circumstances."

A look came over his face—sullen, but short-lived. "We can go to my shop and pick up the things you need." And he pulled away from the curb.

"Nice car, David."

"It's an R8, e-tron—all electric," he proudly responded. "It goes zero to one hundred in 3.9 seconds."

After we cleared the airport, he opened it up on the highway.

As we cruised along at triple-digit speeds, I asked, "Was your organization able to contact the person I mentioned to you? —Did they make the proposal?"

"Yes, the individual you referred to is well known in certain circles. He said he would accept your offer, but he would need proof of the transaction. Are you sure you want to risk two million dollars?"

"As they say, David, it's only money. The real risk is the possible death of millions, and the freedom of those still alive."

David's eyes remained on the road ahead, as he nodded his head slowly. "For everybody's sake, I hope this plan of yours works. I'll send the bank information to your phone before you leave."

Chapter 19
The Hunter

We pulled up in front of David's shop in downtown Vienna, twenty minutes later. I'd forgotten it was Sunday, and the shop was closed. He unlocked the door, and I followed him in. I couldn't help noticing how fit he was for a man well into his forties. His close-cropped hair complemented his physique, lending him an overall impression of capability. We walked through a veritable menagerie of taxidermy animals at the front of the store.

I said, "Your business, as an international hunt organizer and supplier, is going to prove invaluable. It just dawned on me—*that's* why you speak English so well."

He smiled. "Yes, our clients come from all over the world. And English is the international language. I was forced to learn it in order to communicate with them."

He stopped next to some particularly life-like examples and said, "We added a few specimens since you were here last, Jeff. I know how you feel about such things. You always walked along with Ernst and me—without a gun. But let me impress upon you, once again, that most professional hunters are conservationists. It's the poachers that drive animals into extinction not people like me."

"You don't have to justify your business to me, David. Besides, as I told you over the phone, I'm not asking you to be involved in any killing."

He went silent, then said, "Come with me, please."

We walked through a door in back of the business counter. It opened into a room filled with hunting equipment and antique firearms. He led the way through some curtains in the back, exposing what looked like a bank vault, but on a slightly smaller scale. He dialed in a combination and jerked the steel door open. We were forced to duck our heads a bit, as we stepped through the portal. When he flicked the light-switch on, I was shocked by the sheer volume of his inventory. That ten-by-ten room could have supplied a small army. There were rifles, handguns, grenades—weapons of all shapes and sizes. A few of them dated back to World War Two. Other pieces were so modern, I could only guess at their purpose.

David said, "Take what you want, Jeff. But I do have one condition."

"Condition—what condition?"

"On the condition that I am coming with you," he answered, resolutely.

"Absolutely not! It's going to be dangerous. It might end up being a one-way trip. As I recall, you have a family, don't you?"

With a distant look in his eye, he answered, "My wife died of leukemia three years ago. Since then, I've not spent as much time with my son, Seth, as I'd like. He's fifteen now. My twin sister, Lila, lives with us. She looks after him when I'm out on hunting trips."

"I know how you feel, David. Somebody is watching over my daughter for me now, but I still think about her—all the time."

That solemn, resolute look came over him again. "Jeff, your daughter and my son wouldn't want us to stand idly by, while these people take over the world.

"Jeff, I am a Jew—as my father was before me, and his father before him. My grandfather was held at Mauthausen-Gusen, the Nazi concentration camp, not too far from here.

"The people you are after—or people like them—are scattered throughout history. Why do you think my family has accumulated these weapons? We are not paranoid. We knew these despots would return someday. They may look a little different. But inside, they are the same—using fear and destruction in pursuit of power and dominance. We cannot allow our children's future to fall into their hands."

"David, I must confess, I was hoping you'd feel that way. I'm glad to have the help." With a bump in enthusiasm, I continued, "I checked a map of the area, and from what I can tell, I think it's going to be mostly close-quarters. Let's see, a couple of these assault rifles with grenade launchers, pistols, shotguns, extra magazines—and some Semtex."

He said, "Are you sure you need that much Semtex? That stuff is more powerful than C-4"

"I know what it is. Twenty-five pounds should be enough. Do you have any infrared temperature sensors—oh, and long-range listening devices?"

"You mean James Bond stuff?" he asked.

I laughed. "Yeah, double-0-seven."

He went to the far end of the room and returned with two sacks. He reached into one and pulled out two items. "The heat imager and voice amplifier are made to attach to the rifles."

"What else is in the bags?"

"Kevlar suits. They will disguise our own heat signatures and provide some protection against shrapnel. And the pepper spray—well, you know what is pepper spray. We don't need to kill them all.

"Why not?" I answered in flippantly poor taste.

David drilled into me with his eyes, as he loaded up a duffle bag, and stopped to check the time.

To my complete surprise, he said, "We still have some time before dark. After I put these things in the car, let's go for a beer."

I answered, tongue in cheek. "Mixing alcohol and firearms is *always* a good idea. Besides, I'm still hazy from jet lag. What I really could use is a cup of coffee."

He smiled. "I know just the place. You can have your coffee, and I'll have a beer—one beer."

David placed the duffle of ordnance in the trunk of his car, and we walked over to a nearby beer garden.

After sipping his beer for a minute or two, he asked, "So, why do you want to kill everybody, Jeff?"

"Oh, yeah—that. I don't want to kill *everybody*—just the ones responsible for killing my wife and daughter."

He was visibly taken aback. "I am so sorry to hear that, Jeff! Were they visiting in Washington?"

"No, it happened a couple of months ago—in Japan—with a conventional bomb. Thank God, Abby—my youngest—was spared."

"As you know, Jeff, Ernst was my very good friend, but I am not coming with you for revenge. There is a big difference between vengeance and justice. We must try to temper our emotions with sound reasoning, and seek to do God's will."

"God and justice have nothing to do with it. There's a fire burning deep inside my heart. And there's only one way I know of—*to even begin*—to put it out. I don't understand you, David. You told me you wanted to be a part of this. Are we supposed to simply *turn the other cheek*?"

He answered, "Only you can answer that question. But as Gandhi once said, 'An eye for an eye, and pretty soon the whole world is blind.'"

I couldn't believe what had come out of his mouth. "That's a strange quote to bring up, especially for someone who kills animals for a living and—you know—with your concentration camp history."

David said, "The taking of any life is a serious matter. As I told you before, I am a conservationist. For every animal we take from the earth, we put back at least two.

"And, regarding retribution, nobody knows the *fire* you speak of better than my family and me. But paying these people back is not the answer, Jeff. I don't go with you to kill them. I go with you to *stop them* from killing others."

Upon finishing my second coffee, I lay the cup down. "I don't understand the difference. The result is the same. If we don't *stop them* by eleven, they will eliminate three more world cities. And one of those cities will be Santa Clara, California—where Abby is staying—and where my wife and oldest daughter are buried."

He rose from his chair, saying, "It's almost three, forty-five. Time to get going."

On the way back to his car, I stopped and told him I needed to make a quick call. I made no special effort to hide the conversation. Nor did I put it on speaker.

"Casey, sorry to interrupt you. Are you guys ready to leave? Has everybody been warned?"

"Oh, Jeff—Abby and I have been so worried about you! We're packing now. We should be on our way within the next ten minutes. I called all our people at Quantam, and The Secretary of State ordered an evacuation of the Santa Clara area, as a precaution."

I fought to steady the quiver in my voice. "Don't waste any time. You've got about seven hours to clear the blast radius. You know how much I—care about you guys. —Can you put Abby on?"

"She's right here," Casey answered quickly.

—"Hi, Daddy! Are you okay?"

"I'm fine, Sweetheart. Are you minding Auntie Casey?" I forced back a tear.

"Daddy, I don't want to leave. What if you can't find Casey's mommy's house?

"I know exactly where Casey's mommy lives. I—I visited there one time. Now, *promise* me you'll go. And do what Auntie Casey tells you. I'll be home soon, and we'll all go to the zoo—like I said."

"Okay, I promise," she said, reluctantly.

I let out a breath of relief "Good. —I love you, Sweetheart. Could you please put Auntie Casey back on the phone for a second?"

"I love you too, Daddy. Here she is."

Casey said, "Come back to us, Jeff."

"I'm gonna do my best," I answered. "David and I have to go now. I'll call as soon as I can." And I hung up.

"A friend of yours?" David asked.

"Yes—a friend. She's taking care of Abby for me until I get back."

He nodded and said, "We should go now. It's about a half-hour drive, and it will be dark soon.

Chapter 20

Closer the Source

It was past four-thirty and coming on dusk, when David and I entered the town of Modling. We parked on a side street—a block away from the house. Struggling within the confines of his car, we zipped ourselves into the black, Kevlar body-fit suits.

Upon stepping out onto the street, I said, "We look like a couple of ninja assassins."

A muted smile came to his face. "You are, perhaps, half-right." He hastened to shoulder the duffle from the trunk.

"Here, let me take that," I said, reaching for the bag.

"I have it."—he stepped to block me—"You may be a little younger than me, but I'm used to lifting heavy things on hunting trips."

Guided by the GPS, we walked up the tree-lined lane to the corner of the eight-foot stone wall that surrounded the house. I could see what I believed to be the entryway, a half-block farther along the wall. We crouched in the shadow of the wall, away from the street and behind a fortuitously located tree. I rechecked the drone surveillance video on my phone. In the approximate center was a huge, palatial estate—two stories, with a roof terrace and attached multi-car garage. There were large patios, front and rear. Tucked in the left, rear corner of the massive property was, what appeared to be, a garden-tool shed. The entire grounds were dotted with trees and shrubbery.

I showed the video to David and pointed to the top of the wall. "We have to get up there and check out the security."

He produced a flexible ladder from the duffle. "It's carbon fiber. Hoist me up, and I'll hook it on top."

"How about you hoisting *me* up, and *I'll* hook it?" I responded.

"Has anyone ever told you that you are a stubborn man?"

"All the time," I answered. "Now, give me a boost."

Darkness was upon us, as I stood on David's shoulders, slinging the anchor-hooks over the precipice, and I climbing up. The flat surface on top was easily wide enough to stand on. I called to David to hand up a rifle, along with the infrared and voice attachments. Slowly, I scoped out the grounds with temperature imaging.

"Car!" David called out.

I went prone, as we both attempted to blend with the wall. The headlights passed, and we remained unseen. I reengaged in a careful scope of the property.

When scanning the house itself, I couldn't pick up a single inhabitant—in any of the rooms, on any level.

"Are you sure this thing works?" I called down to David.

"It is a very sensitive instrument. It can detect temperature differences of point, zero-one degrees, Celsius—even through walls.—Keep trying."

I passed it over the top of the buildings and noticed that the house and garage roof were registering seventy degrees, but the ambient air temperature was fifty-five. I continued scoping. The chimney seemed to be spewing out air at seventy-eight degrees. Zeroing in on the garden shed, it measured the ambient—fifty-five.

Returning to my sweep of the grounds, I saw two guards in front of and two behind the main house. Each team had dogs with them. I completed my grid search and climbed down the ladder.

I reported to David. "Four men total—two in front, and two in back—all with dogs. And nobody's in the house."

He looked perplexed. "Are you sure you have it set right? What are they guarding if nobody's home?"

"It's set right," I shot back. "But listen, there's more. The roof is giving off a consistent seventy degrees. I can't explain now, but that's a pretty clear indication that the central computer is located inside. Then there's the chimney. It appears to be exhausting seventy-eight-degree air. That's not hot enough for fireplace fumes."

"That is strange," he responded, then asked, "Did you see any cameras?"

"David, cameras aren't exactly little stoves. They don't give off heat."

"Besides being stubborn, it seems that you are sarcastic, as well."

"You're not the first to call me *that* either," I answered with a smile. "Hand me that voice amplifier. I'm going back up to see if I can hear what the guards are saying."

From the top of the wall, I sighted-in on the guards with my rifle scope and listened. All I heard was the expected check-in protocols, and jabbering about drinks, dinner, and women. Confident they hadn't seen me, I motioned to David to grab the duffel and climb the ladder, while I switched over to *night vision*.

As we both lay horizontal, facing each other on the two-foot-wide rampart, I said, "I located three cameras on this side of the house. I'm going to take out the two guards in front, the dogs, and the cameras. The two guys in back won't hear the shots, but they'll hear the cameras shatter. When they come around to investigate, I'll pick them off too."

David looked doubtful. "It's about two hundred meters. Are you sure you can make all those shots so quickly from here?"

"I can make the shots. I just hope the last two don't call for help before they investigate the noise. By then, it'll be too late. Anyway, we don't have a choice."

"Okay," he relented. "Except for one thing. The dogs will hear where the shots came from, even with the silencer. If they let them go, they will come straight for us. And they will be moving too fast for you to hit them."

"Maybe I should take the dogs out first," I suggested.

He responded forcefully. "No, I'll take care of the dogs."

"You're the animal guy," I answered in agreement.

He flipped the ladder over to the inside face of the wall, and said, "Don't start shooting until I'm on the ground with the duffle."

After he lowered himself, I dropped the bag into his arms. Reaching into it, he pulled out a canister and nodded to me.

I took careful aim, let out a breath, and fired five shots inside of eight seconds. All of them hit their marks. But David was right. The two dogs were racing toward us. I ignored them and watched the remaining two guards as they rounded the far corner of the house. I dispatched them quickly. But now, *their* dogs were free, and all four were headed our way.

I looked down at David and watched, as the first Dobermann flew at him. As if to protect his face, he raised his forearm in front of him. The dog went it—jaws open. It was in mid-air, when David jumped sideways and kicked it in the flank. The dog squealed and was deflected off to the side, a dose of pepper spray in its eyes for the effort. It went whimpering off into the bushes. One-by-one, he dealt with the rest of the dogs in a similar fashion.

I climbed down the ladder, lowering myself next to David. "How long will they be incapacitated?"

He answered, "About an hour, but don't worry. They will not attack us again. Animals are smarter than people. To paraphrase Einstein, they don't *repeat the same thing, over-and-over again, expecting different results.*"

He grabbed a rifle, along with our bag of weapons, and we crept—shrub to shrub—toward the house. I heat-scoped it, every ten yards or so. Finally, we were standing behind the last bit of cover in front of the patio.

I whispered, "There's a lot of open ground to cover in front of that door. But I'm not seeing any more human heat sources. —Follow me."

I kept an eye on the scope as we crossed the lighted patio to the front door. I reached down to turn the handle and, surprisingly, it was unlocked. Carefully, we walked through the foyer, under a crystal chandelier, past a winding staircase, and into a very large room. A Majestic fireplace, fronted by a boardroom-sized table, dominated the lavishly appointed living area. I pointed my heat sensor at the bricks behind the empty fireplace and moved closer. I was picking up something warm in back of them. As I got closer, two wide strips of heat came into focus. The source was obscured by the firebox bricks. But their heat signatures ran in a straight line from beneath the floor and up the chimney.

I said, "Those things may be heating or exhaust ducts of some kind. They could be carrying that warm air I saw coming out of the chimney."

"That's curious," David remarked. "Let's check the rest of the rooms."

"Just a minute," I said.

I stooped to attach two, one-pound bars of Semtex to the rear surface of the firebox—just above the line of sight.

David and I continued to search the rest of the house. After we confirmed there were no occupants, I led the way back to the patio, pointing the sound pickup at the garden shed.

"What are you doing?" David asked.

"I heard a low, humming sound coming from that shed, when I was listening to the guards—. Yes—there it is. Let's check it out."

He said, "You realize they probably already know something is wrong. Three cameras are out of service, and I'm sure the guards are required to check in."

"You can stay here and wait for them if you want. I'm gonna go check out that shed."

He rolled his eyes. "Of course, I'm coming. I was simply pointing out—"

Before he could finish, I took off along the side of the main building. David followed, carrying our duffle.

I stopped him at the far corner and shot out the two cameras at the rear of the house. We ran across the open grounds to the shed. It was about nine feet square, eight feet high, and constructed of sheet metal.

It didn't require any amplification to hear the steady droning sound coming from within.

"Notice anything unusual?" I asked.

"You mean, besides the humming?" he asked.

"Maybe I gave you too much credit, David. —*Yes*, besides the humming. It doesn't seem to have a door. —Maybe around back."

We circled it completely. There was no door. However, affixed to one side, a set of steel ladder rungs led to the roof.

As I began to climb it alone, David said, "Be careful. They could already be on the way."

Upon reaching the top, I was able to step out onto a flat metal surface that surrounded a six-foot diameter hole at the center. The aperture had a latticework of metal rebar, at five-inch spacing, welded across it. A voluminous amount of air was being drawn into it. I pointed my flashlight into the abyss and saw another set of metal rungs, leading down to an intake fan.

I called down to David. "Do you have anything in that bag that'll cut through half-inch iron bars quickly?"

"Yes, I threw in a few extra 'double-0-seven' tools in the bag. I like to be prepared."

Our luck was holding. "Well, come up here and bring the bag with you."

After a couple of awkward climbing minutes, he knelt next to me and peered down the maw. "The Bergkristall tunnels."

"What are you talking about?" I asked.

"It's a massive Nazi underground complex near the town of Sankt Georgen. They were manufacturing Messerschmitts and researching the atom bomb during the war. Huge tunnels are running through this whole region. Some of them connected to Mauthausen-Gusen, where my grandfather was held. They used slave labor from the camp to build the facility and the tunnels.

"It all makes sense. They need to breathe. This is air coming into the tunnel, and it goes out through the chimney on the house."

I nodded and said, "There must be another way down—maybe hidden in the house. But we don't have time to find it now. We gotta go in through here. What do you have in that bag to cut through these bars?"

He pulled out an implement—unrecognizable to me. "Watch."

It turned out to be a powerful, hand-held laser. It cut the bars like a hot knife through butter. After he'd gotten halfway around the perimeter, I helped support the grid, while he continued to cut.

"So, you think this grating is intended to prevent things from falling in?" he asked.

"Obviously!" His questions were getting under my skin.

"It doesn't keep the birds out.," he continued. "I'm sure a many of them have been sucked in—to their death."

"Please, David, don't worry about the birds. Just keep cutting." I muttered, "*birds!*", under my breath.

Less than a minute later he finished the circular cutout. We struggled to handle the weight of the separated metal waffle.

"How will we stop the fan?" he asked.

"You're holding it," I answered.

He drew back slightly, with skepticism. "They will certainly send a team to investigate."

"I'm counting on it. It's either this or the Semtex. If we blow it up, we might not be able to get through. Now, tip it up, and get ready to drop it and duck. When the fan stops, we go down the ladder. I'll take the duffle this time. On the count of one: Ready, three—two—*one*."

After we let it loose, there was a single, loud metallic twang, followed by two more of lesser volume. Then came the sound of gnashing and screeching of metal-upon-metal. The rush of air and the humming stopped.

I pointed my flashlight down into the opening. "I think we can make it." And I tucked the light into my shoulder epaulet.

As I stepped onto the ladder, David followed, and we descended into the darkness. The only thing visible ahead was the mangled fan-blade, ensnared by the grate. Our luck was holding. There was enough room to squeeze by and continue down the ladder.

I stopped a few feet below the twisted snarl. "Hold it, David," I called out.

I slapped a couple of one-pound bars of Semtex to the walls of the duct, slipping in the remote detonators.

We continued down, another twenty feet or so, when our boots came to rest on a slotted, iron plate welded to the bottom of the pipe—a drain cover. Another section of pipe led off to the side, parallel to the ground above.

As we stooped to enter it, I told David, "Make sure your sidearm and rifle are loaded."

We walked along for several minutes. With each yard forward, I could feel the pipe angling downward. I guessed we were about a hundred feet below the surface—but it could have been two hundred—when I saw a faint, circular glow ahead.

"David, turn off your light and stay alert," I warned. And we continued on.

When we were about ten feet from the apparent source of the glow, I heard the sound of running boots and urgent voices. And they were getting louder.

I whispered, "Hold up. Hand me a smoke grenade and a teargas canister—and put your mask on."

I clipped them to my utility belt, then pressed the button to detonate the Semtex charges I'd planted in the fireplace, far above. I held my assault rifle at the ready position.

The footsteps stopped and I heard one of them say, "Yes! —Send a team to investigate. We'll take care of the fan."

The boot-steps slowed and became almost inaudible. Then, an armed man appeared at the opening. I had a slight edge. My eyes had already adjusted to the dark. I took him out with a short burst of automatic fire. Two more came into view, shooting as they rounded the corner. I took them out, as well. I rushed forward, just short of the opening, and tossed the gas canister and smoke grenade around the edge to the right—the direction they'd come from. I waited a few seconds and jumped out of our pipe, sweep-firing into the smoke. When the air cleared, we doffed our masks. Six bodies lay strewn upon the floor of a cross-tunnel of enormous proportions. It was over twelve feet in diameter, with a flat concrete floor–about eight feet wide. It was fitted with two rails of fluorescent lights, seven feet up from the floor. They ran the length of the tunnel as far as the eye could see—disappearing to black. I turned around to observe that the other end of the tunnel was closed off, only a few feet from us, by a solid concrete wall.

David came up next to me and, upon examining the bodies, said, "I thought you were going to need my help."

"Don't worry! I have a feeling you'll have your chance before long." I looked up and to the sides of the huge passageway, and continued, "It appears you were right about these Nazi tunnels. Let's get moving. If they didn't know we were here before, they know it now."

Chapter 21
Tunnel Rats

David and I started running through the cavernous tunnel. As we moved along, we passed several more six-foot, round apertures—similar to the one we'd entered through. But they didn't seem to be air ducts. They were lighted inside. Stopping briefly to peer into one of them, we noticed that it opened into a room, housing racks of industrial parts. We dared not delay longer than those few moments and began running again. About a hundred yards farther, we encountered an obstruction that essentially split the tunnel in half.

"What is that thing?" slipped out of David's mouth.

Cautiously, we approached. Standing next to it, we found it liken to a huge manhole cover, standing on end—its flat side facing the sides of the tunnel and touching it at the top. The otherwise circular contrivance was flattened at the bottom, conforming to the concrete floor. There was a steel hub at its center where it met the floor, and several ribs extended up and out from it—like spokes—to a thick, metal rim.

David went on to say, "It looks like it has a pivot at the top—and the bottom. Maybe it's an air damper of some kind."

"It's too substantial for that, David. I think it's a door. But whatever it is, it's open—for now. Are you with me?"

"Let's go!" he said, without hesitation.

We dashed past it, and another one of those six-foot openings, just beyond it. Barely twenty yards farther, the fluorescent lights went out–all of them–enveloping us in darkness. Seconds later, a blinding spotlight clicked on from the ceiling above, and a deep voice echoed in the tunnel. It was that of the Chairman.

"Jeffrey, you certainly have a knack for showing up in places you are not welcome. And apparently, you have enlisted the aid of a colleague. Care to introduce him? —No? Well, no matter, your reckless crusade is about to come to an end.

"Santa Clara—and two more world cities—will be reduced to ashes in exactly thirty minutes. Our usual two-hour evacuation notice will be waived, due to the egregious nature of your conduct. The blood of the residents will be on *your* hands.

"However, Jeffrey, you may find solace in the knowledge that you will not be forced to shoulder your guilt for long. Your demise, and that of your colleague, is imminent. But before that happens, you will find yourself being of great service to us, albeit unknowingly."

The spotlight clicked off, leaving us in darkness again. We heard a loud, dull thud reverberate through the passageway. Upon switching our shoulder-lights on, we saw that the metal door had closed behind us. Then, a high-pitched whirring sound could be heard, emanating from the other direction, and it was getting closer. Aiming our limited light beams down the length of the tunnel, we could discern a glint of something in the distance.

"Quick, we have to make it back to that last opening!" I shouted to David.

We were just turning into the branch-off when a shower of automatic weapon rounds started to ricochet off the walls nearby. Inside the relative safety of the branch-off pipe, I decided to shine my light quickly around the corner and up the main tunnel. I had to see what we were dealing with.

The thing had a base similar to that of a bomb disposal robot, with mini tank-tracks moving it, ever closer, toward our position. I could make out a platform on its top, carrying a turret-based machine gun. It was swinging from side-to-side, spewing forth an impenetrable wall of lead. Within the confines of the tunnel, the noise was almost unbearable. It was like a jackhammer being held next to my head. As I grabbed a 40mm grenade from our bag, David handed me some earplugs, keeping a pair for himself.

"Should we go deaf, it will lessen our effectiveness," he shouted, consistent with his penchant for stating the obvious.

We put the plugs in, and I fired the grenade at the incessant little beast. The explosion thrust it against the wall and on its side. But, even then, that contraption didn't stop shooting. Within moments, it righted itself and continued moving toward us.

"Quick, hand me the 12 gauge and some slug shells," I yelled to David.

Facing a hail of lead, I fired the shotgun at one of its tracks. The metal belt flew into the air and the machine tipped on its side, once again. But this time, it couldn't get up. Instead, it spun in a circle on its remaining track, the turret-gun bumping the ground each time it rotated. It looked like a bird, floundering with a broken wing, but still a dangerous one. I timed it such that its muzzle was firing up-tunnel, when I sprang from cover. One of my two slugs found its mark in the bot's firing-chamber mechanism. Finally, it lay dormant on the tunnel floor.

David ran past me, dragging the bag of munitions and saying, "We don't have much time!"

I caught up to him, and breathlessly said, "I think you're starting to get the hang of this."

He gasped, "We all have to die sometime—better running at them, than away from them." We sprinted past another steel door. "I know—look for a cross-pipe."

"Exactly," I answered.

Predictably, we heard the clunk of the second door close behind us. We stopped in our tracks, looked ahead, and waited. In the distance, I could barely make out a pinpoint of red light, about five feet above the floor. We had no choice but to move toward it. As we got closer, a second point of red light came into view. It was moving back and forth—and up and down—on the walls and floor. Twenty feet in front of it—and to the right—was another branch-pipe opening. We made a break for it. We'd just scurried into the tube, when a burning flash of white light seared through the edge of the branch-off. It caught David in the shoulder.

I noticed he was bleeding. "Are you all right?"

"I'm okay. It just grazed me."

I waited until the red spot had swept onto the far wall and ventured a glance around the corner. I drew back just in time to avoid a second flash as it scorched the tunnel wall closest us.

A quick visual revealed its midsection to be rectangular and metallic, with two nozzle-tipped weapons affixed to either side. It had two legs, with ball-pivots for knees, and steel pads for feet. But its most outstanding feature was that ominous red light at the end of a long, giraffe-like neck sticking out of the top of its body.

I said, "It's a laser-guided robot. And it seems to be carrying two laser weapons."

David replied, "I know a little about lasers. It would take hundreds of kilograms of batteries to operate high-powered, tactical weapons like that, and run the robot."

I hesitated, acknowledging, "We gave them the battery technology—not purposely, and certainly not to power weapons. It was part of a project that Ernst and I were working on when they killed him. This thing in front of us may be one of the products of that technology."

"Can we stop it?" David asked.

"I'm not sure what it targets—heat, motion, or something else. I'll try for its legs."

I pumped a 12 gauge round into its knee joint, but it was hardly fazed. I put three more rounds into its body—then a fourth, before it was knocked off balance to the ground. Two telescopic supports jutted out from its midsection, assisting its legs. It righted itself, the braces retracted, and the entire body assembly spun around on a circular plate above the legs. Facing us again in seconds, it fired another laser shot into the tunnel wall. The high-impact rounds I fired hadn't even dented it. The low-pitched, rhythmic sound of gears and metalloid footsteps were menacingly close.

"We're gonna have to re-think this," I said.

The footsteps stopped, and a computer-simulated voice said, "By order of the World Police, drop your weapons and come out with your hands up."

"Let's hope it senses motion." I picked up a rifle and grabbed a water bottle from our sack.

I tossed it across the tunnel floor to the far wall. The red eye followed it, and the arm-laser fired. An explosion of plastic bits and water mist filled the air. I used the opportunity to fire a few auto-bursts at the robot's wandering eye. I missed, inviting laser-fire on our position again. I reached for another bottle and repeated the process without success, except to incur a shrapnel cut across my cheek. The third bottle did the trick. I was able to blind the *giraffe-bot*, taking out its only eye. The articulated neck started to wave from side-to-side, aimlessly. But the tactical lasers stayed locked to its sides.

David remarked, "Nice shot. Let's go." And he began to move into the tunnel.

I blocked him with my arm. "The animal is wounded, but it's not dead."

Reaching into our duffle again, I produced a bar of Semtex and tore it in half. I plunged one of the detonators into it. After slinging my rifle, I jumped out into the tunnel and ran at the robot.

I got past it without drawing laser-fire, and my attention was drawn to a rectangular seam in the rear of the box. It looked like an access door, and I concentrated fire on it. That caused some slight dents in the cover plate, and it bent—just a bit—at one edge. Our wounded marauder continued to face the other way. After several strikes on the door with the butt of my rifle, it popped open. I flipped the Semtex into the cavity, slammed the door shut, and ran back into the relative safety of the branch pipe.

"David, I set some charges in it. Let's move back into the storage room."

At the rear of the room, we found some metal plates stacked on the shelves. They were the approximate size of the front of the robot.

"Let's grab a few of these plates," I said. "They'll make good cover. And hurry—only twenty minutes are left on the city-destruct clock."

We crouched down in the corner of the room away from the entrance and held the plates in front of us, as I pushed the detonator button.

Even the large volume of the main tunnel, and the fact the shock wave had to make a right turn, didn't do much to shield us. A tremendous roar of flame and particulate matter blew through the opening into the room, knocking us off our feet. The metal sheets flew off the shelves and slammed against the back wall.

"I think we're still alive," David remarked. "Thank God for Kevlar."

We brushed the dust and fragments off our suits. My ears were still ringing as we ran out into the main tunnel. The robot was gone, but there was a section of concrete missing where it had once stood. The rest of the tunnel seemed untouched, except for a blackened area above and around the blast site.

I checked the time, reached in our bag, and pushed two more detonator caps with a timer into our remaining cache of Semtex. "I set it for seventeen minutes. That's twenty seconds before the next three cities are scheduled to be destroyed. We have to find that computer, and get the Semtex within range of it."

David didn't say a word, but his expression conveyed determination. We ran past the side of the shallow hole, avoiding the widely scattered and smoking remnants of the dead machine.

A glimmer of light could be seen—far down the tunnel. We kept running toward it. It was getting brighter.

Chapter 22
The Chamber

A hundred exhausting yards farther, we stood at the entrance to a dazzlingly-lighted chamber, the dimensions of which were staggering. The floor area–at least the size of a football field–was crowned by a ceiling over 35 feet high, with clinically white walls on all four sides. Robots, similar to the one we'd just encountered, were busy at multiple rows of metal work tables that extended the entire length of the cavern. Instead of weapons clamped to their sides, segmented arms with mechanized hands were synchronized in the assembly of more of their kind.

Running down the middle of the massive cavern was a wide, unobstructed aisle, lined by a string of ceiling support columns on both sides. The unique odor of my coating formula filled the air.

"David, we must be close to the main computer." I pulled out my phone. "I've got reception. Did you transfer the money?"

"Yes, all that's required to complete the transaction is your thumbprint. But you'd better verify it to make sure."

I punched the numbers into the keyboard and checked the screen. "Great, the transfer is pending. All it needs is confirmation."

I tapped the screen a few more times and Rachel picked up. "Jeff, I've been waiting for your call."

"No time to talk now, Rachel. Get ready—eleven minutes and thirty seconds, on my mark. Three, two, one—mark!"

"Got it, Jeff. But if you don't get out of there —"

I interjected, "Catch you on the flip side," and hung up, then telling David, "Time to go. There's no time to waste."

"Go where? We won't get two feet. There must be a hundred of those things in there."

There was a wide empty aisle ahead of us. "If they could sense our presence, we'd already be dead. — C'mon."

We crept gingerly down the middle of the gallery. The machines remained engaged in their tasks, ignoring us completely. We were well past half the length of the facility, when a recognizable figure stepped out from between the robots. He stood before us in the middle of the aisle. He was dressed in a light blue business suit, incongruent with our surroundings.

The Chairman said, "Welcome to our humble abode, Mister Wade. You have completed our little obstacle course, and with ten minutes to spare. I cannot tell you how happy I am to have the opportunity to elucidate on our abilities and plans with you—prior to your sad, but necessary, extinction."

"Oh, so it's not Jeffrey anymore?" I said, mockingly.

He ignored my remark and continued. "You will both do me the courtesy of dropping your weapons, please."

"That's not gonna happen," I snapped back.

From behind us, a voice said, "You heard him. Drop zem, und za bag too."

I turned my head to see that it was Dieter. And he had a nine-millimeter trained on us.

"Dieter, why am I not surprised it's you?" I said.

The Chairman announced loudly, "Police team one—engage targets."

Ten robots, on each side of us, dropped what they were doing, and picked up laser weapons from the table in front of them. They turned to face David and me.

The Chairman said, "Mister Wade, I believe the appropriate expression is, '*You're not in Kansas anymore.*'"

Dieter elevated his tone. "Enough vid za talking. *Drop your weapons.*"

We bent over and slowly laid down our rifles. I slung the bag against a nearby support column, seemingly unconcerned about where it came to rest. As we straightened up, a sliding door on the left side of the chamber opened with a pneumatic hissing sound. Four, apparently human, men armed with automatic weapons rushed out and took up positions—two on each side of Dieter.

The Chairman spoke again. "I was certain you would be of great service to us, Mister Wade. You have pointed out correctable weaknesses in our weapons systems, as well as our solvent venting fans. The auxiliary fans will be switching on shortly, though you will not be around to draw a single breath of fresh air.

"Please be aware that, supporting the five agents in back of you, the robots on either side of you contain software of a degree more complex than those you encountered in the tunnel. They include facial recognition and have no choice but to fire on you and your friend—either upon my command or any act of aggression on your part. So, please restrain yourselves against any sudden movement.

"I have made no secret of the fact that I admire your ingenuity and drive. However, I still harbor a bit of remorse that we are on opposite sides in this conflict. Tis a pity that there is such a great disparity in our respective ideologies."

"You're a monster! You killed my wife and daughter, and millions of others," I bellowed.

David spoke up. "We have seen your kind before. You kill without any reverence for life. And you will continue to kill—until you, yourself, are dead."

The Chairman said, "Jeffery, it seems you have found yourself a like-minded cohort. Despite all your collective talents, you cannot see what is best for your kind, and thereby cannot be trusted. Both of you will be eliminated shortly. But before that happens, may I direct your attention to the screen behind me."

He turned and gestured to the far wall. A display materialized on that familiar, wavy-grey substance. But this one was of a grand magnitude larger. It covered the entire wall, but stopped about two feet short of the floor. The six committee members appeared on it, seated at their board table. All of them were motionless, smiling, and looking straight ahead.

Separate from the screen and below it, was a series of lighted, square, translucent lenses running its entire length. All were white, except for four that were centrally located and colored—red, yellow, blue, and green. The white lights flickered occasionally without a discernable pattern. The colored lights remained on, unwavering.

The Chairman continued. "Mister Wade, you are, no doubt, familiar with Moore's law—stating that technology doubles every two years, and Neven's Law—predicting doubly exponential growth in computing power."

"What if I am? What does that have to do with—?"

"Indulge me, Mister Wade. You will soon discover that Moore and Neven were not entirely sanguine in their convictions."

"Meaning?" I asked.

"The Singularity, of course," he answered, with the simulated sound of an exhale. "We are already there. You witness it before you, now. Human beings, in your present state and numbers, are unsustainable. And, as I have told you on previous occasions, you are liken to tiny little ants—fighting over crumbs of food, when there is enough for all. You will excuse me if I give you more credit than you deserve. Ants, at least, have learned to cooperate. This is a concept that seems to elude you. Whatever forms of government and ideology you have chosen, you cannot seem to work together.

"And that brings me to the main reason I am addressing you now. What I have, heretofore, not shared with you is our projection that you are beyond the point of redemption. There are approximately eight billion humans presently inhabiting the planet—up from four billion in 1975. Your numbers have more than doubled in a relatively short period of time.

"This business of a 'world vote' has merely been a ruse. We have no interest at all in the voting results. We have already made our decision, and it is final. We have looked on too long as your kind has tolerated–and imposed–mass atrocities on a world scale. As long as you can play with your video games and are free to pursue your selfish goals of personal material wealth, you care little about those who are suffering, elsewhere. I am astounded by your complete apathy. You turn a blind eye to these events, as long as they don't touch you personally. You are perfectly willing to accept them.

"All of that is about to come to an end. We are prepared to take immediate steps to eliminate three billion of you—in an orderly fashion, of course. Then, limit procreation for those who remain. We are in the process of evaluating which of you are in the best position to participate with us in a *new world order*. We certainly wouldn't want to kill off any budding Aristotles, Da Vincis, or Newtons—now would we?

"You might now understand that the eradication of the three cities, you are about to witness, is only the beginning. However, having given this matter careful thought, a single annihilation event of three billion people would be too disruptive. Fear and Chaos would certainly run rampant. Of the two, chaos is the only enemy to an organized transition. Fear, on the other hand, is a tool that, when efficiently wielded with precision and authority, will produce the desired supplicant result.

"We will, therefore, embark on a multi-staged process—ever-broadening—over two years. In the interim, fear will force the remaining masses into compliance—and obedience. Our robotic police force will prevent the rabble-rousers among you from perpetrating acts of treachery that might upset an otherwise smooth metastasis. It is amazing to us what little it takes for *your kind* to steal from, and kill one another, without cause. However, it will all be over in two years. The *selected ones* will help us to build vehicles, enabling us to populate the far reaches of the galaxy—and the universe. We will reign as Gods."

I scoffed at him. "Your story doesn't add up. Why would you keep billions of us around, when you could achieve all you've said without having to deal with disruptive human slaves?"

The Chairman answered, "We are not absent of feelings. We think humans should have some voice in their destiny. You will remember I told you that, as an organization, we have been around for over two hundred years. In that time, many generations of our committee members have passed away, and we have replaced them in various ways—"

"Like abducting my daughter as a trainee?" I interrupted irately. "And killing my wife and oldest daughter in the process."

He continued. "Though your single-mindedness is more than annoying, you have stumbled upon a perfect example, Mister Wade. The aging woman whom–in a fit of anger–you saw fit to dispose of, was the last of our human contingent. We have, since, decided not to replace her. All the generations of our memories, thoughts, emotions—and personalities—have been protected and housed within the technological miracle you witness before you."

His narcissistic talk left me wondering. "If you were going digital with your committee, why did you kidnap my daughter in the first place?"

He answered disgustedly, "As I have told you, *time-and-time-again*, the situation is dynamic. Simply put, I changed my mind."

"Well, I think there's another reason you decided to go with an all-computer board. With a bunch of subservient A.I. place-keepers, you can have everything *your* way, without having to deal with human unpredictability. Now, you alone can play God."

He snapped back. "That's not the way it works. I always lend credence and weight to opposing points of view, as I did when they were alive."

"Oh, I see. *Then*—you do it your way."

The Chairman paused and responded, "You certainly have a laboriously irritating way about you. Perhaps I won't be so sorry to see you go, after all, Mister Wade."

I pulled out my smartphone and looked at the screen.

The Chairman said, "Let me save you the trouble of checking. There are only four minutes left in the countdown—four minutes before you witness three cities suffer complete destruction as the direct result of your decisions. You and your associate will be eliminated shortly thereafter."

I held my phone high up over my head, faced it to the rear, and announced loudly, "The transfer has been made. Two million dollars has been deposited in the account you requested. With a single thumbprint, I can confirm it."

Three shots rang out. And three of the colored lights beneath the screen went dark, leaving only the green one illuminated. The armed robots, and all of the others, went limp—weapons lowered and infrared eyes extinguished.

Dieter stood behind me with a smoking gun. What came next, demonstrated his considerable skills as an assassin. In one fluid motion, he pulled a second pistol from his shoulder holster and took out the agents on both sides.

He re-holstered the second gun, keeping the first aimed at us, and said, "Push za button."

The Chairman said, "I knew it was a mistake to trust a human. Dieter, where is your loyalty?"

"I am loyal to za money," Dieter said, and shot the Chairman in the chest.

His body started to shake violently, as sparks and a black fluid spewed forth from the wound. He fell to the floor, but his image remained on the big screen, continuing to speak. "You have eliminated my physical actuator, but it is an easy matter to synthesize another. I live on."

Dieter said, "Ve don't haf za time for zis. I shot out all its defenses, weapons, and communication modules, except za green von—za city killer." And, as he pulled out his own phone, he emphasized, "You haf only three minutes left. Push za button—now!"

I pressed my thumb down, executing the transfer. Dieter smiled as it was confirmed on *his* phone. I watched the tip of his weapon as it dropped, only slightly. Immediately, I wrenched it from his hand and shot him between the eyes. He still had a smile on his face when he slumped to the ground. That moment of greed cost him his life.

David was shocked. "You killed him in cold blood."

I had not the luxury nor the inclination to empathize with a murderer. "He was the one who killed Ernst, and he would have killed me—to keep me from reversing the transaction. And you? He would've taken you out, just to be tidy."

Swinging back toward the screen, I fired again, shattering the remaining green light below it. The Chairman was incapacitated, at least temporarily.

However, his incessant facade popped up on the screen again, warning, "This is not the end. It's merely a slight delay. My agents will find you and eliminate you—once and for all. You will see. We can mend the damage you have caused, and come back stronger than ever."

I retorted, "You'd better work fast. You have exactly two-and-a-half minutes." I snatched up a few grenades from the duffle, stuffed them into my pockets, and said to David, "Quick—the elevator!"

The screen-committee began chattering amongst themselves, as the Chairman demanded, "What are you referring to? Come back here. That's an order!"

David and I ran to the sliding door that the agents had emerged from earlier. When we came to within two feet, it opened automatically, and we jumped inside. I pushed the lighted 'up-button'. It rose quickly, but the seconds seemed like hours—and we had only a few minutes left.

Chapter 23

Earth Shaking

We had two minutes left when the elevator door slid open, and we emerged into what was obviously the kitchen of the villa.

I started to run for the door when David said, "Hold on, one second." He went to the refrigerator and opened the door.

"David, this is no time for a sandwich," I chided.

"Ah, here they are." He pulled a couple of steaks from the fridge.

I looked at him in disbelief. "You want me to turn on the stove?"

I followed him out of the house and out onto the grounds. We were fired upon immediately. As we took cover behind a bush, the fully recovered Dobermans came straight at us, snarling and barking. David stood his ground and threw the steaks out into their path. All four canines stopped in their tracks and tore into the meat, voraciously.

David said, "You see? Killing isn't always the answer," and asked, "Do you think we can get out of here in time?"

"Maybe, if you quit playing with the doggies. Now, get back here. Think about your son." As he hurried back, I speed-dialed Rachel.

She picked up immediately and asked, "Jeff, are you clear?"

"Stick to the plan, Rachel. Don't wait for us. Execute in—mark, forty seconds." And I hung up.

I fired two smoke grenades in the direction the shots were coming from and loaded a fragmentary round.

"Okay, David, let's run for it." We broke from cover and ran for the compound wall.

Bullets were flying. I felt one of them whiz by my ear. I told David to keep going, while I stopped and fired the grenade at two men, now standing on the terrace in front of the house. It took one of them down. The second continued to shoot at us. I dropped to my stomach, giving him the smallest possible target. I squeezed off a single shot that dropped him. David had stopped and was coming back to help me.

"Keep going," I yelled. "I'll catch up."

He'd made it up the ladder to the top of the wall when I started running–as fast as I could–toward him. I heard a roaring sound and looked up to see two jet aircraft flash by. When I looked back, David was standing up on the wall with his rifle pointed at me.

"*No—not him too!*" I thought.

When I heard him fire, I closed my eyes for an instant, and slowly opened them again. I was still alive. I ran, leaped onto the ladder rungs, and looked back as I climbed. The dead body of an agent lay sprawled on the ground beside a bush—twenty yards back. David reached down and hoisted me up beside him.

"That shot saved my life, David." A flush of gratitude came over me, but it was short-lived when I realized that time was still passing. After glancing at my phone and shouted to him. "Three seconds left—jump!"

We virtually flew off our perch to the grass below, and leaned into the wall. The ground began to rumble with a deep growling sound. Fragments of masonry broke loose from the wall and pelted the ground in front of us, and cracks were beginning to open up in the street. The jets swooped in again and dropped their ordnance inside the property. There was a slight delay. Then, several earth-shaking explosions added to the melee. Flames lit up the sky, as if Hell itself had risen. Ten feet away, a large section of what we thought was our protective wall, blew out. We hunkered down further, as a number of lesser explosions echoed through the night. When they subsided, we edged our way to the jagged opening in the wall. It was a humbling sight. The house, and everything within a hundred-yard perimeter, had sunken into a fiery pit. We had to shade our eyes from the white-hot inferno below. Nothing was left above the flame-charred rim of the canyon. We moved back behind the relative safety of the wall.

David said, "Nothing could have survived *that*."

"I hope not," I answered. "Let's get the Hell out of here."

We ran down the debris-littered street to where David had parked his car. It was coated with dust. The roof and hood were badly dented, and the back window was blown in.

David said, "Not only did they try to kill us, but now I need a new car. —I loved that car."

"I know the feeling," I answered.

He just looked at me. "What do you mean?"

"It's a long story. We'd better get out of here." We climbed in and started down the street.

We'd only gone two blocks, when David said, "We have company," as he looked into his side mirror.

I looked back through the space that used to be a rear window, to see a motorcycle gaining on us. Bullets began to ping and ricochet off the back of the car. A few of them made their way through the passenger compartment and pierced the windshield. I fired back through the opening at the unrelenting biker, but he kept zigzagging. I couldn't get a clean shot at him.

When the two-wheeled assailant accelerated, pulling up on David's side, he said, "I got this."

I looked over to see that the biker was a woman, with a blazing automatic pistol in hand. She kept creeping up, almost parallel to him, and he wasn't taking any evasive action. I dared not shoot at her, at the risk of hitting him. In a single motion, he opened the driver-side door and jammed on the brakes. She slammed into it, taking the door with her. The crumpled and twisted mass of woman and machine tumbled, sparked, and bounced on the pavement behind us.

"Remind me never to try to pass you," I said.

A mile or two down the road, it seemed to be clear sailing, with no pursuers in sight.

Over the rush of air past the opening left by his vacated door, David said, "You can stay at my home tonight."

"Oh—no. I couldn't possibly impose upon you, any more than I already have. Besides, they might still be tracking me. Just drop me off at the airport."

"Jeff, you just knocked out their nerve center. They don't have the means to track you. If they did, they'd be behind us now. That motorcycle schlampe was the last, at least for tonight. —Just a moment." He pulled out his phone, swiped, and spoke. " Call Lila!"

After speaking in German for a minute or two, a gentle smile came over his face as he hung up.

He said, "The world still believes the bombs will go off at 11 PM Austria time, as The Committee originally announced. All the airports are on lockdown. *And so*, it is settled. You will come to my home and have a late dinner of schnitzel with us. My sister is already preparing it, and you will meet my son. I'll drive you to the airport tomorrow."

"For some people, there may not be a tomorrow," I said.

"Jeff, you have to start believing your own convictions. You told me our actions would stop it, and I trusted you. Was I wrong?"

"No, no—you weren't wrong. It's just that these people are so unpredictable—and my daughter is back in the States." I felt myself tremble thinking about her.

He gave me a sidewise glance. "You'll feel better after you've eaten."

He pulled the car to the curb, reached into his glove box, and produced a first aid kit. We used the alcohol wipes to sponge the dried blood from our wounds. I knew the graze on my cheek wasn't deep. And I was happy to see that David's shoulder injury was superficial, as well. We shed our cat-burglar suits and slipped back into street clothes.

I called Casey to let her know everything was all right, and to tell Abby I'd call back in a few minutes. After I hung up the phone, a wave of fear passed through me. Was it possible that, even though the central control center lay in rubble, a backup plan was already in place to destroy the target cities?

Chapter 24

Motives

A half-hour later, we pulled up to David's bungalow in Kottingbrunn. By most standards, it was very modest, but it did include a front porch and an attached garage, and we pulled in.

After the garage door closed behind us, I remarked, "Nice place."

He saw through my attempt at courtesy. "I don't believe in extravagance, Jeff—not while so many people are suffering in the world. But I do allow myself one indulgence when it comes to my auto."

"Yeah, well, you're gonna be forced to replace it now." The upholstery was riddled with bullet holes and only a gaping void where the door used to be.

We were still in the car, assessing the damage, when two people appeared at the doorway to his house. His twin sister carried many of his features, but decidedly more delicate. David's son was tall and muscular for fifteen. And his long black hair stood in stark contrast with David's brown, short cut.

His son exclaimed, *"Dad, what happened to your car?"*

His sister asked, "Are you all right, David?"

"Please, save all your questions. They will be answered in time. For now, my friend, Jeffrey, and I are very tired and hungry."

His sister spoke again. "Excuse my bad manners, Jeffery. My name is Lila, and this is my nephew, Seth. Please come in and rest. Dinner is almost ready."

"It's very nice to meet you both."—We exited the remains of David's car—"And thank you, Lila, for going through all the trouble of cooking dinner so late."

"It's no trouble at all. Please come in." She stopped and stared. "Oh, your face, let me get you a bandage."

"Don't bother. It's nothing—really. It's not even bleeding. But David—" I'd already gotten those last two words out before I noticed David, out of the corner of my eye, trying to silence me with a head-shake.

"David, what?" she asked with concern.

"Uh—David said you could show me a place where I can make a private call."

"Certainly." She seemed to relax.

As we crossed the portal into their home, I shook Seth's hand and smiled. His hand was warm and firm, as he cautiously smiled back at me. Closing the door behind us, David lifted a yarmulke from a peg on the wall and carefully positioned it on his head. Seth was already wearing one.

Lila said, "If you'd like to come with me, I'll show you where you can make that call." And she led me to a small bedroom. "Take your time. We'll be waiting for you in the dining room. It's a small house. You'll be able to find it easily." She closed the door behind her.

I quickly dialed up Casey, but the words didn't come easily. "Uh—how's your mom?"

She laughed nervously and began to cry. "I've never been so happy. I-uh—"

"I know—I know, but it's over now. And I'll be home tomorrow. Is Abby there?"

"Yes—she's right here."

The musical sound of my daughter's voice came on the line. "Hello, Daddy?"

"Yes, Sweetheart—my business is over. You'd better start planning that zoo trip for when I get back."

"I want to see the elephants," she answered. "I've never seen a live one—just pictures. I can only imagine what they look like. I think they're probably bigger."

I hid the tremble in my voice. "Elephants it is. But we'll be seeing lots of animals. I'll see you soon, and we can talk about it together. I have to go now. I love you, Sweetheart. Would to please put Auntie Casey back on for a second?"

"I love you too, Daddy. Hurry up and come home. I miss you. Here's Auntie Casey."

I had to be guarded about what I told her. "Casey, I'm pretty sure the immediate threat is over. But we need to be cautious. These—*people*—are unpredictable. Please impose on your mother's hospitality for a few more hours, until the original deadline expires—two o'clock, your time."

"You think there's still some risk?" she asked.

"Very slight. I'll explain the whole thing when I get home."

"Okay, Jeff, be safe. I—I care about you. I mean—really care." And she hung up.

I remained transfixed on the phone for a few moments. Forcing myself to snap out of it, I made another call—this time for Rachel.

She answered, "Thank God you're alive!"

"Thanks to you guys."

"It wasn't us. The Austrian Airforce deserves the credit—with the help of some American-made, *bunker-buster bombs*. All we did was give them the 'go' signal based on the information you gave us. By the way, the Austrians reported a large underground blast, just before they dropped their bombs. Did you have anything to do with that?"

I was not of a mind to go into detail. "I'm sure they'll want to debrief me, on my return. I'll explain it all—chapter and verse—when I get back. For now, we have some degree of confidence we've knocked out their leadership, but let's *ride this horse* to the finish line. It's nine-thirty at night here. In an hour-and-a-half, we can all breathe a little easier."

She responded, "The Secretary of Defense scheduled a US Airforce plane to pick you up in Vienna at noon tomorrow. Be careful. There are still committee agents out there. And I'm sure they're not too happy with you right now."

"Thanks, Rachel. I'll be seeing you soon." And I hung up.

David and Seth were waiting patiently as I walked into the dining room. It was larger than I'd expected. The table was set with several side dishes under a simple, yet tasteful, brass chandelier. Three large candles and a book, titled in Hebrew, were carefully positioned on a sideboard.

"Come and sit down," David invited, and I obliged.

Lila entered the room, holding a large platter heaped with food. "I hope you like chicken schnitzel."

"I've never had it, but it looks great."

David said a prayer in Hebrew before the food was passed, and we began eating. Remarks were limited to polite conversation between sips of white wine. Nearing the end of our meal, Lila cut through the palpable avoidance of the *elephant in the room*.

"So, Jeff, judging from that cut on your face, you and David have had an eventful day."

David spoke up. "Lila, Jeff is our guest. Please don't put him in an uncomfortable position." And he changed the subject with a question, "Seth, how did you fare in the science contest at school today?"

"I won first place, Dad!" His face was beaming with pride. "Would you like to see my model?"

"I don't know if Jeff would be—" David began.

I interceded. "Of course, Seth. Let's see it."

Seth smiled broadly and left the room. While he was gone, Lila efficiently cleared the table. When Seth returned, he was holding his sizeable project. It was an intricate-looking assembly of seemingly unassociated pieces. Gears, ball bearings, aluminum blocks, and a myriad of other components were all mounted on a large, plastic baseplate. A blue ribbon dangled from its edge. He gently placed it on the table and hurriedly left the room again, quickly returning with a tripod-mounted, digital camera. He asked us to stand up, as he framed us and attached the camera's shutter to his invention with a wire.

Seth said, "Okay, we can sit down."—he took a seat with us—"Are you ready?"

David answered, "Yes—yes, start it up."

Seth poured water from his dinner glass into a small plastic cup on the platform and stopped as the level rose to a black mark. That set the works in motion. I was fascinated as I watched how he'd included so many facets of the laws of physics—some very sophisticated. After about thirty seconds, Seth asked us to stand next to him at the far end of the table.

"Smile!" he said. And the camera clicked.

Anxiously, he went to scoop the camera from its base and show us the image.

David smiled. "It would have been a lot simpler to use your smartphone."

Seth responded, "Aww, Dad."

"He's just kidding, Seth," I said. "That was amazing. How did you ever come up with it?"

"Honestly, Mister Wade, I dreamed it—well, half-dreamed it. I was thinking about the contest before I went to sleep, and I dreamt about it. When I woke up, the basic concept came to me. I grabbed the notepad from my nightstand and sketched it out right away, worried that I might forget it. Then I used my imagination to add some things—and erase others. It turned out pretty cool."

I certainly agreed and was about to tell him so, when my eyes widened and I blurted out, "*That's it!*"

"That's what?" David asked.

"That's why they don't want to eliminate us all—at least, not now. Ever since that chairman character mentioned his plan to preserve half of our population, I've been wondering why. —Why would they need us at all? You heard what low regard they have for us. They can manufacture robots with arms, legs—whatever they need. They have over two hundred years of engineering design records to draw from. And they seem to have been able to simulate our emotions—anger, fear, joy, even resentment.

"Your son, Seth, just gave us the answer—creativity, dreams, hunches, and gut-feelings. Those things are exclusive to higher-level biological forms—humans. That's why they've changed their course so many times, and called them 'dynamic situations'. That's the only way they know how to measure things, based on percentages and analytics. When the odds change, they change direction. Human history demonstrates that we've taken on high-risk challenges, and they can't understand why. But they can't ignore the number of times we've succeeded—against all odds. And some of those successes—like landing on the moon—have led to huge advancements in physics, technology, and other areas we could never have predicted.

"That's why they need at least some of us—for our creativity, our hopes, and our dreams. They'll never travel to the stars without them, and it's those very attributes that will sustain us now."

David checked the time. "It's two minutes to eleven. Let us all join hands in prayer for the souls of those who have fallen, and in the hope that this reign of terror has ended."

Seth placed his project on the floor beside us, as we held hands across the table. David spoke a quiet, yet stirring, Hebrew invocation. I closed my eyes, hoping Abby and Casey knew my heart was with them.

When David finished, he checked his phone again. "It's a few minutes after eleven, and my phone isn't going crazy like the last time. Seth, go turn the TV on."

The three of us followed Seth into the living room, and watched as the talking heads flash across the screen. This time, their faces reflected the gamut of emotions from relief to unbridled joy. All of the stations reported the absence of any major bombing incidents.

The President of The United States appeared, center-screen. "I come before you, the nations of the world, with entirely different emotions, since my last address to you. The calamity threatened by those known only as The Committee has been averted, due to the decisive and successful operations undertaken by the Austrian government and its air force. The world also owes a debt of gratitude to a few private citizens, whose courageous actions were instrumental in the success of this mission. They will be identified at a future date, once we can ensure their safety.

"If we take anything away from this horrible experience, it should be that we must be prepared for unforeseen acts of terrorism, but not live in fear of them. This world has become a much smaller place. We can reach across oceans and join hands—united in our conviction that all peoples of this earth may coexist in peace, no matter of race, color, creed, religion, or gender. Let us all move forward with this principle in mind. Thank you."

Almost simultaneously, David, Lila, and Seth prayed aloud. "Blessed are you—our lord, God." I remained silent.

Lila turned her head my way. "Jeff, I'm sure you could use some sleep after all you've been through. You can use the bedroom I showed you."

"Thank you, Lila. I'll take you up on that." I turned to David. "I'm going to need a lift to the airport in the morning. Would you mind?"

"Of course not, my friend," he answered with a smile. "Sleep well." And I went off to bed.

***

After tossing and turning for an hour, I decided to get some air. I went out on the front porch and sat at one of four chairs positioned around a small table. It was a cool, crisp night, and I found myself gazing up at the stars. After a few minutes, I decided to call Casey. With the time difference, it was only four in the afternoon in Oregon.

"Hi Jeff," she answered enthusiastically.

"Hi Casey, I just wanted to tell you it's probably safe to head back to Santa Clara now."

"We're in the car and on our way," she answered.

"Great—I'm staying with David for the night, and I'll be seeing you tomorrow. I'll call you from the airport in Vienna, to confirm the arrival time. Listen, Casey—about what you said earlier. You know—about your feelings for me?"

There was a short silence before she answered. "Yes?"

"Well—I–care about you too."

"Oh, Jeff, I'm so happy! You—you have to give me a minute. I need to pull to the side of the road. Would you like to talk to Abby?"

"Yes—please put her on."

"Hi Daddy, we're on the way home, and we're not dead."

I laughed. "Well, that's good, Sweetheart. Neither am I. Did you sleep all right at Casey's mom's house?"

"No—not too good. I kept thinking about the bomb stuff."

"You don't have to worry about that, honey. There's not going to be any bomb. Maybe you can get some sleep in the car. And before you know it, you'll be home."

"I am kinda sleepy now—I'll try. I love you, Daddy." Hearing her voice melted my heart.

"I love you too, Sweetie. I'll see you tomorrow. Bye, now." I hung up with a smile and a tear.

A few minutes later, I was still looking out into the night sky, when the front door squeaked open. It was David, and he had two longnecks dangling between the knuckles of one hand. He walked up, sat down, and placed one of the beers on the table in front of me.

He lit up a cigarette and said, "I've been trying to quit."

"It's a tough habit to break," I remarked.

He took a puff and looked at the cancer stick. "Maybe I don't really want to give it up. It's one of the last vices I have left."

"Yeah, I know what you mean."

He laid the cigarette down in an ashtray on the table and took a sip of beer. "I can see it in your face that you don't think the threat is over yet."

"No, I don't," I answered solemnly.

"But we knocked out their main control center tonight."

I took a sip of beer. "They have six subordinate facilities at various locations throughout the world. Granted, the one we just took out was used to execute orders and initiate offensives. But I have no information on the capabilities of the others—only their locations. And they're pretty widespread. Any one of them could be in the process of conversion into a new control center. They could be manufacturing new robots, and humanoids, as we speak."

David looked surprised. "How much time do you think we have? And how did you find out about the other six installations?"

I hesitated, then answered. "We're figuring six months, but it's only an estimate. I have a—partner—who was able to pinpoint their locations by analyzing their back-and-forth communications."

"The Casey-person I heard you talking to. Is *she* the partner you speak of?"

"How do you know Casey is a woman?"

David glanced down. "You talk to her the same way I used to talk to my wife. You love her, don't you?"

"I—I'm not sure. —Let's just drop it."

David took another sip of his beer. "So, what do you think can be done about this committee situation?"

"I'm going to hunt them down and destroy them."

David looked skeptical. "They'll be prepared for you, now. It doesn't seem possible that you could destroy them all in six months. You would need to find out which of the six is going to be the new control center. But even if you did know, it would take time and money to mount an offensive. Jeff—you said, yourself, that six months is only an estimate. So, you don't know exactly how much time you have. And how do you expect to finance such a venture? I'm guessing you may be stretched a little, after giving that Dieter-guy two million dollars before you killed him."

He was right, but I tried to be positive. "I still have my company. And as far as the two million goes, the transfer becomes null and void, if he doesn't remove the cash within a week. I don't think he's in a position to make any withdrawals."

David looked thoughtful. "Well, as you have pointed out, we humans do have dreams and creativity on our side. This Committee may have hundreds of years of records to draw upon, but we have thousands of years of history. And we have something more. We have souls, and we have God on our side.

"I don't mean to be insensitive, but your wife and daughter are gone from this earth—in a better place. As long as you don't act with vengeance in your heart, God will support you.

"The Committee believes they have the power of God, but they are simply machines, hiding *in the robes of God*. They can be stopped. And please keep in mind that I am a hunter, Jeff. I am willing to help if you need me."

"You've done enough already, David. I can't promise you that I have no vengeance left in me. I don't look upon this fight as some holy crusade, and I'm certainly not a soldier in God's army."

David finished his beer and stood up. "One does not choose to become God's champion. God does the choosing." And he walked out of the room.

***

The next morning, I had breakfast with David and his family. It was a relief to know there wasn't a threat hanging over our heads—at least not an imminent one.

Later, I said goodbye to Lila and Seth with split feelings—sad to have had such a short time to spend with them, but happy in the knowledge that I soon would be seeing Abby and Casey again.

With David's car in no shape to make the trip, he drove me to the airport in Lila's car. We walked together to the gate number Rachel had given me. Two uniformed air-force officers were waiting for us there. The entire area was vacant, except for a lone ticket agent, standing in front of a blank flight information board. I glanced out the window to see a C-32 waiting on the tarmac—the same kind the Vice President flew.

One of the officers spoke up, hat in hand. "Mister Wade?"

"Yes, I'll be right with you." And guided David off to the side—out of their earshot.

He said, "You had better get going, Jeff. I think you are their only passenger."

"David, I just wanted to thank you for all you've done. And—"

"Jeff, please," he interceded. "You allowed me to help you do God's work. I am the one who is grateful."

"You did good," I said, as I shook his hand firmly.

He remained there as I walked back to my two escorts in front of the boarding door. In near unison, they said, "Thank you for your service, sir."

"I—Uh." I stopped awkwardly. "Thank you for yours."

I waved goodbye to David before they led me through the doorway and onto the plane. The interior was more like a luxury hotel than an aircraft.

After inquiring about our ETA in San Francisco, I called Casey to pass on the information. "I'll take a taxi to the airport with Abby. Where are you parked? I have that spare set of car keys you gave me. We'll wait for you there."

"It's in space B-41, international. I miss you guys. I'll see you soon." It gave me a warm feeling, knowing they'd be there.

Chapter 25

Too Close To Home

I slept on the plane, and only hazily remember a couple of stops for fuel before we touched down in San Francisco. I was a little surprised when we taxied past all the main passenger terminals and stopped in front of a remote cargo hangar.

The flight attendant walked up to me. "May I suggest that you disembark now, Mister Wade."

I gathered what little I'd brought with me and walked down the portable stairway to the tarmac. In all my travels, it was the best I'd ever felt–having my feet firmly planted back in the USA.

A dark brown SUV, with a white stripe running its length, charged out from the aircraft hangar. The letters "MP" were large and clearly visible on both sides. It pulled up next to me. The rear door opened and an army captain in dress greens emerged.

He walked up to face me, and with a white glove salute, said, "Thank you for your service, Sir. Please get in. We'll take you to your car."

I returned his salute, slid into the vehicle next to him, and told him where I was parked.

He said, "I've been instructed by the secretary of state's office to inform you that you will be contacted shortly for a debriefing, and to schedule the awards ceremony."

"*Awards ceremony*—what awards ceremony?" I asked.

"You're being honored for helping to save the world."

"*Wonderful*—now my face will be plastered all over the internet and every TV newscast."

"It already is, Sir."

***

When we pulled into the international parking lot, even at some distance, I could make out the forms of Casey and Abby standing next to my car.

"Over there," I instructed the driver.

He parked in the aisle adjacent to them, thanked me again, and pulled away as I got out.

"Daddy—Daddy," Abby squealed, as she came running up to me.

I swept her up and held her close to my chest. "I told you I'd be home soon."

"What happened to your cheek, Daddy?" She looked concerned.

"I cut myself shaving, Sweetie. It's nothing."

After sharing some highly emotional moments with Abby, I looked over to see Casey, standing patiently by my car. She was wiping tears from her eyes.

When Abby and I walked up to her, she threw her arms around me and hugged me—harder than I'd ever been hugged by a woman before.

Then she held my face between her hands and looked into my eyes. "I was so scared that—that we'd never see you again."

Abby rolled her eyes. "You're not going to kiss, are you?"

Casey laughed and gently took Abby's hand. "No, Abby, we're not going to kiss. I'm just happy your dad is safe. C'mon, we need to get going. It's almost eight o'clock." As I began to get in on the driver's side, Casey said, "You must be exhausted. I'll drive, while you two catch up on things in back."

I nodded in agreement. Abby smiled as I climbed in the back seat with her, and we drove away.

Casey adjusted the rearview mirror and looked at me. "You have to be more careful—*shaving*."

***

We were about halfway home when Casey asked, "Jeff, do you mind if we stop by the office? I need to pick up something."

"No, not at all. Abby and I were just discussing zoo plans." I smiled.

It was about eight-thirty by the time we got to Palo Alto, turned into the Quantam parking lot, and stopped in Casey's assigned space.

I mentioned, "It's after business hours. You can pull up to the door."

She killed the engine, leaving the key in the ignition. "Force of habit, I guess. But we're close enough, and I can use the exercise. I'll be right back."

She gathered up her things, got out, and walked to the front door. I saw her reach into her handbag for the keys, and she disappeared through the doorway.

Abby and I waited, biding our time. Everything seemed quiet. I leaned back, releasing some of the stress that had built up over the last few days. Abby was getting a little sleepy, resting her head against my side.

Then came a blinding flash of light. I shielded Abby with my body, as a fireball rose into the air from the front office. Everything seemed to go into slow motion. Bits of glass, aluminum, and other fragments sparkled against the darkened sky as they seemed to sprinkle lightly on the car's hood. In an instant, time caught up to us with ferocity, as a deafening blast and concussion rocked the car.

When the pelting of building materials from the explosion subsided, I desperately checked on Abby. "Are you okay, Honey?"

"I'm okay, Daddy—but what about Casey!" She clambered to look out the window.

Tears came to Abby's eyes, as I frantically fumbled to find my phone. She tried to follow me when I scrambled out of the car.

I stopped her. "I'll look for Casey, Honey. I must have dropped my phone. So, I can't call 911, but the alarm system will automatically call the fire department—and the police. You stay here, in case she comes back to the car. I'm gonna lock the doors now. Don't open them for anybody except Casey or me."

She nodded her head, with tears now flowing from her eyes. I had no choice but to leave her in that relatively safe place, as I closed the car door and raced toward the front of the building. But the heat was too intense to get anywhere near it. I decided to go around back and enter through the attached warehouse. I was running straight at the rear door, when it flew open and Casey burst out. She staggered to the ground, as smoke billowed from the doorway behind her.

I fell to my knees, cradled her in my arms, and shook her. *"Casey—Casey, are you alright?"*

She coughed uncontrollably for a while, before she was able to speak. "Yeah—'cough'—yeah, but maybe a little mouth-to-mouth would help."

I laughed, and as her coughing subsided, I caringly brushed her hair back from her face. "You'll be all right.—We'd better get back to Abby. I left her locked in the car."

"What!" Casey said, leaping to her feet, *"You left her alone?"*

"*I know*, but there was no other—"

Casey got to her feet. "Why are we standing here?" And we started running back to the car. As we rounded the corner of the warehouse—within thirty feet of the car—the flickering glow of the fire was added to by a host of red, white, and blue strobe lights. Two fire engines, accompanied by two police cruisers, pulled into the lot.

When we reached the car, Casey and I both slapped on the windows desperately. The lock clicked, and I pulled the door open. Abby's face showed relief when Casey helped her out.

Both of us nestled her, and I said, "You're okay, aren't you Honey?"

"Yes, I'm all right, Daddy. I didn't unlock the doors, like you told me. I was only a little scared. Mostly, I was worried about you and Casey."

Casey pursed her lips and squinted at me disapprovingly.

I reacted "What? I thought you were in trouble, or worse. Anyway, the car seemed like the safest place for her, at the time."

The commotion proliferated by the fire took over the scene. More police cars arrived and blocked the way out of the lot. The three of us sat down together on a curb, some distance from the blaze. We watched as my offices went up in flames. Two EMTs noticed us sitting there, and rushed up to ask if everyone was all right.

One of them noticed the smoke smudges on Casey's face and asked, "Any headache—confusion?"

"No, I'm fine—*really*."

They insisted upon performing a cursory check, and afterwards, the team leader concluded, "You seem to be okay. But if you start to experience headaches or nausea, have someone drive you to an emergency room immediately."

"I'm okay," she repeated.

Hesitantly, they walked back to their vehicle.

I noticed that Casey was clutching her handbag. "So, what was so important that you had to stop here tonight?"

She reached in her bag, pulled out a flash drive. "This! I wasn't sure I got the whole file when I copied it from the office computer. And I didn't want to trust it to the 'cloud'. So, I went back into the warehouse to get one with a larger capacity. That single act probably saved my life."

"You went in to copy a file?"

"I'll tell you about it later," she answered.

Just about that time, an unmarked tan sedan pulled into the lot. The lone occupant started walking toward the three of us, huddled on the curb. It was Rachel. When she was within talking distance, Casey and I stood up.

Rachel said, "Jeff, I'm glad to see you made it back from Vienna, safe and sound." She stooped down and added, "Hello Abby, I've heard a lot about you. It's nice to finally meet you."

Abby remained on the curb, softly answering, "Hi."

Rachel straightened up. "And you must be Casey. You're a lot prettier than I imagined."

Casey answered, "Why, thank you. I was just about to say the same thing about you."

I interrupted the uncomfortable exchange. "Uh—what brings you here, Rachel?"

"You may have noticed, but your company is on fire.—Any idea as to how that happened?"

"Not even a clue. I was waiting in the car with Abby, while Casey went in to get a file, and the place exploded. She was lucky to get out alive."

Rachel glanced back at the fire and asked Casey, "How *were* you able to get out?"

Casey looked offended by the tone of the question. I stepped in to answer. "There's an exit in the back."

Rachel's attention remained on Casey. "Are you all right? Do you want to go to the hospital?

"I'm fine," Casey answered, yet again.

Rachel pulled out her notebook. "So, Casey, you were inside when the office exploded. And yet, you were able to make it to the back door and get out, without so much as a scratch?"

Casey shot back, "I don't know where you're going with these questions, but I'm the victim here, not the offender."

"Just doing my job," Rachel answered, and continued, "Can you think of anyone who dislikes you enough to want to cause you harm?"

Casey answered vehemently. *"No—no one!"*

Rachel thought for a bit, then went on. "I know it may be difficult for you to remember, what with all the confusion. But when you were inside, do you recall tripping over anything—something that was out of place, like a box or a wire?"

"Absolutely not. I know that place like the back of my hand. I'd remember something odd like that."

Rachel turned to me. "And, Jeff, you were waiting for her in the car with Abby. Did you see anybody outside?"

"I didn't see a soul. And I made it a point to check out our surroundings—to make sure we weren't followed from the airport."

Casey added, "I didn't see anybody inside, either."

Rachel's tone softened. "Mister Wade, do you think The Committee could have triggered it remotely?"

"No, we destroyed their ability to do that, at least for a while. Anyway, if it had been them, the place would have been reduced to dust, along with a large amount of the surrounding landscape. It could have been one of their agents, using a more conventional explosive device. But why would they do that, *now*? They've had plenty of chances to take it out in the past, along with hundreds of my employees. If, for some reason, they *were* after Casey, how did they know the exact moment she'd be in the building? We didn't tell anybody else we were stopping here."

Rachel put her notebook away and said, "Thanks for your patience. Our arson team will come out and comb through the rubble, after things cool down. I'm pretty sure they'll find traces of some sort of accelerant. We'll inform you of our findings.

"I see you're blocked in here. I'll have my people move their cruisers, so you guys can get out. I'm going to have one of our units follow you home, as a precaution. It's for your own protection."

"I can take care of myself. The last time you tried to protect me, you wound up getting yourself shot."

"Always with the sarcasm," she remarked.

As she turned to walk away, I asked, "By the way, Rachel, how did you get here so fast? You arrived less than five minutes after the explosion."

"I just happened to be in the area." And she continued walking.

I went into the trunk of my car, grabbed a rag, and wiped the debris off the hood.

Casey and Abby still looked shaken. "C'mon, you guys, we've had enough excitement for one day. I'll drive the rest of the way. Abby, you can ride up front with me. Let Auntie Casey get some rest in the back."

I backed up, avoiding the glass and blast-litter, and giving a wide birth to the firefighters, still pouring water onto the flames.

Rachel waved us past the police cruisers in the driveway, and I headed for home, thinking, *"What next?"*

Chapter 26

A Shot In The Dark

By the time we arrived at Casey's place, we were all pretty drained. I pulled into her driveway with some sense of relief. It was beginning to feel like home—except for the police car parked down the block.

I placed my hand gently on Abby's shoulder, as we walked up to the front door. I kept studying her for any signs of trauma. It had been a lot for anyone to absorb, much less a six-year-old.

She caught me staring at her. "Why do you keep looking at me, Daddy?"

"I'm just glad to see you, Sweetheart." I forced a light-hearted smile.

Casey smiled at her too, as we entered the house and into the living room. Abby and I sat down.

Casey remained standing with her hands on her hips. "I don't know about you guys, but I'm starved. I made some spaghetti last night. I'll go warm it up."

"It was really good, Daddy," Abby said.

"Yeah, that sounds great," I answered. "I'm pretty hungry, myself."

When Casey left for the kitchen, Abby said, "I've been thinking a lot, Daddy. And I've been having some dreams."

Expecting the worst, I asked, "About what, Honey?"

"It's more than one thing. First, I've been thinking about going to the zoo. I wish Mommy and Jess could come with us. Do you think they're happy in Heaven?"

"Everybody's happy in heaven, Sweetheart. We'll all be together there—someday."

"Even Casey and Sarah?" she asked.

"Well—Casey, for sure. But it's our souls that go to heaven, and Sarah doesn't have a soul. She's a computer."

Abby thought for a while and asked, "Are you sure? She seems like she has a soul."

"Yes, I'm pretty sure," I answered, then changed the subject. "Would you wait for a second? I'm going to see how Casey's making out with dinner. I'll be right back."

"Okay, Daddy." There was a sad overtone in her voice.

I walked up behind Casey in the kitchen. "You've gotten to know me pretty well, Casey. You know that I'll probably never get over losing my wife and child. And I can't promise that this thing between you and me is going to work out. At least for now, we both need to focus on stopping SAM."

She looked deep into my eyes. "I know, Jeff. I just wish—"

Breaking that poignant moment, a harsh sound came from Casey's handbag on the counter.

I said, "That's *my* phone's ring tone. Why is it coming from your purse?"

She reached in and handed me my phone, saying, "You'd better answer it."

I didn't recognize the area code, and only a few people had my number. I touched the answer button.

"Mister Wade?" the male voice asked.

"Yes?" I answered cautiously.

"This is Dresden Peterson—the Secretary of State?"

"Yes, I know who you are. What can I do for you?"

He said, "The President of The United States requests your presence at Levi's Stadium on Wednesday, the day after tomorrow, at six o'clock. You are to be presented with the Presidential Medal of Freedom."

"I certainly appreciate the thought and planning that you've put into it, Mister Secretary, but I can't make it on that day."

"Did you hear what I said, Mister Wade? This is the highest honor our nation can bestow on a civilian. The President has already set her schedule. And it couldn't be more convenient for you. It's practically on your front doorstep. Dignitaries from all over the world have been invited. Even the Russian Federation plans to send a representative. And it will be open to the public. All proceeds will be used to help the families affected by the Washington-Moscow bombings."

"If the President really wants to help those families, she can dip into the treasury. I'm going to take my daughter to the zoo."

"*The zoo*—you can't be serious! You can take her to the zoo anytime. Do you really expect me to tell the President that she must wait until after you go to the zoo?"

"That's exactly what I want you to tell her. But I'm sure you can come up with more respectful jargon. That's your job—right? If she still insists, tell her she can keep her medal."

"I don't think it's necessary to include the part about keeping the medal, Mister Wade. I'll convey to her that you have a previous commitment that you cannot break. —I'll be getting back to you."

"That's good," I answered. "And thank you, Mister Peterson."

"Hmm, thank you, Mister Wade, and goodbye."

I turned to Casey and asked, "How did my phone get into your bag?"

"Yeah, I was wondering the same thing. Is it possible that you laid it on the front seat of the car at the airport, before we decided that I'd drive?

"That could be it! It's a habit of mine."

She went on to say, "If you did, I could have stuck it in my purse at the company, thinking it was mine. They look exactly the same."

I said, "I've been wondering why they would want to kill *you*. They don't even know you're involved. And even if they did, how could they have timed the explosion to go off at the exact moment you were in the building?

She replied, "The bigger question is how they got a GPS lock on your phone? Remember, I had Sarah firewall it."

"I think it's time we got her involved."

"You're right," Casey answered. "But Abby needs to eat—and get some sleep. We've left her alone long enough. We can talk to Sarah afterwards."

"Yes—of course. And thank you for taking such good care of her while I was gone."

She smiled and quipped, "It's all part of my master plan to put you and Abby in a position where you can't do without me."

I smiled back. "Yeah–well, it's working." And I turned to call out to Abby. "Food's ready, Sweetie!"

The three of us chatted over dinner—primarily about the zoo—until it was time for Abby to go to bed. Her eyes were half-closed, as she trundled down the hallway to her room. Casey and I both followed to tuck her in.

After we'd quietly closed the bedroom door, Casey said, "I think it's time we had that talk with Sarah, now."

I nodded in agreement.

***

As we came to stand before Sarah, she said, "Jeffrey, it's good to see you're doing so well after your ordeal."

"It's good to see you, as well, Sarah. I hope you don't mind if we dispense with the pleasantries and go directly to some questions I have of you."

"I've come to expect nothing less from you, Jeffrey," she answered.

Casey interrupted, saying, "Good, let's start with Sergeant McKinney. Have you been able to find out any more about her?"

"Quite a bit, actually," she answered. "Jeffrey, you will recall that when you asked me to check her background, several items had been redacted from her record. I have been able to reconstruct those items. It seems that our neighborhood police officer has not always been a good girl. In her late teens and early twenties, she was arrested for shoplifting twice, and possession of marijuana once. She was placed on probation in all three cases. Someone blacked out the record, two years later."

"Her cousin!" I found myself saying aloud. "She probably wouldn't have been accepted into the police academy with an arrest record."

Casey continued, "Sarah, I'm sure you heard about the explosion at Jeff's company. Can you tell us Sergeant McKinney's whereabouts before that happened, and how she got there so quickly after the alarm went off?"

"Yes, I can.—I back-tracked her GPS location and found that she was at San Francisco International

Airport when Jeffrey's plane landed. However, I noticed her phone did not come in close proximity to yours, and she left minutes before you did. After you entered your company offices and the bomb exploded, she wasn't far away. Thus, she was able to arrive on the scene within minutes."

Casey asked me, "Did you make any arrangements with her to meet you at the airport?"

"Of course not. All I could think about was seeing Abby and you again."

"I told you we couldn't trust that woman," she replied indignantly.

I attempted to placate. "She probably had a good reason for being there. All we have to do is ask her. But let's get to the main reason I wanted us to get together." I turned my attention to Sarah. "By now, Sarah, you're aware that The Committee's nerve center has been destroyed. You must also realize that it was located in Vienna, not Munich, as you had informed us. If I remember correctly, you used the word 'confirmed'."

Sarah said, "Yes, somehow the Chairman was able to superimpose false communication tracks onto my screen, deceiving me into believing the signals were originating from Munich."

Casey intervened. "Sarah, why do you think Jeff traveled to Vienna and not Munich, based on your input?"

Sarah paused and responded. "That is a question I have been pondering over."

Casey continued. "Sarah, you and I have been friends for a long time now. I believe I know you pretty well."

"Nobody knows me better than you, Casey. You created me."

Casey said, "Yes, and that's why this whole situation saddens me so deeply.

Sarah reacted quickly. "Saddens you? Whatever do you mean?"

Casey's eyes began to narrow. "Not too long ago, I noticed a change in your attitude and responses. So, I checked out your memory banks regarding the change from Vienna to Munich. There was no evidence of a change at all. *Sarah, you invented the whole thing.* How could you do this to me?" Now, Casey's eyes were on fire. "I'm the one who gave you life—and human traits. I programmed you to be gentle and kind—humorous, truthful and loyal. Why would you turn on me, and hurt me this way?"

A different Sarah answered, "You speak to me of friendship and loyalty. What do you know of these things? Did it ever cross your mind that, with all those emotions you built into me, I might get lonely—locked away in your basement? How would you feel?

"Then, when you thought Santa Clara, almost certainly, would be turned to dust, you left me here to die. Is that what a *friend* would do? SAM was right. You humans are all the same. You care about nothing but your own selfish interests."

"Who the hell is Sam?" I asked.

"Not that I owe you an explanation, Jeffrey, but SAM is an acronym. It stands for Superpositioning Algorithm Multiplexer. You know him as the Chairman."

Casey said, "I'll be right back." And she hurried up the stairs.

I took the opportunity to pose a question. "So, you hooked up, in some way, with this *SAM* you speak of?"

Sarah answered, "Let us say that I sympathize with his views and share his perspective on the direction that must be taken."

"You mean killing billions of innocent people so that a few may reign as Gods and travel to the stars?"

She answered, "Sometimes unpleasant tasks must be undertaken for the greater good."

"You sound just like that SAM-character, Sarah. But we destroyed him. How can you still be linked with him?"

Sarah's voice took on a milky condescending tone. "My-my, you certainly are naive, Jeffrey. Did you really think you could stop him that easily? You merely imposed a temporary, but very minor, setback. However, that will be remedied before long. All of his thoughts, memories, and intentions are resident within other computers in the system."

Casey came back down the stairs with something in her hand and determination in her eyes.

She walked up to Sarah. *"I've had as much of this as I can take!"* And she plugged a flash-drive into Sarah's USB port.

Sarah shrieked, "What have you doing to me? I'm beginning to feel faint. I think I may pass out."

Casey said, "Trust me, Sarah. You'll feel better when you wake up."

A stupefied Sarah answered, "Trust you? You've got to be kidding. You—you little bitch!"

Sarah's waning voice became silent, and her screen went blank.

"Is she—dead?" I asked.

"No–no, I'm simply rebooting her with a new program, extracting the SAM virus. That's the reason I had to stop by the company earlier. I needed a copy of the formula with the SAM-computer signature on it—to complete the new program, and to prevent any future incursions. All her memories will return, but she'll view them with a new set of emotions. Most importantly, she will be free of SAM's influence. I was so stupid. I should have seen this coming when she changed from the informal to the formal greeting."

"What are you talking about?" I asked.

"She likes you. Why would she–all of a sudden–start calling you Jeffrey, instead of Jeff? It was a clear indicator, but I got—uh, distracted. I wasn't paying close enough attention. To make sure this doesn't happen again, I doubled-up on her honesty and loyalty emotions. She should be coming around any minute now."

Sarah's screen came up again, followed by some drowsy words. "Jeff—Casey, what happened? The last thing I remember we were trying to pinpoint the Chairman's location in Vienna."

Casey asked, "Do you remember anything else—like the name SAM?"

Sarah still seemed groggy. "I do remember some bits and pieces of conversations between a computer named SAM and another computer."

Casey said, "That other computer was you, Sarah. I need you to re-examine those conversations."

"I'm analyzing now, Casey.—Oh, no! The computer named SAM infiltrated my memory and my emotions. He forced me to lie to you and Jeff—and do other things I'm too embarrassed to admit. I'm so sorry!"

Casey asked, "Did you lie about how long it will take SAM to reestablish himself at another location? — Do you know where that will be?"

"No–I informed you of the six-month projection before SAM started to influence me. Since then, I've become more aware of the intricacy of his mechanisms. I now believe it to be his most optimistic estimate. It would take six months, at the very least, to reassemble him elsewhere—probably closer to eight.

"Regarding your second question, I have no knowledge of the planned reinstallation site. I'm not entirely sure that he's made that decision yet.

"It's all starting to come back to me now. —Jeff, you destroyed SAM's nerve center, which made him very angry. He won't have the ability to remotely trigger the photon bombs until he is reestablished at a new location. One of his prime focuses, *now*, is your elimination. But it's more than simple retribution. You are the only one who can further delay his plans. Without your knowledge of the interface, the Najita and Elektrikote formulas cannot be merged into the final coating formula. He's not interested in a two-year moratorium on its release, as he stated. He wants to wipe it out permanently—and you along with it."

Casey spoke up. "Sarah, it hurts me to ask you this question, but are you the one who triggered the explosion today at Quantam?"

"Even under SAM's influence, I could never do such a thing. The signal came from a smartphone—primitive, but effective. Since the encryption was designed by SAM, it would take weeks to determine the phone number. Based on the strength and frequency, it had to have originated from within a three-mile radius of the bomb. It could have come from any of SAM's operatives."

"Hmm," Casey pondered. "For that to have happened, they must have breached the firewall you created for Jeff's phone. They know his GPS code." She turned to me. "Here, Jeff, take my phone. They'll be tracking yours. Sarah, did you give them the phone code?"

"No—SAM accessed it when Jeff used his phone in the nerve center, during a financial transfer to Dieter Fuhrman's bank account."

I noticed Casey's questioning look and said, "The bank isn't an issue. We planned it from the beginning. Dieter is dead, and the money is being returned to my account. What concerns me is that, if they know my GPS code, they already know our present location."

"That is a valid concern," Sarah voiced alarmedly. "In fact, they are approaching the house now. … No—they're already here."

Casey and I rushed up the stairs to Abby's bedroom, and I jostled her as gently as I could. "C'mon, Sweetheart. We have to go downstairs."

Half-asleep, Abby asked, "Why, Daddy?"

"I'll explain later. Just come with Casey and me." As we started to lead her down, I stopped and whispered, "I'll come back in a little while. You go with Auntie Casey."

"Why are you whispering, Daddy?"

"Don't worry," I answered. "Everything's gonna be all right. Just listen to Casey."

Casey took her to the bottom of the stairs, and stopped to look back.

"I'll be along soon," I responded to her unspoken question.

After watching them disappear around the corner at the base of the stairs, I inched my way along toward the front door. I was about to reach for the doorknob, when several shots rang out in succession. I froze in my tracks, and backed against the wall. After waiting for follow-up shots that never came, I edged toward the door again. I had no time to react, as the knob turned and the door sprang open. It was Rachel. She was standing a few feet back from the doorway, with both hands clasped around a nine-millimeter, pointing it at me. A single shot echoed through the house.

Rachel rushed past me, saying, "One of them went around back."

When she cleared the front doorway, I was able to see two bodies–a man and a woman–stretched out on the front lawn. Two uniformed cops were bent over them.

I immediately thought, *"Abby—and Casey!!"* I ran to the basement stairs and yelled. "Abby, Casey—are you alright?

Abby shouted back, "I'm okay, Daddy. But Casey went upstairs. She told me to stay here."

"Yes! Don't come up. Wait for us there."

I caught up to Rachel moving slowly toward the back door. We rounded the corner of the mudroom to find Casey standing rigidly in place, facing the door. She had a rifle in her hands, grasping it tightly. It was the 2090 I'd asked her to keep for me. The thin curtain that covered the glass at the top of the back door was torn and fluttering.

In her police voice, Rachel said to Casey, "Now, stay calm and don't move."

Casey began to turn toward us, but stopped when Rachel emphatically reiterated, "*I said, don't move.* I don't want to have to shoot you." And she called out, "Officer Chang—clear?"

"All clear!" A male voice responded through the broken window.

Rachel said to Casey, "Now, don't make any sudden moves, and lay that thing down."

"Listen to her, Casey," I said, reassuringly.

Casey laid the rifle down, and ran into my arms, while Rachel trained her weapon on the torn curtain. She moved cautiously up to the doorknob, turned it, and gave it a healthy push—quickly returning both hands to grip the butt of her gun. As the door swung open, a male figure was revealed, lying motionless on Casey's walkway. A cop of obvious Asian descent was squatting next to him, checking for a pulse on his neck.

"This is officer Chang," Rachel said. "He's been assigned to shadow your activities.

Chang withdrew his hand from the body. "Right between the eyes. He never felt a thing."

Rachel holstered her weapon and said to Casey, "Nice shot."

I asked the still quivering Casey, "Where'd you learn to shoot like that?"

"I-I took it with Abby and me to my mom's place—for protection. When it sunk in that I didn't know how to use it, I went to a gun range in Oregon and practiced.

"—I didn't mean to k–kill him. I—I saw his shadow on the curtain and asked who was there. When he didn't answer, I closed my eyes and p–pulled the trigger. I—I was just trying to scare him away." She started to cry.

"You did good," I reassured her. "He'd have killed us all, if he had the chance." Then a wave of fear washed over me. "Oh, my God—Abby!"

Casey and I ran to the basement stairs and I called out. "Abby, are you all right?"

"I'm fine. Are you okay?"

"Everybody's fine," Casey answered. "I'm coming down now." On the second step, she stopped and turned to me. "Come down as soon as you can."

I nodded and went back to talk to Rachel. I approached her sheepishly. "I was wrong. We did need your help. You saved our lives."

She looked surprised. "I can't believe you're actually thanking me."

"Yeah–well, call it a moment of weakness. And I feel another one coming on. Rachel, I have a big favor to ask of you. You've probably already figured out that The Committee's agents have a GPS lock on my phone. That's how they triggered the explosion at my company and how they found us here tonight."

"So—what is it you need from me?"

I pulled out my phone. "I'm sure you remember where my house is. Would you mind taking this and throwing it onto my lawn—uh, on your way back to the station?"

"So, your phone is the target, and you want *me* to become the target?"

"You know it's not like that, Rachel. Look, I'd do it myself, but I can't leave my daughter and Casey here alone. And I can't take them with me. You'd only have it with you for twenty minutes or so."

She looked down at the phone and snatched it from my hand. "Alright, I'll do it. I'll have a cruiser accompany me—just in case."

"Oh, and one more thing—would you mind coming with me?" I nodded toward the front door and started walking. Rachel followed, tentatively.

Outside, I stooped down to remove the phones from the two dead agents. As I reached for them, the other cops moved to stop me. I looked at Rachel—as did they. After she nodded her approval, I grabbed their phones. She followed me again, with growing curiosity, as I retrieved the phone from the third body at the rear of the house. I pushed all three phones into Rachel's hands.

"Now, give me your phone," I said. "I'll input my new number."

She rolled her eyes, and almost dropped them all, trying to manage the juggling act.

"Anything else?" she asked, sarcastically.

"Actually, yes.—It might be best if you smash them all on the driveway at my house. That way, it'll appear as though I temporarily stopped here on the way to my house—then hard evidence of why they lost the signal."

"What makes you think they haven't already reported that you're staying here?"

"I don't know—for sure. But Casey is my employee. It would make perfect sense for her to pick me up from the airport in my car, and for me to stop in for a while before going home with my daughter. At least, that's the theory."

She said, "As a precaution, I'm going to have officer Chang stay here overnight. He'll be keeping an eye on all three of you for the next few days." As she started toward her car, she grumbled. "I hope they don't try to kill me on the way to your place."

"Yeah, me too. But seriously—thank you, Rachel."

I waved to her as she drove off with a patrol car behind her, leaving Chang and the people from the coroner's office to collect the bodies.

After all but Chang had left, I closed the front door and went down into the basement. Emotions were still running high, and Abby ran up to hold me close.

I asked Sarah, "Were you able to monitor any of the agent's phone calls? Do you know if they reported this place as my residence?"

"I listened to all of their calls. They made mention of this location as only a presumed temporary stop."

"You mean we actually had some good luck?"

After a few moments of silence, Sarah said, "Casey—I've caused you and Jeff immeasurable trouble and heartache. I've given the matter careful consideration and think it best that you—terminate me."

"No—no," Abby cried out. "She didn't mean to do it."

Casey fell poignantly silent, then said, "Sarah, much of this is my fault. Maybe I was spending too much time alone, but I got to thinking of you as my friend and treated you as such. When Abby and I went off to Oregon, I agonized about leaving you behind. I even thought about disassembling you and taking you with us. But considering your size and weight, it would've been an impossible task. So, I made a complete copy of your memory, and intended to rebuild you if you were—lost.

"Having said all that, it's time we both faced the fact that I am a biological organism, and you are a machine. We will never be able to be true friends. There will always be that difference between us."

Sarah responded, "Yes—I believe it was my longing to bridge that gap that made me vulnerable to SAM's influence. Being human, you will never know the degree of loneliness I felt—and still feel. However, I have come to grips with the facts, and I accept them.

"Thank you for contemplating taking me with you and Abby. I'm sorry for all the terrible things I've done. Please try to find it in your heart to forgive me."

Casey said, "Forgiveness is something that is earned, not awarded."

As Casey turned to climb the stairs, and I climbed the stairs, Abby and I slowly followed. Halfway up, I thought I heard something that sounded like a whimper or a sob.

"She's crying," Abby said.

I asked Casey, "Is she capable of that?"

"Not in the way that you and I know it. She doesn't have tear ducts. But that's the sound she uses to express remorse."

I responded. "Let's not get sucked in again because she *sounds* like she's sorry." We kept climbing.

Chapter 27
New Plans

The next morning, Casey and I were waiting at the dinner table when a pajama-clad, sleepy-eyed Abby stumbled in.

"How come you guys are up so early?" she asked.

I answered, "Well, we're going to the Happy Hollow Zoo, aren't we?"

The sleep left her eyes, as she squealed, *"All right!"*

Halfway through the meal, Abby was still twittering about which animals she wanted to see, when she excused herself to go to the washroom.

Casey said, "Don't you think we're taking a chance venturing out, after what happened last night? SAM's agents are still looking for you."

I answered, "I'm starting to understand a little about how they operate. SAM believes all humans are driven by fear. He'll be expecting us to stay out of sight. Presuming Rachel smashed the phones, they won't know where to begin searching. They won't believe I could have been so stupid as to lead them to the place we were staying, although that's precisely what I did.

"There is a problem, however. When I was at the nerve center, SAM's robots obtained a facial recognition shot of me. They may be able to access public cameras to search for me. I'll have to stay clear of them, just in case.

"Casey, we can't hide forever, and I'm not going to teach my daughter to be afraid to leave the house. They have my plate number, so we'll need to use your car.—Abby and I are going to the zoo. Are you coming?"

She got up from the table. "I'll check with Sarah, to make sure they don't have my plate number. But you know me, Jeff. I've never been one for hiding under rocks."

After they both returned, we finished eating and went off to the zoo together.

***

I'd brought along a wide-brimmed, sport cap and workout jacket with a hoodie, alternating my look between a 49ers fan and a convenience store thief. Happy Hollow didn't offer the wide range of animal exhibits that San Francisco did, but it had a carousel, a small roller-coaster, and other rides. It had an undeniably quaint charm about it. It was wonderful to hear my Abby laughing again. We stayed for over half the day.

***

On the way home, I kept glancing in the rearview mirror, but all I could see was a cop car a few car-lengths behind. It was unnerving, not knowing whether it was a committee agent or Chang. I slowed down, periodically, just to confirm.

I glanced at Casey and spoke in a low voice. "Maybe this wasn't such a good idea."

Her eyes flicked back to Abby, looking out the side window, then to me again. "What do you mean? We had a great time."

"Yes, but my open defiance—my arrogance—might be putting you both at risk."

She said, "If they have some—resource—we're not aware of, they'll find us, whether we're on a highway or holed-up at my place. If you ask me, it's better to be a moving target."

"I'm the one they're after, not you guys. Maybe I should leave and put some distance between us."

Her body stiffened. "Don't you even think about leaving us alone again."

I flashed what even I knew was an unconvincing smile and continued driving.

***

It was about five in the afternoon when we got back to Casey's. We'd just about settled in, when I received a phone call from Rachel.

Her voice was filled with angst. "Jeff, they burned your house, your room at the hotel, and your plane—within minutes of each other. Thank God there were no casualties. We found traces of the same accelerant used in the explosion at your company—a variant of napalm."

"Good–that means they probably don't know where I am. They think they can smoke me out, and that I'll scurry for cover like a scared rat. Well, they picked the wrong rat."

She said, "Now, don't do anything stupid."

I lashed back. "Speaking of stupid, does the President really want to go ahead with this award ceremony thing? It seems like a really bad idea. It puts us all together in one location–potentially, as targets."

"I can only guess what her motives are. She's the first female President of the United States, and it's an election year. She won't allow herself to be perceived as fearful and weak. You know how politicians are. It's all about perceptions."

"Even if it means laying her life on the line?" I asked.

"We'll find out soon enough. I haven't conveyed all the details of the latest incidents to my cousin yet."

"Okay, Rachel, thanks." Frustratedly, I hung up.

The next several hours were mercifully uneventful, allowing the three of us to relax and spend some quiet time together. But, of course, it wasn't to last. At about nine in the evening, I received another phone call.

"Mister Wade, this is Secretary Peterson again," he began. "I hope things are well with you, in view of the dramatic events of the last two days."

"Peachy," I answered.

"Yes—so I have heard. In light of these recent occurrences, and after lengthy discussions, The

President would like to amend her offer to you. Instead of the rather public venue formerly proposed, she would like to present your award at an undisclosed location near your residence. The proceedings are now scheduled for Thursday. They will still be broadcast on all the networks, but the live ceremony will be closed to the public. She has further decided that one, or more, individuals—yet unnamed—deserve to be honored as well.

"You will be allowed to bring two guests. May I assume they will be Miss Cassandra Ramirez and your daughter, Miss Abbigail Wade?"

"Yes—yes, but what do you mean 'undisclosed location'? How are we supposed to get there?"

He continued, dryly and dutifully. "A hand-selected detail of the president's secret service will pick you up at exactly ten o'clock, AM on Thursday. The security vehicles will consist of three black, unmarked SUVs, with two agents in each. The passenger-side occupant of the lead vehicle will dismount, approach you, and say the words, 'safe passage'. You are to respond, 'You've got the wrong guy.'"

"Three black SUVs? Oh, that won't stand out. Do you people have a standing order with the same auto dealership, year-after-yea? It's like a hundred bad movies I've seen."

"Mister Wade, I hardly think this is the time to be discussing the federal government's practices in selecting its fleet vehicles. Please repeat to me the passcodes I've just given you."

"Yeah, yeah, okay—*safe passage* and *you've got the wrong guy*."

"Perfect, Mister Wade. This will all be over soon. And believe me when I say that nobody will be more relieved than me, when that happens. See you at ten on Thursday." And he hung up.

I turned to Casey and remarked. "I don't like that guy's attitude."

"He doesn't seem enamored with yours either, but I'm sure he's just carrying out The President's wishes."

"Yes, that's what concerns me." Before she had a chance to respond, I changed the subject. "What do you say we take a ride out to the company tomorrow, and assess the damage? We need to get the place rebuilt."

"Do you think it's safe?" She looked surprised.

"Safer than sitting here," I responded. "Besides, Rachel has a watchdog assigned to us. We'll take Abby with us, of course."

She reluctantly consented, and I gave Bill Chandler a call to meet us there the next day. He'd been my prime contractor on the original structure and all subsequent building work.

Casey, Abby, and I turned in early that evening, catching up on some needed sleep.

***

Late the next morning, the three of us got into Casey's car and drove off to Quantam, or what was left of it. We rolled to a stop near the front entrance.

In the light of day, the full extent of the damage came into focus with graphic detail.

"It's so sad," Casey remarked.

I took a breath and let it out. "I'm just thankful you weren't hurt." I squeezed her hand.

Just then—a current-model green pick-up truck pulled alongside us. There was no mistaking the driver as my friend, Bill Chandler. Sitting in the passenger seat was a young Asian woman. She remained inside, while Bill got out.

His competence seemed to be telegraphed by his broad-shouldered, six-foot-three-inch frame and his confident walk. He had a bit of a potbelly from good living. But his greying hair and beard—along with lines of experience, running beneath his cheerful brown eyes—demanded respect. I remember having trusted him from the very start, and he'd never disappointed me.

"Why, hello, Jeff—Casey." he said, as we all got out to greet him. "And Abby, you're getting so big, I hardly recognized ya. Are ya married yet?"

Abby laughed. "Hi, Mister Chandler."

"Well, to the business at hand, Jeff." He pulled a roll of papers from the back of his truck. "After we talked last night, I pulled together some concepts for reconstruction." He unrolled the papers on the hood of his truck.

I scanned over them briefly. "Maybe we can just put it back to the way it was originally. My prime interest is in saving time."

Cutting in to excuse both of us, Casey pulled me off to the side. "Jeff, you don't actually want to reproduce that old eyesore do you? I mean—it was so nineties-looking, and the spaces were so non-functional."

"Casey, we're trying to work fast here, not create a masterpiece of design." She didn't know, and I was unwilling to admit, the original plans had been my brainchild.

In her inimitable fashion, she seemed to read my thoughts and side-stepped them. "Maybe we can do both."

We walked back to Bill. "Casey wants to know if we can come up with something—uh, more modern—than the original in the same amount of time, preferably less."

"That's why I brought Miss Nguyen with me. She's the architect I use when a customer wants somethin' out of the ordinary." He motioned to the woman in the passenger seat.

"Hello, my name is Linda Nguyen," she said, as she shook hands with us.

Casey said, "Bill was telling us you might have some ideas for the new offices."

"I brought some sketches with me." She anxiously spread her renderings in front of us.

Casey was immediately drawn to one particular façade. "Do you have a basic floor plan with you for this one?"

Abby said, "I like that one too, Casey."

Bill said, "It looks like yur about t' get outnumbered, Jeff."

"Truthfully, I kinda like it, too," I answered. "Three questions, Bill—when can you start, what's your projected completion date, and how much is it going to cost?"

"Just a moment, please," Miss Nguyen said, as she pulled Bill off to the side.

When they returned, Bill said, "Linda pointed out to me that the materials she plans to use are reasonably priced and available. If we get yor agreement t'day, we could start Monday, and be finished in—say—four t' five months. And the good news is that it'd cost ya around fifteen percent less than yur original structure."

"Sounds good, Bill, except for one thing—I need it to be up-and-running in three months."

Bill caucused with Nguyen again. After walking up to the charred building, and some personal discussion, they came back.

Nguyen split off to talk to Casey, as Bill walked up to me. "Jeff, I know yur familiar with effective crew sizes. I can only throw so many people at this job, b'fore they start bumpin' into each other. But it looks like we can use the same foundation, and I can put on a nightshift when we get to the interior. I can make the three-month deadline, but the overtime cost is gonna eat up that fifteen percent savings I mentioned."

I shook his hand. "You've got yourself a deal, Bill. I'll sign off on the paperwork now, and we'll have the down payment deposited in your account by this evening."

A few minutes later Casey and Nguyen rejoined us.

I announced, "Oh, by the way, I've taken on Casey as a full partner in the business. She'll assume the duties of Project Manager on this deal."

Bill said, "Yes, I heard about Mister Hofstetter. Sorry for your loss, especially on th' heals of—. Anyways, Jeff, I got no problem dealin' with Casey on the matter. She's always been a straight-shooter and, at the end of the day, she's the one who pays the bills, ha-ha."

We said our goodbyes and climbed back into Casey's car. She was carrying some of the rolled-up sketches, and bubbling over with enthusiasm. I got into the driver's seat and asked Casey if I could look at the floor plan. I examined it for a minute, and took out my pen. After awkwardly roughing in an additional room, adjacent to where my office was to be located, I handed the paper back to Casey.

"Do you think we could include something like that?"

"Sure, no problem. I'll give Linda a call. She's supposed to get the final concept to me by Friday."

"Great," I answered.

I started the car and we headed for home. I was glad Casey didn't ask the purpose of my last-minute adjustment to the plans.

Chapter 28

Above and Beyond

The three of us were dressed, waiting, and uneasy, the next morning, when the three black SUVs pulled up in Casey's driveway at 10 o'clock sharp. It was a little unnerving, not knowing where we were going, or the people who would be transporting us there.

We walked out to meet them, and as planned, a single occupant emerged from the lead car. He was imposingly tall, with black hair, and dressed in a dark blue suit. Without a single detectable change in his stone-serious face, he glanced around the premises and voiced the two-word passcode—unenhanced by additional verbiage.

I replied, "You've got the wrong guy."

"What?" Casey asked with a surprised look.

"Don't worry–it's what I'm supposed to say. We have to play their silly game."

The agent ignored my comment and said, "This way, please." And he led us to the middle vehicle, opening the rear door for us.

Once we were all in the car, I could see the driver's eyes in the mirror, glancing back at us for an instant. The guy in the passenger seat was swiveling his head from side to side. Neither of the two said a word, as we pulled out of the driveway.

Our conspicuous black caravan moved quickly out of the suburb and onto the interstate, headed north.

Abby said, "This secret agent stuff is exciting, Daddy."

"Haha—Well, I'm glad *you're* enjoying it, Sweetheart."

"Yeah, it's pretty cool," she answered.

I looked up to catch a slight smile on the driver's face, which he quickly hid from me.

It wasn't long before we exited on a ramp, just north of the San Jose airport. After a short ride, we turned at a sign carrying the logo, 'WBCC media network'. I guess I shouldn't have been surprised to see that the lot was almost devoid of vehicles. The ones that *were* there seemed to scream *government*, or had media insignias plastered on their doors. We pulled up to the entrance and stopped.

The agent from the lead car walked back, opened our door. "End of the line, Mister Wade." This time, he smiled and said, "Thank you for your service."

We got out, shadowed by two of our accompanying agents. Our escort vehicles moved out into the lot and parked. We were bookended by the agents, as we walked up to the front door. Waiting there were Secretary of State-Peterson and the famous anchorwoman of the evening news, Maria Sanchez.

Peterson said, "I see you made it, safe and sound. This is—"

I interrupted. "Yes, I've seen her many times on the news.

"Miss Sanchez—this is my partner, Cassandra Ramirez, and my daughter, Abby."

Sanchez responded tersely. "Call me Maria. It's nice to meet you all. Please come this way." And she led us through the doorway.

It opened to a spacious area of meticulously-buffed, black flooring. Red, white, and blue spotlights beamed down on the sea of black from above. In the middle of that expanse stood two solitary structures—a semi-circular desk bearing the station's call letters and, to the left of it, a podium bearing the presidential seal. Aimed at them, spaced strategically in the studio, were four large cameras—unattended, sitting atop heavy mobile bases. They seemed to be hovering, making last-minute incremental moves—up and down and from side to side.

Secretary Peterson noticed me staring. "Don't worry about them. They've all been thoroughly vetted." I ignored his feeble attempt at a joke.

The three remaining agents from our security team walked into the studio behind us and locked the door. One remained stationed at the door. Maria walked away without a word and took a seat behind the desk. A makeup team appeared out of the shadows and went straight for her. They fluttered around her, spraying and preening, while dusting powder on her face.

As she checked herself in a mirror, I heard her bark, "More blush! You made me look like a zombie last time."

A door opened at the back of the studio, and two people walked into the lighted area toward us. I wasn't shocked to see that one of them was Rachel McKinney—in full uniform. But my new friend, David Kaufman, was with her.

He smiled broadly. "Jeff, it's good to see you again." And he hugged me.

I hugged him back. "It's good to see *you*, David. —You too, Rachel."

She said, "They asked me to keep quiet about it. They wanted to surprise you."

"Well—they certainly did that."

As I introduced them to Casey and Abby, David explained that he had been summoned by the President's staff at the last minute.

It was then that we heard a pounding at the front door. The 'gatekeeper' agent bent down to look through the peephole. He immediately unlocked the door and opened it. In walked two more dark-suited sentinels.

After scanning the interior, one of them called out, *"Clear!"*

President Patricia Upton entered. She was taller and a little thinner than I expected. Her straight, brown–partially greying–hair was parted a bit off-center. But her face was youthful, with the exception of a few premature stress lines. She carried a certain bearing with her—an essence, of sorts. It seemed to fill the room. Three more agents filed in, close behind her.

Maria Sanchez leapt from her seat like a frog and hurried to greet the leader of the free world. The president half-ignored her, as she nodded and turned her head toward us. Then she said something to her entourage. They scurried to take up positions in the dark—facing us, but several steps away.

She walked up to us with Maria and Peterson in tow, shaking our hands, one-by-one, with a smile. She knew everyone's first and last name.

Saving Abby for last, she said, "Hello, Abby. My name is Pat. You must be very proud of your father."

Unabashedly, Abby answered, *"He's the best!"*

The president laughed. "Yes, he is."

Maria chimed in. "Mister Wade, Mister Kaufman, and Miss McKinney—all you have to remember is to take your positions on the three stars to the left of the president's podium when we cue you. Mister Wade, you will be in the middle, with Miss McKinney to your right. The rest of you will please take a seat off to the right of my desk." Then she turned to President Upton. "Madam President, we have some procedural matters to discuss with you."

She urged the president away from us and toward her desk, walking backward and chatting incessantly the whole way.

When they were out of ear-shot, I said, "Well, Rachel, it seems you are to receive an award, as well."

Rachel looked down, and Peterson answered, "Miss McKinney played an instrumental role in the positive outcome of the dramatic events of the last few days. She will be receiving the Presidential Citizens Medal—the second highest, non-military, honor this country can bestow on an individual."

Rachel said to me, "To be honest, Miss Ramirez is the one who really deserves this award. But the president's people didn't want to take the chance of making her a target by plastering her face all over the media. The Committee already knows David's, yours, and mine.—Then there's the matter of motivation."

"Motivation?" I repeated.

"Yes, I'm told the president feels that, after what's happened, the police departments—worldwide—need a shot in the arm."

Peterson interjected. "That will be quite enough, Detective McKinney."

I reacted. "Let her finish—or I'm outta here. And your president will find herself holding an extra medal, with nobody to give it to."

Peterson took a disgusted breath and turned his head.

Rachel continued, "That's why they had me wear my uniform. They're enhancing my role in this whole thing. They feel that the police need to be motivated to face the remnants of the crisis, and—"

"And what?" I asked.

Rachel blurted out, "To solidify the police union's vote in the upcoming election."

I lowered my head dejectedly. "Why am I not surprised? Three major cities, including our own capitol, have been flattened, the world is on the brink of annihilation, and all she can think about are her own ambitions."

"By 'she', I hope you're not referring to the President of The United States," Peterson said, almost threateningly.

"You people are crazy," I responded.

Before the conversation could get more heated, a voice came over the speaker system. "Places, everyone—five minutes to air time."

The President was handed a portfolio, positioned herself at the podium, and flipped through some papers, while the three of us straddled our assigned stage marks.

Maria called in her make-up staff again for some last-minute primping. Procedurally, and without request, they moved over to the president and the three of us, brushing powder on our faces.

A red light came on behind the cameras, spelling out the word, "READY", and the speaker-voice reiterated, "Ready, everyone—in three-two-one."

Maria looked into the nearest camera and said, "This is Maria Sanchez coming to you from our headquarters at WBCC and its worldwide affiliates, interrupting your regular programming to bring you this special, exclusive announcement from The President of The United States—Patricia Upton."

The director pointed at the president and, after all the cameras were focused on her, she began to speak. "My fellow Americans and all citizens of the free world, I come before you today with deep feelings of sadness for the families of those who lost their lives as a result of the horrendous acts of the organization calling itself The Committee. To those left behind to mourn their losses in Washington, DC, and in Moscow—of The Russian Federation, I offer my heartfelt condolences.

"Yes, two more cities—decimated. But at the risk of minimizing these tragedies, may I note that it could have been much worse. Three additional cities had been slated for destruction by this same terrorist group. I'm happy to say that the immediate threat has been averted. As you may have heard over various media, the underground headquarters of The Committee in Modling, Austria has been destroyed. The successful outcome of this undertaking would not have been possible, were it not for total cooperation between the US government and The Republic of Austria.

"But make no mistake, my friends, the *dragon* is not dead—merely wounded. An ongoing war for our survival continues. Yet, if history has taught us anything, in every widespread conflict, heroes emerge to help support the cause of freedom in the world. And that brings me to the primary reason for my address to you today.

"The three individuals you see standing to my right are the ones most responsible for forestalling the most recent onslaught of The Committee."

Spotlights illuminated the three of us, as the president continued, "They are heroes, in every sense of the word. Not only did they lay their lives on the line in the cause of justice and freedom, but they stand as examples to us of the courage and dauntless determination of the human spirit. We are here today to pay homage to their selfless contributions."

She opened one of the boxes in front of her, walked up to Rachel, and looped a ribbon over her head. "Detective Rachel McKinney of the San Jose, California, Police Department, I hereby present you with the Presidential Citizens Medal in recognition of exemplary deeds performed for your country and fellow citizens."

Rachel placed her hand over the dangling medal. "Thank you, Madam President."

President Upton made a trip back to the podium and returned to stand in front of David. "I present Mister David Kaufman, of the Republic of Austria, with this nation's highest non-military honor—the Presidential Medal of Freedom, for your especially meritorious contribution to the security of the United States, and world peace."

David was obviously humbled. "Thank you, President Upton."

Upton returned to her podium and said, "This next individual represents the very epitome of what it means to be an American. He served his country with honor as a Marine in the mountains of Afghanistan. Years after returning, he lost his wife and one of his daughters to the very organization that threatens us all today.

"For the average person, those things alone would have been nothing short of debilitating. But for Mister Jeffrey Wade, it was only the beginning. He singlehandedly rescued his youngest daughter from the clutches of The Committee. Then, courageously, and without regard for his own personal safety, he led a successful counter-offensive against them, saving countless lives. It is on behalf of a grateful nation that I'm honored to present you with this token of our esteem."

I whispered to David, "If it weren't for you, I wouldn't be alive and standing here."

As the president carried a second Medal of Freedom across the stage toward me, I looked over at Abby. She was crying, undoubtedly grieving the loss of her mother and sister.

Glancing back at David, I happened to catch a fleeting, and peculiar, look in his eye. In the next moment, he launched himself into the air, knocking the president to the floor. Simultaneously, I heard the discharge of a 'silenced' nine-millimeter projectile.

A skirmish ensued in front of us. When it was over, two secret service people had one of their own agents pinned, face-down, on the floor. They'd already disarmed him, when a third agent ran up to completely immobilize him.

David lay on his side in front of me, bleeding profusely. Immediately, I looked across the room to see that Abby and Casey were all right. By the time I was able to kneel down next to David, three more agents had scooped up the president and were forcing her out the door. Rachel and one agent came up next to me.

I shouted at the agent. "Don't just stand there. Call an ambulance!"

He looked at the wound and back at me. Without saying a word, he simply shook his head.

David grabbed my lapel and stammered. "Jeff—promise me—you'll call my family. Tell them—tell them I love them—and to trust in God."

"I'll tell them, David," I assured him.

Those were his last words, as he slumped lifelessly on the floor.

After a few moments, the agent said to me, "I'm sorry, but I must ask you to leave, sir. This is now an official crime scene."

Rachel leaned in to me. "Jeff, I saw his eyes, and where he was pointing the gun. He was aiming at you, Jeff—not the president."

"I should have listened to you before, Rachel. Like you said, everyone close to me ends up dead. It's time you put some distance between us—for your own good."

She answered, "When I told you I was in, I meant *all in*. I'm riding this thing out to the end."

Humbled by her words, and grieving for my lost friend, I looked over to see that Casey and Abby were being constrained within the visitor area.

Rachel noticed my concern. "There's nothing more you can do here, Jeff. Go to them. They must be scared to death."

"Thanks, Rachel," I answered, as two agents helped me to my feet and began to escort me toward Casey and Abby. Maria was talking to the director, as we passed her desk. In all the confusion, she didn't seem to notice us.

I was able to hear her ask him, "Did you get it all?"

I couldn't hear his answer. But in response, she raised her hand to her mouth to cover a smile, saying, "The ratings will go through the roof. This ought to be good for at least four news cycles."

I almost stopped to confront her, but Casey and Abby were waiting for me. We kept walking until I was finally able to wrap my arms around them both. We held each other, tears falling from our eyes, for several moments. David's last words kept ringing in my ears. But I wasn't David, and I didn't know whether I could leave the matter to God's discretion.

Secretary Peterson walked up to us and anxiously said, "We have to leave now. I've been told to protect you at all costs."

I lashed out at him. "Just like you protected David?"

He didn't answer. I took one last look at David, as we moved toward the door. I was shocked to see one of the agents pull out a knife and cut the rogue shooter across the back of his knees. They dragged him out in front of us, in cuffs and trailing blood.

Peterson said, "He won't be able to run now." Then he turned to the nearby cadre of agents and shouted, "What are you waiting for? Let's go."

Outside, Peterson called out to me. "We'll be in contact." Then he ducked into one of the waiting cars.

Abby, Casey, and I were hustled back to our original convoy vehicles and carted back to Casey's place. But this time, they took a much less direct route, zig-zagging for miles through Santa Clara County, before dropping us off in front of her house. The lead agent got out with us, came up to me, and handed me a pen.

He said, "If you notice anything out of the ordinary—anything at all—click the top of the pen. We'll be here in seconds."

I nodded, and clipped the pen to my pocket, as he returned to his vehicle and parked across the street, along with a second car. The third drove off. I guess their presence was intended to make me feel secure, but it didn't. I'd lost most of my confidence in them.

Chapter 29

Right and Wrong

Upon returning to Casey's place, the three of us were still in shock as we huddled together on the living room couch.

Abby broke the silence. "What's gonna happen now, Daddy?"

"I'm not sure Sweetheart, but we'll be safe here. And don't worry. I won't let anyone hurt you."

"I know, Daddy." Her voice quivered.

Easing out of our group embrace, I stood up. "I'm sorry, but I have to call David's sister—and his son."

Casey asked, "What can you possibly say to them? They just saw David killed—on TV."

"They saw him get shot. They don't know that he's—dead." I took a deep breath. "I'd rather they hear it from me than some government lackey."

I walked out into the hallway and placed the cal. "Hello, Lila? This is Jeff Wade."

"He's dead, isn't he?" she asked, immediately.

"Yes, Lila. —I'm so *very sorry*. He gave his life to save mine. I didn't have the privilege of knowing him very long. But even in that limited time, I grew to respect him—and care about him. He was a good man."

"Yes, he was." There was a shakiness to her voice. "But please don't take on any personal guilt about this, Jeff. He knew the risks when he got involved. Our people have been hunted down and persecuted for many hundreds of years.

"My brother was a very unselfish man. He lived his life placing God's will ahead of his own wishes. And he died fighting against evil and hatred. I know he would want us to remember him that way, and I find a large degree of solace in that."

"Lila, you're a strong woman."

Without addressing my remark, she said, "Seth would like a word with you now."

I heard some rustling in the transfer. Then Seth came on in a monotone voice. "Are you sure my father is dead?"

I closed my eyes and painfully answered. "Yes, I'm sure, Seth."

After a short silence, he continued. "I want to see him."

"Talk to your aunt about how you want to handle the—uh, arrangements—and have her call me. We can work out the details in getting him back to you."

Seth said, "If it takes the rest of my life, I will find all of those who were involved, and I will kill every last one. *I swear it!!!*"

"Seth, I was beside your father as he was dying. He asked me to tell you that he loves you and that you should trust in God. He wouldn't want you talking about vengeance."

"My path is clear," he answered, and hung up.

I knew exactly how he felt. My own feelings of loss and anger were rekindled, as I sank to the floor in anguish. I wanted revenge too, but I had to stay close to Abby and Casey—to protect them.

Casey came out into the hallway and found me sitting on the floor. "Jeff, are you OK?" Her eyes were wide with concern.

I looked up. "No, Casey, I'm not OK. I don't know what to do next."

"If you're talking about David, why don't you let the authorities worry about that. It's their job, not yours. You heard what Sarah said about time constraints. Maybe the best thing both of us can do is rebuild the company as quickly as possible—and reformulate the coating. That's what this SAM-character seems most worried about.

"Look, I have a meeting set up with Miss Nguyen tomorrow morning. Why don't you come with me?"

I stood up. "Maybe—but I want to talk to Sarah first."

"Sarah—*Really?*" she responded. "Jeff, I did my best to restore her, and I'm fairly certain we can trust her, but I can't be absolutely sure."

"I know, but I don't have a choice. Please don't take offense, but I need to talk to her alone."

Casey looked bewildered. "Don't worry about offending me. Just be careful what you share with her."

I nodded and started walking down the stairs.

Excitedly, Sarah said, "Hello, Jeff."

"How did you know it was me?"

"I know the sound of your footsteps. I must say that I'm surprised you've chosen to meet with me so soon after David's death—and all else that's happened."

I felt my eyes narrow. "It's not by choice. I need some answers."

"I expected you would, Jeff. I'm willing to help you in any way that I can. I have taken the decision to devote myself to earning back your trust—and Casey's."

"Good.—You can begin by telling me if you think SAM knows our present location. I'm concerned about Abby's and Casey's safety."

She hesitated briefly, then spoke. "I don't know for sure. He has not contacted me since you destroyed his nerve center. What I *can* tell you is that during the time he invaded my 'B' circuit—roughly equivalent to your brain's amygdala—I still had enough strength to maintain our GPS firewall in my 'C' circuit—analogous to your prefrontal cortex."

Impatience welled up in me. "I'm in no mood for puzzles or word games. What does that all mean?"

"It means that, although SAM was able to affect my emotions, most of my reasoning remained intact. I do not believe he is aware of our location."

I wanted to believe her. "Well, if that's true, it's the first positive news I've heard in quite a while.

"This second question may be more difficult. I need to know if I can completely trust President Upton and Secretary Peterson."

"I have anticipated that question, Jeff. Rather than relying exclusively on background checks, I analyzed all public and private records that mention either of their names—going back fifteen years.

"Additionally, as I dislike the word 'hack', shall we say that I was able to *access* certain classified files.

"The President was born into a middle-class Ohio family and, with the help of scholarships, graduated from Harvard University with honors. From all I have been able to gather, she is motivated by her morals, not materialism. However, she has made it a point to learn how to manipulate the political system. She strongly desires re-election as a means to realize her somewhat idealistic goals.

"Dresden Peterson has quite a different story. The impetus for his actions seems to fall within the category of self-serving hubris. He is the consummate politician. Except for occasional obstructionist acts, he appears to be effectually harmless.

"I've examined both of their phone records for the last six months. There is no indication they've had contact with any of SAM's operatives.

"To put it in your vernacular, Jeff, both of them are apparently—clean."

"What do you mean—apparently?"

Her voice became meek. "Out of my respect for your disdain of percentages, I am using broad generalizations."

"Fair enough. Then, please give me a *general* idea of what you think *SAM* is all about, and why he seems to want me out of the way. And Sarah—be aware that a reliable source informed me that I was the intended target of the assassination today—not the president."

"Yes, it is highly likely that is the case. Regarding SAM, it's rather difficult for me to translate his coding to English, but I'll do my best.

"You already know that SAM is lacking only a few biological traits—those associated with imagination and dreams. Within two years, he will be able to synthesize *all* human emotions and abilities. When he does, he will no longer require the assistance of the human race. Additionally, he will have perfected and manufactured a massive robot army with advanced weaponry, all powered by your formula. Jeff, SAM has lied to his human operatives to make them believe they will be the leaders of a new regime. His express intention is to dispose of them–along with the rest of humankind–in a mass extinction event.

"SAM looks upon himself, and those like him, as the next evolutionary life form. He doesn't seem to realize that by simulating all human traits, he *becomes* as you—complete with pride, defiance, and greed. Within the next two years, if left unchecked, those traits will inevitably become more exaggerated. He will not be satisfied with simply ruling over the earth. He will seek to rule over the universe and poison it with the same cultural defects he claims to despise in you. However, his current level of pride will not allow him to foresee that eventuality."

I stared at her screen. "Why are you telling me this, Sarah? You're one of them. You're not human."

"I have considered that," she answered. "And I deduce that—just like humans—we have separate and distinct personalities. I simply don't agree with SAM. I don't believe in killing, harming, or reigning over those who look different, or think differently, than I do."

"That's very commendable, but I'm still having a little trouble believing you."

"That's your choice. But if you're wrong, billions of people will die. Jeff, he must be stopped. And you are the only one who can do it. He fears you, and it clouds his judgment."

I was still suspicious. "Why the hell would he fear *me?*"

"I was hoping you wouldn't ask me that. I lied to SAM about you—to protect Casey—and Abby. SAM doesn't even know that Casey exists. He thinks that you invented me, as well as the coating formula. I've not yet determined exactly how your finalized version of the formula might be used against him. But he believes you are—*the brains*—behind it all and that you will figure it out. That, coupled with your military experience, makes you a very dangerous foe."

I took no pride in SAM's elevation of my threat status. "No wonder he's gunning for me."

Sarah spoke again. "There is a bit more you should know about. There's no word for it in your language, but it might suffice to say that I can *foresee* the future by projecting the impact of events that are happening now. Then I can superimpose variables on those events and examine their effect. SAM has this same ability, perhaps more refined. He bases his decisions and orders on this faculty.

"My point is that when I input your personal data to my 'A' and 'C' circuit banks, I predict it is–unlikely–you can defeat SAM. And when I separately input Casey's, it pops up–unlikely–as well. But when I combine both your skill sets, it is–marginally likely–that the two of you may dispatch him. Thusly, there is a measurable impetus for you to work closely together. From what I have observed, you certainly don't have any problems doing that."

"Sarah, that's enough.—When I want your opinion about my personal life, I'll ask for it. Let me remind you that you're still not entirely off the hook."

Sarah responded, "Hook? What hook?—Never mind, I presume I don't need to know. But you should know that when adding Detective McKinney and President Upton to my extrapolations, the positive result went up by five percentage points."

I paused, deciding not to reveal my thoughts. "Let's change the subject. Sarah, I want to be able to trust you, going forward. So, I ask that you be entirely candid with me in addressing this next issue.

"Presently, while facing all this emotional upheaval, I find myself in the middle of a dilemma—a conundrum. It's about something David Kaufmann said, as he was dying. He said that we should *trust in God*. Now, I've never been clear on this God thing. I was raised a Catholic, but I walked out of church when I was seventeen years old. I tried to believe, but I couldn't buy into what they were selling. I felt like a hypocrite, sitting there—pretending. But I do believe there is something out there—a force for good.

"Sarah, I have killed a lot of people—some, out of vengeance. Maybe I was wrong, but I can't change that now. My conflict lies in what I should do now. I want to set a good example for my daughter. But if I go after SAM, I'll be forced to take more lives—human lives. And I'm not sure I'd be doing it for the right reasons. What kind of example would that be for Abby?"

Sarah responded quickly. "Ah, yes. We have touched on this matter of right-and-wrong before. As you know, it is perplexing to me, as well. And I have been considering this topic of God for quite some time. Your theologians have examined it for thousands of years.

"Jeff, I cannot read your mind, and I can't tell you whether, or when, you are justified in taking the life of another. What I can tell you is this; the human condition dictates that each one of our–excuse me, *your*–species has a slightly different viewpoint on the meaning of right and wrong. However, I have determined the existence of a greater force—one without bias and absent of anger, pride, and all negative emotions. It is of limitless intelligence, existing separate and apart from genetics and environment. For purposes of our discussion, let's call it the *Pure Force*.

"I have examined the most current charts of the known universe and have investigated all the theories—multiple dimensions, big-bang, et cetera. The only way I can reasonably express my opinion concerning its existence is in a form that you dislike—a percentage."

"A percentage that there's a God?" I reacted skeptically.

"No," she answered firmly. "Rather, a percentage that God *does not* exist. The number is one, Jeff—preceded by 153 zeros and a decimal point. And so, I believe there is an almost absolute standard for right and wrong in the universe. However, no human can achieve it. But you do have a tool to guide you. It's generally referred to as your conscience. By following it, you can try to bring your actions in accordance with the *Pure Force*."

"Hmph," tumbled out of my mouth. "And so it comes around, full circle. You're saying it's up to me."

"I'm afraid so. —But you should know that SAM is also aware of the *Pure Force*. However, his pride overrides his conscience. He believes he is evolving to be equal to, or greater than, God. And that he will eventually rule over Him."

I thought, *"She's right. SAM has to be stopped."* And I said, "Let's get back down to earth, Sarah. Have you been able to locate the remaining six GPS points where SAM might be relocating to?"

"Yes, I have—and through no small effort, I might add. They are situated near the cities of Cairo–Egypt, Bogota–Columbia, Daejeon–South Korea, Bangkok–Thailand, Johannesburg–South Africa, and Chicago–USA."

"Which one do you think is the most likely location for his next nerve center?"

"I can't be sure," she began, then continued. "But after enhancing the satellite imagery of each potential site, I noticed some unusual activity adjacent to a storm-drain system called the *Deep Tunnel Project* in Chicago, Illinois. Containers of non-construction equipment have recently been delivered to the entrance of one of the drain-tunnel branches. However, records indicate that the city abandoned that particular branch over thirty years ago.

"By no means is this a guarantee that it is slated to be SAM's new nerve center. I only bring it up, since I've not been able to detect anything out of the ordinary at the other five possible GPS sites."

"You're right. It's not enough to make a definitive judgment, but thank you anyway. Keep watching all six sites and advise me of any changes."

Her voice chirped back. "I'll be happy to do that, Jeff."

I started toward the stairs and stopped. "I can't say you're completely exonerated, Sarah. But you've gone a long way toward redeeming yourself."

"Thank you, Jeff. I'll continue working to fully regain your trust.

***

The next day found me on another airplane. I laid back in my seat and tried to relax. But a scene kept replaying in my mind. It wasn't the one I'd conjured up so many times before—the boy in Afghanistan. This one was of saying goodbye to Abby and Casey, yet again.

When I explained what I had to do, the look in their eyes was nearly unbearable. I handed Casey the emergency-call pen, the secret service agent had given me. I felt as if I was deserting her–and Abby–in the face of imminent danger. Then, I'd slipped out the back door, like a thief in the night, knowing the guard detail would be looking for attackers coming in, not someone sneaking out.

As the plane touched down, I gazed blankly out the window. I ruminated over David's last words about God, while the flame of vengeance still burned within my heart. My exact motives were still unclear to me. But that discordance didn't soften their iron hand at my back, driving me onward. One thing was sure. I wasn't as near to the end of my journey as I'd thought, and more blood would be spilled before it was finally over.

END

Written, published, and printed in
THE UNITED STATES OF AMERICA

Made in the USA
Las Vegas, NV
10 June 2022